Acknowledgements

Thank you to Steve and Laura. I'm so glad our paths met.

DARK PRISONER

THE KRUTHOS KEY

Foundations Publishing Company
Brandon, MS 39047
www.foundationsbooks.net

Dark Prisoner – The Kuthros Key
By D. Thomas Jerlo

Cover by Dawne Dominique
Edited by Steve Soderquist
Copyright 2017© D. Thomas Jerlo

Published in the United States of America
Worldwide Electronic & Digital Rights
Worldwide English Language Print Rights

ISBN: 978-1-64583-021-4

Dedication

To my older brother Roland, who never had to opportunity to finally read this one as a real book. Thank you for always believing in me. I miss you so much.

Table of Contents

PROLOGUE

"How many centuries must I rely on your incompetence?"

Manifesting his mage'ic across the many leagues to ensure that imbecile servant, Isafel, carried out his instructions was a tiring process.

As Balthazar paced, a sphere of fire erupted around his ankles, doggedly trailing him like an insolent child. With each step the flames grew, fed by his fury when dealing with this particular demon.

The depth of his anger reached through the darkness in which he existed in fiery hues that danced across the obsidian walls of his prison. He manipulated the flames, binding them to his will, for they were the lone source of his power here but not near enough to escape. No. Never that. He needed two things to destroy this damnable internment.

The Kruthos. And the key to unlock it.

For a thousand years he fed his vengeance, and with every passing minute he added more tinder.

His frustrated growl chased through the empty corridors of the cavernous chamber. Other distorted cries soon joined in. Closing his eyes, he whispered, "Yes, my children. Our time is near. Soon."

Balthazar focused inward, searching for his special child; the one he'd created for just this purpose. It had been no easy task creating his offspring. He took from the earth clay to fashion their bodies. He then infused them with his malice and as much of his mage'ic he could spare. But one in particular was his prized possession. The one he'd given a name.

The one able to break through the Divenean prison that held him. Until Isafel.

From earth and water, saliva and blood, he'd infused all his cruelty to birth this particular spawn. The creation process had nearly destroyed him, but a hundred years of sleep was spit in the wind compared to the thousand he'd been trapped in. The other children that came after were minor replicas. Not so smart or gifted as Ilio.

The Diveneans who'd imprisoned him thought to render him useless. But his will and desire for revenge made him stronger, wiser and more cunning.

Balthazar shivered at the memory of the suffering he had to endure. Every ounce of pain had been worth it. He couldn't rely on Isafel alone. That demon always had an agenda of his own.

He watched through the eyes of his special child, waiting and biding his time.

Soon the wretched human race would be no more. *Soon...*

CHAPTER ONE

In the billowing dust kicked up by the human's boots, Isafel hovered close by, unseen. Down the hewn stone stairs, he followed the blasphemous path of footprints the man left behind.

This was the Keep of Komis'Na, a forgotten prison for wayward mages whose crimes had been so vile that they'd been locked away, never to be seen again.

The demon shuddered at the memories of his imprisonment in the cells below, however short they were.

The Diveneans had thought him and Master too dangerous to be held captive here and had devised other oubliettes for them.

Isafel pushed aside the useless memories and continued after the human. Ever downward they went until they reached the dark, empty catacombs of the dungeons.

He waited, and watched.

The tang of human sweat mixed with apprehension swirled through his senses. Yes, the blood-bag sensed *something* following him. Isafel almost laughed aloud at the fear he could still manifest in these weak beings. In his absence that hadn't changed in the least.

Such a pity he couldn't bring the mortal over to their side, for the human reeked of cold corruption and greed. But he had his orders, and little time. Rendering exquisite pain like that should be savored.

When he spoke, Isafel's disembodied voice echoed through the underground chambers. "Do you have it, man-thing?"

The curious human halted just outside a cell, his beady gaze darting through the murk in an attempt to locate the source of the voice. "I have what you seek."

Fear vacillated in the air.

Isafel hovered closer. The sloshing of blood in the man's body made him lick his lips. The want to gut and gorge on the disgusting fleshy lump pulled at him, but the importance of his task stayed his hand. His hunger had to wait.

The human glanced left, then right, shifting from foot to foot. "I've brought one half, as per the agreement."

The lie was blatant and easily detectable in the quickening of the man's heartbeat. Isafel slithered deeper into the shadows and sent tendrils of his misty body to snake around the human.

The man recoiled at his touch, confused at what he could feel, but not see.

There was much cunning in this human, but Isafel knew the flaws of mortals. If reckless enough to bring one half, they were foolish enough to bring both. Greed did not breed intelligence.

"I know of no such pact," he whispered close to the man's ear.

The human hissed and drew back. "We had a deal."

Always an emotional race... and such easy prey. Fascinated, Isafel watched a glistening trail of sweat run down the man's brow. "There's time enough to speak about such matters. Come," he said, moving closer, but still unseen. "You have travelled far. Sit and rest your weary bones."

The man stumbled to a decrepit chair that had once been used by a former prisoner. Isafel smelled the mage's putrefied body buried shallowly in the dirt floor beneath the human's boots. Sadly, the ensuing years had rotted away whatever meat had been left on them.

But there were more important matters to contend with than his appetite. "Tell me. What is it that my master seeks?"

The human's nostrils flared. "Not 'til you seal your bargain with me. I've traveled far and kept it safe. You promised—"

"YOU DARE TO BARTER WITH ME?"

Gaps in the ancient stone widened as Isafel's voice echoed through the Keep like the breaking of brittle bones.

The man cowered and grappled with a pocket in his cloak. "N-No!" His clumsy fingers pulled out a lock—old, rusty and worthless—few knew the significance of that derelict piece of metal.

The Kruthos!

The man held the object tightly in his fist. "It's just a lock, and if I brought it you promised power—"

Blood cascaded into the air and splattered like a macabre fountain. In the silence that followed, an unintelligible gurgle whispered down the stone corridor as the man's severed head flew off his shoulders and bounced across the room to land with a resounding *thud* against the wall.

Enthralled, the demon watched the man's eyes as he passed from this realm into another. The human élan—the light of the man's loathsome life—flickered for a few moments more before extinguishing completely. A jagged trail of blood leaked from the corner of the man's repugnant mouth to join the larger pool forming in the ochre dirt beneath the matted hair.

It was moments like this Isafel wished he was again human, for then he could siphon the sweet marrow from those piteous bones and savor the piquant taste of blood. Alas, such pleasures had become nothing but fleeting memories. And he had no use for memories. A thousand years was a long time to be denied such delightful delicacies.

Soon...

In the stillness that followed the sudden violence, Isafel glided to the headless corpse and took that which had once belonged to another. He slipped the Kruthos into the fold of his robe before beginning a manic search of the man's pockets for the key. When he found nothing, he ripped the corpse limb from limb, shouting in frustration.

"He was smarter than he looked," the demon grumbled as he cast down a severed arm in disgust.

Where was the Kruthos' key?

One thing was for certain. He'd been too impatient. He should have stayed his hand and found out more.

Isafel threw back his head and howled. He'd have to face Master's fury, but unlike mortals he looked forward to the pain. To feel anything brought him that much closer to his goal. When he became flesh and bone once more, then he'd rule this pathetic world. And nowhere would be the one he called Master.

Soon...

Like a sigh of death, he vanished through one of the many lichen-covered cracks in the stone.

CHAPTER TWO

Beneath the dense leaves of a towering goldenwood, Suna leaned against the tree trunk and shuddered uncontrollably. She'd been but a child learning the Divenean ways when she'd last felt such intrusive mage'ic travelling through her body.

Who'd found her?

Who'd dared to search?

Who knew?

"RELEASE ME!" she cried out.

Evil simmers beneath the bowels of Etharia, and if all comes to be as I have seen, no living creature shall ever live free. Suna Di'Viao, heed my words.

She struggled in vain to escape the trap that had ensnared her mind so easily. Only another like her had the ability to do so. But she was the last of the Divenean race. Wasn't she?

You've made a mistake. I'm not who you're looking for.

An invisible blow struck just below her sternum to snag the air from her lungs. She struggled to breathe.

Then true pain came.

Visions more horrendous than any she could have imagined slammed into her awareness.

She saw the world ravaged by drought and pestilence. Landscapes turned into decayed wastelands with bloated carcasses of dead livestock dotting the countryside like an obscene painting. Menacing skies flashed jagged, red streaks of lightning that cut through thick, inky cloud cover.

Recoiling in horror, she watched as ragged children sobbed as they searched for their parents who lay flayed and unrecognizable at their feet, their bodies sundered by forces not of this world.

A crescendo of screams cleaved through her soul and drove her to the brink of madness. Blood flowed like swollen rivers across the war-torn lands.

She cried aloud when she saw the kingdom of Dunkerk nothing more than smoldering ruins—a city never before taken by an enemy.

The scene shifted to one of roiling darkness that slithered into every crevice of her being; a putrid presence of absolute evil. She witnessed an army of black wraiths wielding the depraved mage'ic. Demons raped the landscape of Etharia, destroying and massacring everything in their path. They ravaged and depleted the world of all that was good until only pain, ruin and death remained.

Suna crumpled to the ground and sobbed.

Then the mage'ic left her as suddenly as it had invaded, but still she shivered uncontrollably. Forcing her eyes open, the stark sunlight scorched away her sight, but not the images she'd just seen. They'd been seared into her soul.

In a fog-like stupor, she attended to the meaningless chores around the quiet glen she called home for the last thirty-odd years. Her head throbbed. Even chewing a handful of zelato leaves refused to ease the unrelenting thudding in her skull.

Worse of all, those horrid visions haunted her every step and refused to give her peace.

And one question consistently niggled at her: *Who has found me?*

As she repaired a damaged portion of thatch on the roof of her small cottage, the usually warm, serene winds that blew in from the south now carried the stink of something left rotting in the sun.

Here in Kanora she thought she'd be safe, secreted away from the outside realms. Now her world had been splintered apart, and she knew not who or why.

She picked wild mushrooms and beets for dinner, even though she had no appetite. The urge to glance over her shoulder never ceased. She despised the unyielding pull of stalking eyes.

For the rest of the day, her uneasiness festered. Her headache intensified. When a fiery magenta sunset filled the western sky, exhaustion sent her straight to bed.

As she fell into a deep slumber, the stranger came again, but this time he whispered words of hope instead of despair. She sensed a familiarity in the strands of mage'ic that wound around her, but far too long had she hoped she wasn't the last of her kind. Her Divenean ties had been severed by her own volition. She'd tossed aside duty and the three gods she'd once served for reasons of her own, yet she sensed he knew of her failings and they were inconsequential.

Feel the shifting of the soil and sands. Follow the subtle hints it leaves behind. The knowledge it reveals," the voice explained. *The strength contained here has persevered for centuries. It has always been a Divenean's inherent duty to guide and protect the people of Etharia. This is your destiny. Do not deny who and what you are. Listen closely, Suna Di'Viao… not with your ears, but with your heart. Long have you hidden, but no more.*

You've made a grave mistake, she argued. *I'm not the person you're looking for. My powers won't help you. Find someone stronger. Someone who won't let you down. Aren't there others you can haunt?*

For many years she'd wondered if any of her kind still existed, but she'd sensed no others like her, nor heard from her Fold again. It'd been a wayward hope that she'd clung to like a piece of driftwood in a churning sea of solitude. Then again, it wasn't like she'd gone out and searched for them.

When only silence followed, she prayed the stranger had vanished, until...

Without you there is only oblivion.

The stranger's voice grew fainter until it was nothing but a lingering ghost whose presence on this plane of reality was destined to fade.

Go to the city of Odarian.

This was utter madness. But no matter how much she wanted to disbelieve, instincts told her that all would come to fruition if she denied this summons. She was born of a race that couldn't ignore such impending horror. And if no other Divenean existed, then this task fell upon her shoulders and hers alone.

No matter where she attempted to hide, duty bound her to these lands. It would find her no matter where she hid. The sole purpose of her existence was as a protector of Etharia. She couldn't deny it any more than if she could stop breathing.

Go to Bailor's Inn. You will find an ally in the madness about to transpire.

A shimmery image of a man's features passed through her mind like a sigh on the wind. She had little fondness for cities or their inhabitants anymore, preferring the isolated life she'd chosen. The life she deserved.

As if reading her thoughts, the stranger replied. *You will never be alone again, Suna Di'Viao. This I promise.*

His final words endured long after he faded into oblivion.

CHAPTER THREE

Against the backdrop of a smokeless campfire, the old man appeared unaware of who hid behind the thick copse.

Something about this traveler's scent piqued Isafel's interest.

So he watched.

He waited.

He assessed.

The surrounding leaves, once vibrant and green, fell in the presence of his evil mist. Fluttering to the dew-covered grass, they withered and died like everything else that crossed his path.

Strange though it was, something elusive whispered through the dark canals of the demon's mind. Something familiar. Something painful. With it came an uneasiness. Isafel had little use for memories or emotions, and faint though it was, a wariness crept over him; however, curiosity drew him closer.

"You shall come no further," the old man ordered.

Isafel froze for a breath of time, stunned that this man-thing dare speak to him in such a manner. He manipulated his dark mage'ic out from the mist of his body to ensnare and question the stranger who raised these perplexing thoughts. Afterwards he'd feast upon the human's soul.

But as soon as his corruption touched upon the warmth of the human flesh, his spell curved inward and vanished.

Hissing in fury, Isafel rushed forward, but a mage'ical force held him stationary. In the deepest, darkest recesses of his mind, a voice took hold.

"You will leave. Now."

Only one race had the gall, and power, to do this. Sudden recognition of who sat before the fire clouded all judgment. With a deafening howl, Isafel broke the spell and lunged forward, eager to claim vengeance for his thousand year imprisonment by that damnable Divenean race.

He got no more than a few feet before a sphere of pure, blinding light trapped him within its center. Intense heat saturated every inch of his cold, dead body, weakening and shriveling his mage'ical abilities like the leaves littering the ground beneath him. Crippling pain thrashed through his filmy body like a relentless storm. A pain he recognized—and had escaped.

A Divenean! Those mages have all but vanished.

"Our time has not yet come, dark minion. Leave now or suffer the consequences."

Isafel stopped his struggles. "You would set me free?" He snarled in disbelief and waited for the deception. *He will not destroy me?*

"I have neither the time nor the will to deal with you now." Without turning, the man flicked his wrist over his shoulder.

Isafel hurled through the bleak sky like a shooting star. As he soared, he screeched out his unbridled rage.

* ~ * ~ *

Karel despised expelling such wanton energy. He'd sensed the demon watching him for some time, but refused to make the first move. Still recovering from his recent channeling, this visit from Balthazar's minion didn't bode well with his already stretched thin disposition. He had only to look once at that vile creature's skeletal face and there would have been no holding back his fury—he would have destroyed the odious servant where he stood.

He'd worked too long placing these pieces meticulously together. As much as Karel loathed releasing him, Isafel's role in the scheme of things to come had not yet come into play. The gamble he'd placed upon Etharia was out of his hands.

Fate now ruled the future.

He threw another piece of wood into the fire and thought about his dreams that had tormented him far longer than he cared to admit. He should have listened to the warnings sooner. If it meant allowing evil to wander recklessly in the world for a little while longer, so be it. He vowed to see this to the end.

As he glanced up at the luminous crescent moon, he beseeched the gods to guide and protect those he'd carefully chosen, for they too had parts to play in what was about to transpire—the two who bore the heaviest of burdens.

The Divenean and the Guardian.

I should have told her.

It was for this reason he ensured Suna wouldn't be alone.

Sleep was a long time coming for Karel Di'Vennor.

* ~ * ~ *

Isafel hurled through the ebony skies until the distance between him and the mage was enough to weaken the bands of mage'ic that bound him. When the spell shattered like frozen glass, he shrieked out his defiance into the empty night. Flocks of silver senthals burst upward from the trees below, their startled screams responding to the sudden violence resonating in the air. With a sweep of his arm, they plummeted to the ground like burning stars, their feathers in flames, and every one dead.

Somewhat satiated at the loss of unimportant life, he floated to the ground. *Another Divenean? That accursed race is no more.*

Once freed from his prison, he'd searched for revenge, but not a whiff of a Divenean did he find. It was their spells that had held him and Master captive. With them gone, how else was he able to destroy his prison and escape?

Vengeance had been so close. *The mage could have destroyed me. Why set me free?*

A familiar tightening of evil filaments coiled and twisted repulsively around his awareness. Choking. Suffocating.

Balthazar's depraved voice moved through his mind. *You have delayed, Isafel. Do not fail me.*

Isafel knew whom Master spoke of. Unfortunately, the Guardian was now out of reach. There would be others, true, but that soldier he'd so carefully chosen had been an impeccable human to consume and manipulate. Something about the man called to him like a siren. Alas, such pleasures would have to wait. He had other tasks that needed attending.

To appease his frustration, he set the forest below to flame before vanishing in search of better prey.

CHAPTER FOUR

It was several days later when Suna made camp about a league from the towering gates of Odarian. She wondered, and not for the first time, how she was to fulfill a quest she didn't understand. Whenever she closed her eyes, those visions rushed through her with a cold, merciless foreboding. It tagged after her, nudging and prodding her closer to her destination. She didn't have to like this decision, but since she'd left the safety of her glen, the disquiet she sensed in the winds only confirmed the warning she'd received.

In the isolation of her private glen, she hadn't noticed the world had changed. Or perhaps it she who had.

Crouching on a small rise overlooking the Tamara Pass, which entranced the towering foliage of the Zandarian Forest, twilight faded into depthless night. No stars dotted the opaque sky and the silence hung like an unnatural hum, hastening the unease she'd felt since beginning this journey.

As shadows thickened and settled around her, an oppressive weight added to the heaviness already pressing on her soul. Although some things appeared unchanged in her absence, she sensed the crackling of something demented lingering in the air—ancient mage'ic that twisted and danced like dry parchment caught in a flame.

Such things have no business in this world.

She concentrated her inner sight to the west, where stagnant mist hovered above the marshy horizon bordering the mountains; to the east, mustard sands blew like listless apparitions across a desert-like terrain. The differences between the two landscapes was bewildering enough, but to a Divenean it confirmed that something more lay beneath the surface.

An ebbing of tides to come.

"Well, Suna," she grumbled under her breath. "It's the reason why you're here, isn't it?"

The burn of leg cramps brought her back to reality. She rose and stretched out aching muscles. She'd covered at least a league and a half this day, bringing her that much closer to the gates of Odarian.

She gathered some brittle twigs and picked several tufts of dried tinder moss to kindle a semi-smokeless fire. The wool blanket she draped over her shoulders scratched her skin and did little to keep out the approaching evening chill.

After a meager dinner of dried mushrooms, garroots and beets, she settled down next to the fire, but sleep refused to come. The image of a strange key kept her awake as it had since agreeing to this asinine quest.

She rolled onto her back and stared up at the night sky, lost in her thoughts.

A Divenean's foremost duty was the protection of these lands and its people. No matter how hard she'd hid from her past, duty had found her. She'd been a fool to think otherwise. The stranger with the mage'ic words and visions had lacerated her, adding to wounds permanently engraved on an already scarred soul.

As she lay within her blankets, her fire nothing but glowing embers, she tried to relax. Then, just on the cusp sleep, her instincts stirred.

In the stillness of the night, a subtle sound of movement on her left roused her awareness. She cracked open an eye and peered through the gloom.

The intruder stood upright about four feet tall and gnarled like some ancient oak.

Easing out the dagger she slept with into the palm of her hand, she feigned a mumble and rolled over. The creature stopped. Long, torrid minutes passed before she heard him begin to close the distance.

Adrenaline coursed through her as she leapt to her feet, turning in its direction with fluid agility. She had her dagger poised beneath its thick throat before it had a chance to cry out. A rancid stench burned her nostrils and almost made her retch the contents of her meager dinner.

"Say who you are or you'll die," she hissed.

Labored, raspy breathing came as a reply. Although small in stature, she sensed its iron muscles tighten. Unsure as to whether she could physically wrangle with it, Suna released her quarry, threw the blade to the ground and outstretched her arms.

Mage'ic snaked forth from her fingertips, ribbons of iridescent light that bound the misshapen creature into bands of conjured iron. Before her spell touched him, the imp held up its twisted arms like a shield. Stunned, she watched her spell dissolve as soon as it touched the mutant's pale flesh. *What manner of creature is this that can defend itself against my power? Have I become so weak?*

She formed her hands into a partial circle and devised a ball of air in which to ensnare the creature. It became immobilized for mere seconds before her spell dissipated into nothing. Alarmed by its uncanny ability to defend itself against her gifts, she waited for an opportunity.

The creature gave a cheeky grin.

Suna staggered back a step at the malice in its eyes. Now she wished she'd picked up her sword instead of the dagger. She didn't need to read its mind to know it meant to kill her.

As nonchalantly as possible she bent, snatched a handful of dirt and waited.

The creature circled her, sniffing the air through the green mucus that flowed freely from a nose that looked more like a snout. Death reeked from its every pore.

This spawn was an abomination to the lands.

As it shuffled closer, Suna saw her opening. She lunged and threw the handful of dirt into its face. With it momentarily blinded, she raced for her pack and grabbed her rope, muttering a spell to bind the fibers.

The imp spun and faced her, his gaze blazing with hatred.

She ran full tilt and jumped. The bottom of her boot landed solidly against its bloated forehead. The neck popped back. Bones snapped. The gruesome sound echoed in the sudden silence that followed.

The imp wobbled and turned, its bulbous head hanging at an awkward angle, but it was still breathing. Its eyes, however, were filled with pain.

Will nothing stop this thing? With it somewhat disorientated, Suna wrapped the rope around the creature and knotted it. She then threw it to the ground like a rat-filled sack of moldy grain.

It grunted once, but didn't fight, as if aware of the spell she'd encased in the rope. The more he'd move, the tighter the strands would become.

He lay compliant, spitting out dirt that formed a slimy puddle onto the ground by his twisted head.

She wiped a layer of his sticky phlegm off her forearm and shuddered. With a twist of her mind, she willed her dying fire to life. Now she truly saw what lay at her feet.

This land professed many different forms of life, but this thing? It had to have been birthed from the very fires of condemnation.

The creature lay docile except for the occasional grunt and labored breathing. Although not quite human, it was easy to discern its male attributes.

Ill-sewn burlap cloth covered stout legs that were of different lengths. The filthy shirt of cheap woven gauze reached his knees to hide his short but wide torso. Piss stains darkened the fabric in front of the crotch. A large hump stretched from one shoulder to another. Dwarf-like arms bent at odd angles, and fine, gray hair like molten ash covered his misshapen head. His face consisted of mismatched bones, as if someone had beaten him so severely that they'd healed like a permanent deformed puzzle.

This aberration of life came into existence as he was now—not a birthed creature of nature. In retrospect, he looked like something a feeble-minded infant had created out of clay.

"Say your name," she demanded, unable to keep the revulsion from her voice.

Green slime continued to ooze from his nose. When his tongue snaked out and lapped at what had dripped onto his lips, she shuddered again. Both his cheeks were speckled with the disgusting stuff.

When he answered, his voice held a nasally, child-like cadence. "I meant no harm."

He refused to make eye contact, which unnerved her. Merely looking at him made her struggle to keep the contents of her dinner down where it belonged. "Why were you skulking around my camp?"

"Food. I was looking for food."

Suna dug the toe of her boot painfully into his ribs. "Say your name!"

He offered a sullen pout.

She dug at him again.

"I... I'm Ilio."

She folded her arms across her chest and glared. "And where do you hail from, Ilio?"

When he refused to answer again, she prompted him with another painful kick.

"No memory," he mumbled.

The defiance in his tone was difficult to miss. Suna conjured her quickening, a unique form of her mage'ic which enabled her to see a person's élan. In horror, she peered at the creature's distorted aura of tempered shades of gray and black roiling together like a maelstrom. Reeling from the evil she sensed, she strove to move her mind closer to discover its origins. With a startled hiss, she drew back, nauseated by being that close to its vileness.

So it's begun. Can I let him go with a clean conscience knowing what he is? The dark gifts created this creature, but do they rule him? Who would do this? And more importantly, why? What has this Ilio done wrong except come into existence?

Reluctantly, she released her mage'ic with a laden sign. *The world has most certainly changed in my absence.*

"What shall I do with you now?" she murmured.

However malformed his ears were, he heard every word. "I did you no wrong,"

Undercurrents of contempt lingered in his words. She'd crown herself queen before she'd trust this loathsome creature. "You'll be traveling with me to the city of Odarian."

Did she dare bring him within Lord Mollster's walls? But what choice did she have? Perhaps it was just as well. Ilio's fate would be decided by someone other than herself.

Saying nothing more, she picked him up like a festive goose and carried him to a blackbirch tree a safe distance from her camp. Grunting from the effort, she pushed his twisted back into the knotted bark, all the while whispering halting spells in the strands of the rope to ensure the fibers didn't crush any vital organs.

When he was safely secured, she stood and snapped her wrist left. The rope tightened. She enforced the spell stronger than necessary. Something about the imp felt *wrong*. Instincts screamed to kill him outright, but he'd done nothing wrong except try to appease his hunger.

Still, she couldn't help but wonder what kind of food he'd been foraging for.

She returned to her pack and retrieved a piece of beebread. When she attempted to feed him, he spit it into her face.

Nothing is ever easy, she thought with a heavy heart. She returned to her blanket and settled down to catch whatever hours of sleep she could before sunrise.

∼∼*

Ilio tried to remain as still as possible as he searched for a chink in the spell binding the rope. All the while he fumed. *How dare she do this? I wanted one finger. Just one. She has many.*

No. This wasn't part of the plan. He should have stayed away, but for the painful rumblings in his guts that had plagued him for three days, he'd made a mistake.

Like a fleeting caress, he sensed the approach of a familiar presence. The forbidding voice screeched into every dark crevice of Ilio's mind.

Master will not be pleased.

The imp cringed. *Why have you come?*

Phaaa! Humans are so predictable.

Chills sped up and down Ilio's crooked spine.

But you? You were created of better things.

Master's angry with me? He tried to stay still, but he couldn't stop shaking. The rope tightened. If he didn't calm down, he'd soon be unable to breathe.

Isafel's shadow moved like gelatinous oil through Ilio's mind, infesting every corner so that nothing belonged to him anymore.

Master has plans for you. This you know.

The rope then loosened and dropped soundlessly to the ground. Ilio almost sobbed with relief.

You will fulfill that which he has commanded of you. Now go! I grow weary of this tedium child-sitting.

The imp jumped to his club feet and stopped with a glare in Suna's direction. *Let me have her. Just a taste.*

Do you have wool for brains?

He cowered. Isafel sat at the right-hand of Master. As such, he demanded immediate obedience.

No harm is to come to her, Isafel explained. *Not yet, anyway. Master has other plans for her. Now obey me.*

The demon shadow disappeared from his mind as fast as he'd arrived. Assured that Isafel was truly gone, Ilio turned back to the woman. A small bite couldn't hurt. If she screamed, he'd leave her breathing—barely.

Before he took a step in the human's direction, he was suddenly face-first on the ground unable to move. Every muscle in his body went rigid and burned as if his insides were on fire. The agony was unbearable. Tears trickled down his cheeks as he gasped for air.

Isafel's silky, malicious voice returned, taunting him with increased bouts of pain so intense that even breathing became torture.

You dare disobey?

The shadow released him and with it, the pain. Ilio jumped to his feet and ran from the camp as fast as his contorted legs could carry him.

* ~ * ~ *

Suna woke the next morning to find the creature gone and her rope lying limp on the ground with nary a cut on it. The hairs on the nape of her neck stood on end. There were few in the lands that had the power to nullify a Divenean's mage'ic, and even fewer still that could do it without her being aware. Now she truly regretted her decision—she should have destroyed the little miscreant.

He had every chance to kill me and take what he wanted. Why didn't he? Well, I'll certainly not make this mistake twice.

She snatched her pack off the ground and began to walk, more determined than ever to reach her destination and be done with this damn quest.

CHAPTER FIVE

Suna passed through Odarian's city gates amidst the claustrophobic crowds and a myriad of foul smells that grabbed her like a noose around her throat.

In the distance, on the tallest turret of the castle, the standard of Odarian moved sinuously in the breeze—two emerald hands grasped together and wrapped with red vines and thorns on a light grey background. It had been a long time since she'd seen this particular standard, or any of the other five kingdoms.

Carefully dodging freshly dropped dung from horses, she wrinkled her nose at the onion-like smell of human sweat. People jostled and pushed her rudely out of the way without so much as a glance or an apology.

She'd just arrived and already she yearned for the quiet simplicity of her glen. Tugging down the rim of her hood, she forced her feet forward.

Since beginning this journey, she'd sensed the unbalancing of the lands. And Ilio had confirmed her worse fears. Where he was now was anyone's guess, although she had an uncanny sense she'd be meeting him again.

The air, although currently entwined with the stench of a city, smelled corrupt, like some kind of malevolence was attempting to bully its way through the undercurrents of life.

She squinted through eye-watering stenches at the confusing crisscrossing pattern of streets and the numerous shopkeepers standing outside brightly painted establishments screaming out prices for the various wares they sold. Haphazardly dressed children with dirt-streaked faces ran in wild abandon, screeching louder than the vendors. Horse drawn carts moved at unhurried paces, blocking her path repeatedly.

Frustrated, Suna crashed into the back of a heavyset man who'd stepped out in front of her.

"Excuse me, sir?" she asked, tapping his shoulder.

When he turned, his bloodshot gaze leered over her. A slow, sly grin curled the corners of his mouth.

She took a step back, her left hand instinctively reaching up and resting on the pommel of her sword hidden beneath the folds of her red, dusty cloak. To a marked swordsman, the gesture should have initiated a responding defensive stance, but this man was no swordsman. However, he was no less dangerous either.

"Well now, where might you be heading, sweet little thing," he said. His sour breath of cheap ale and a lifetime of garlic wafted across her face. Bits of last week's dinner still clung to his unkempt beard. When he grinned, she saw his two front teeth were black with rot.

His display of ill manners sickened her more than his appearance, but she needed information. Worse was the harsh intensity in his eyes that held more than mere appreciation of her womanly form. She sensed the lingering effects of koffea in his system, an herb that's either smoked or ingested to create a euphoric state of mind.

The little voice inside told her to walk away, but she needed directions. "I wonder if you might tell me where to find Bailor's Inn?" she asked as politely as she could muster.

A koffea addict was known to make its user unpredictable, so she took several more steps back and balanced onto the balls of her feet.

"Now why would you wanna go to a place like that, little girl. I got me a better inn. There you can dance on the table and make me rich." He made a move in her direction.

She held her ground. "Sir, if you would be so kind—"

"That I'm not known for," he growled and grabbed for her arm.

Suna pulled out her sword with her left hand, hoping to cause as little damage as possible. Refraining from releasing mage'ic into the blade, she backhanded him across the head with the flat of its steel.

The man stumbled and blinked several times, more shocked than injured. Then he turned, furious, and charged at her.

With the grace and agility of a desert Menjio dancer, she sidestepped out of reach. He landed like a boulder onto the street, but quickly jumped to his feet, moving faster than she thought possible for someone his size. In his meaty hands, he brandished a deadly honed knife. His bloodshot eyes burned with violence.

Realizing he was now intent on harming her, she released a touch of power into her blade to give her arm more strength.

With Ilio, Suna had discovered her mage'ic had weakened, which was just as well. No one would be able to tell what she was other than an experienced swordswoman. Still, she was drawing a crowd, for there were few swordswomen in the lands.

Many onlookers were curious about the tiny woman who had the audacity to defend herself against such a brute of a man. Others watched for the sheer entertainment of bloodshed. Scuffles of this nature would bring guards. And soon.

She drew her cloak like a shield around her and bounced her sword into her right hand. Crouching, she waited.

Filled with reckless anger, the man lunged at her, swinging his knife in a clumsy attempt to open her guts. She leaned to the left and swung her blade up. The clean arc of her sword cleaved his left arm off just below his shoulder. She stood on the other side of him before the severed limb hit the ground, his lifeless hand still clenching his knife.

A unified gasp rose from the gathered throng, followed by several daunting seconds of silence. All eyes turned to her. Suddenly, voices pealed in the distance.

Hellfire. Guards!

As panic ensued, she searched for an escape.

Her adversary stood stone-still as the confusion erupted around him. When he fell to his knees, she turned and ran, but she sensed his shocked stare boring into her back.

Suna disappeared into the mayhem of the crowd. She ran until the clusters of people grew thin before she forced herself to a brisk walk, packing away her cloak into the small travel sack slung across her back as she went. She regretted using mage'ic within Odarian's walls, but she'd been left with little choice… even if it had been just a small spell.

The rashness of her decision had surprised her, but that little voice inside warned it wouldn't be the last time. She needed her identity to remain a secret for as long as possible.

As she continued walking north, the bawdy taverns and shops became tidy residences and stores with a respectable inn scattered in between, obviously a more affluent neighborhood. The nauseating smells she'd encountered earlier soon disappeared. After stopping a kind-looking woman, she asked for directions to the inn.

It was another five blocks before a sign caught her eye. Shaped like a bell with white lettering that read *Bailor's Inn*, it hung above a brightly painted red door.

She passed through the entrance and paused to admire the cleanliness of the large drinking room with gleaming tables of lacquered snakewood occupied by a few patrons and a musician playing a lute in the corner of a small stage. Directly in front of her, behind a massive bar, stood a giant of a man with red cheeks and an incessant smile that crinkled the corners of his blue eyes. As she approached, he greeted her with a gracious nod.

"I would like a room, please. And a bath. Preferably as hot as you can get it. I assume you're Master Bailor?" She wearily slid a silver dellion across the burnished bar. "I don't know how long I'll be staying. I'm waiting for someone."

The innkeeper's rumbling reply accompanied his easy-going smile. "I'm indeed Cam Bailor, at your service, m'lady. Waiting seems to be the thing to do these days," he said with an incorrigible wink. "I've had him here for three days doing the same, amongst other things that a lady like you shouldn't be privy to."

Suna's gaze followed Bailor's toward the drinking room where a man leaned back against the wall, relaxing on two legs of a chair. From a pipe perched like a reed of grass at the corner of his mouth, a white cloud of smoke swelled above the stranger's head.

Suna had found her ally.

CHAPTER SIX

Feran despised the symphony of pounding anvils in his head. And entirely his fault, too. When would he learn to stop drinking like a fool? Obviously, never.

He cracked open an eye and squinted against the stark morning light creeping through the slats of the inn's small window. With a groan, he eased himself up on his elbows and waited for the sea of nausea to stop churning in his guts. Sendra, the delightful serving wench who'd waited on him the night before, was gone from his room, but a torn remnant of her bodice that hadn't freed itself quickly enough for him lay on the floor as evidence of the fun he'd had and was now paying dearly for.

The memory of last night's tryst made him attempt a smile, but he ended up swallowing a mouthful of bile instead. Grimacing on the sour taste, he swung his legs over the side of the bed, planted his bare feet on the floor and cradled his head in his hands, vowing for the hundredth time never to drink again.

He stood, swayed and waited for the familiar light-headedness to pass. When it had somewhat subsided, he took a tentative step forward. He'd fallen once before trying to attempt this feat in a similar condition and the small scar above his right eye was evidence to the fact. Self-inflicted wounds like those were difficult to explain, especially when achieved by sheer stupidity.

Another day had passed and his mysterious companion was still a no-show. For three days and nights, all he'd done was eat, drink, bed a few wenches—and wait. If this didn't stop soon, his new occupation would be Cam's tavern jester.

"What in the devil's lair am I doing here?" he grumbled past the throbbing between his eyes.

The chill in the air made him remember his nakedness. He managed a step toward the dresser when pain exploded in the big toe he'd just stubbed on his scabbard. "Bullocks and bitches!" He picked up his weapon and threw it onto the bed.

When he reached the basin, he splashed the chill water onto his face. The stinging shock of reality numbed what few remaining brain cells he had left. "I'm bloody well retired. I answer to no one but me. Then why are you here, you ijit?"

Shaking his head, he turned away from the pale reflection in the looking glass on the dresser and dried his face. "Now I'm talking to myself."

Strange as it was, he'd undertaken this quest of his own volition. His conscience had agreed to it, not him. Then there were those nightmares of his. "If I had better sense, I'd tuck tail out of here and not look back."

Frustrated, he searched the sheets for his clothes. He knew it would be another night of drinking in order to quell the 'other' dream that had now come to haunt him.

* ~ * ~ *

With a small twig he'd taken from the bottom of a broom leaning against the wall beside him, Feran picked at a fragment of Sellie's delicious spiced beef that had gotten stuck between his teeth and emitted a satisfied burp in the process. His hangover had now dulled to a livable ache in between his eyes. He'd switched to mulled wine in the hope of easing some of the discomfort he'd been experiencing the last couple of mornings from Cam's potent black mead.

As the bard played his lute softly in the background, he heard the musician's cup clinked as a patron threw in a coin.

Feran filled his pipe and reflected on the music. *Almost good enough for court,* he mused.

He placed the end of the twig into the lit candle on the table and brought the small flame to his pipe. He watched it dance as if in time to the bard's clever notes. When he exhaled, a thick cloud of sweet, pungent pipe weed filled the space above his head. Sighing contentedly, he waved the twig in the air to extinguish it, placed it on the table and resumed his usual waiting. The door to the inn opened and through the haze of smoke he saw a woman enter.

Tiny and graceful in stature, supple leather boots rose to her slender knees. Her form-fitting breeches of brushed brown hide matched a jerkin that laced neatly across a small, but curvaceous chest. Her bare arms revealed well-honed muscles.

His attention strayed to her left thigh, but not in appreciation of her womanly form, although from his vantage that was indeed impressive, but rather at the scabbard and sword that hung comfortably off her hip. Women didn't customarily wear weapons, at least not in public view. Being a seasoned soldier, he wondered where she'd obtained such a fine piece of weaponry.

As she approached the bar to speak with Cam, he watched her mannerisms and the way she carried herself. He had little doubt she knew how to use that weapon, and use it well.

An authoritative confidence exuded from her. Faren couldn't hear her words, but soft, feminine undertones reached his ears. Sensing his eyes upon her, the woman turned and stared directly at him. His heart lurched in his chest the instant their gazes met. A spark from his tobac flew into the air and landed squarely on his pants. He brushed away the ember before it burned a hole and proceeded to place his pipe on the table.

Now this is going to be interesting.

Without an invitation, she approached and seated herself across from him, pausing to glance over her shoulder at the door before focusing on him.

Now that's a familiar habit, he thought as he followed her line of vision to the entrance and back.

He squinted to study her as shrewdly as she studied him. The scrutinizing heat of her dove-blue eyes singed him. It was as if she was memorizing every flaw he had, and possibly any future ones. He'd be the first to admit that he certainly wasn't much to look at, but appearances were deceiving. And indeed, she sat before him as a perfect testament to that fact.

In silence, he met her steely stare with a blasé nod. Then he felt it. A definite surge of energy rustling in the air around him. *A mage?* Whatever she'd seen made those beautiful, full lips of hers thin. That intrigued him to find out why.

"You're late," he said as he righted his chair down onto its four legs. He picked up his pipe, relit the tobac, took a deep breath, and exhaled a large plume of smoke toward the ceiling. *Now why in the Seven Hells would I be allied with her?*

The woman took a cursory stare around the room. "I encountered an, um, obstacle along the way."

He stood and pushed back his chair. The wooden legs screeched across the planked floor. "I don't want to talk about… you know, here. Let's go for a walk." He tapped out his pipe and placed it into the red velvet bag attached to his belt.

She bolted to her feet. "I'd rather we not do that."

"Something wrong?" he asked, trying not to grin.

"It has to do with the obstacle I just mentioned. I don't think it's a good idea if I'm seen right now." She pursed her lips and refused to say more.

What kind of trouble could she have gotten into if she'd only just arrived? She exuded an innocence, but in a dark, mysterious package that took his breath away. He'd never met a woman like her and his need to know more had planted its seed.

"Do tell." He resumed his seat and waited for her to begin.

She sighed and recounted her encounter with a brute he knew all too well. When she finished, he whistled between his teeth. *Blood and guts. How did she take Mellor on and win?*

He shook his head. There was definitely more to her than meets the eye. "Okay, let me flutter a guess here. Big guy? Bushy beard? Rotting teeth? Smells like a soiled nappy?"

The woman nodded, her eyes widening at the accuracy of his description.

He blew out a sigh. "That'll be Mellor Bunderman. Unfortunately, the guards aren't going to be your biggest worry." Leaning close, he lowered his voice. "He has friends, strange as that may sound. If he survived, there's going to be retribution. First things first. You're going to have to change how you look."

She blinked several times before mustering, "Excuse me?"

He eyed her up down. "You're about a four, right?"

She leaned back in her chair with a scowl. "A four what?"

"Size."

"I'm a two, but who's measuring?"

Feran tried not to chuckle. *A slight touchy, she is.* "Go upstairs to your room. I'll be back shortly." He stood and leaned close. "Bailor will have to be told of this."

She started to stand, but he pushed her gently downward into her chair. "Don't worry. He's a good man. He and I are old friends. Your secret's safe, I promise. We'll need an extra set of eyes to keep a lookout for Mellor's associates. They're well known around the inns and their proprietors for, how shall I put it, their upstanding manners?" He scratched his head. "You know, it was only a matter of time before someone bested Mellor. I'm just a little surprised it was you. I'll be back before you know it."

* ~ * ~ *

As Feran navigated the streets of the garment district for one particular dress shop, he mulled over the strange encounter. The more he thought on it, the more baffled he became. *If she's a mage, then what am I needed for? What's my purpose in all this? And more importantly, what exactly can she do with that mage'ic of hers?*

A sense of impending doom worse than any of his nightmares chivied his every step.

CHAPTER SEVEN

Suna watched the man stop and share an intimate conversation with Master Bailor before exiting the inn. As the door closed behind him, she realized they hadn't exchanged names, nor did she have any idea where her room was located. She rose and made her way back to the bar.

Master Bailor stopped his cleaning of a glass and smiled. That toothy grin of his warmed her heart. "Could you direct me to my room?"

He pointed toward the back of the inn. "Down the hallway on your left there. You'll see some stairs. Follow them up. Your room is the last door on the left beside the staircase leading outside. One of my gals is filling a tub for you now."

She didn't know this man from a burrow hole, yet she sensed she could trust him. A stranger willing to keep a secret safe for someone he or she didn't know was a rare find indeed. She murmured her thanks and went to find her lodgings.

As she climbed the stairs, her thoughts strayed to her companion on this mysterious quest. She found herself drawn to him in a peculiar way. His square jaw and angled features created a ruggedly handsome picture. His shoulders were broad and well defined, almost soldier-like. Next to her, he stood a full head taller, which was odd as she was considered taller than most of her analogous persuasion.

More unusual was the authoritative air that flowed about him; a man who is used to giving orders and having them followed without question, even though he looked like nothing more than a drunken vagabond. When she'd used her quickening, she'd floundered in chaos at what she'd seen. The swirling rings of fiery reds mixed with amber and bolts of greens and an array of earthly browns and taupe's were nothing short of astounding. Only once had she'd seen a similar aura, but never so many hues in one person before.

This now made two peculiar viewings.

The more she thought about him, the more she came to realize that he and Master Bailor were gems cast in a sea of sand. Both rare finds indeed. No matter how dark and dismal her thoughts had been of late, hope managed to find a crevice and push its way through.

She found her room just as a young maiden was scurrying out the door. After administering an awkward curtsy, the lass turned and raced down the hallway without so much as a backward glance. Suna stepped through the door to find a welcoming copper tub on wheels situated by a small window, its pane of glass filmed with fine mist from the steam rising from the water. The subtle vapor of freshly gathered rose petals and jasmine imbued the small but tidy room. She breathed deep, closed the door, locked it, and undressed.

After placing her sword on the floor within easy reach, she eased her body into the almost scalding water and submerged herself completely. Soon, the dust and aches of her travels dissolved away.

She soaked until the water cooled and her skin had pruned. A knock sounded at the door as she was drying herself off. Wrapping a sheet around her body, she moved cautiously to the door. "Yes?"

"I've got something for you."

She recognized the voice and opened the door a crack.

The stranger's mischievous grin greeted her. He pushed a tissue wrapped package in between the small space and stood back. "I'll meet you downstairs when you're… properly attired." The sound of his whistling faded as he left down the hallway.

She relocked the door with a rueful shake of her head and took the package to the bed. Her blade cut effortlessly through the strings holding the packet closed. Nestled inside was a simple cotton dress of muted saffron. She donned the garment. To her surprise, she found it fit perfectly, although the neckline was a tad low for her liking.

Finding a dress was a simple enough task, but one that fit her tall build was a little unsettling. She then caught sight of herself in the looking glass by the dresser.

With a sigh, she sat down at the dressing table and began the tedious job of brushing out her hair. In order to conceal its length, she created one thick plait and wrapped it like a crown on top of her head. She worked tenaciously with the fickle pins she'd found in one of the drawers, remembering a time when handmaidens attended to this chore—the memories of a previous life she didn't miss. When she finished, she stared critically at her reflection. Now she looked like any other pampered city dweller.

She turned away from the mirror and made her way downstairs.

* ~ * ~ *

Feran waited for her at his usual table. With the smell of honey roasted onions and stewed spiced beef wafting out from the kitchen area, he wondered whether his guest was hungry. Taking a man's arm off, especially someone like Mellor, would have spiked his appetite for sure.

When the woman came down the stairs and crossed the room, every male in the room turned her way.

Whoa, she cleans up pretty good. As she approached the table, he stood and dipped his head. "I see I measured your size accurately." He eyed her up and down before settling on the two delightful mounds of pale flesh trying to push their way out of the gathered bodice.

Just as a flush crept into the woman's cheeks, Cam Bailor's wife, Sellie, stood at the side of their table.

"Well lookie what the timbercat dragged in," Sellie drawled. Her blue eyes were larger than her husband, but they glowed just as bright and warm as Cam's did. "You favor us with your beauty, you do. You must be hungry, child. There's a fresh pot of stew—"

"The best you've ever tasted," Feran cut in.

Sellie slapped him firmly across his shoulder. "Let me finish talking, you scamp." She shifted around to the woman. "You be wary of this one, girl. Mark my words. His charms have landed him in more hot water than he'd care to confess."

With a theatrical roll of his eyes, he placed his hands over his heart. "You've wounded me, Sellie."

"Thank you. The stew will be fine," Suna replied.

The bar keeper's matronly figure jiggled with laughter as she made her way toward the kitchen.

"Feel better?" He kept his tone moderately subdued. After all, they had important things to discuss. He wished he could stop staring at her hair and the way the light danced within its dark copper-like strands.

"Yes. Thank you. How much do I owe you for the dress?"

"Nothing. Call it a gift for what you did to Mellor."

He paused, wondering how to tell her about the trails of gossip that had followed him back to the inn. Even in here he'd heard snippets about the woman who'd bested that ruffian. Bending his head closer to the table, he spoke softly. "You've caused quite a stir."

She leaned back, her eyes narrowing.

"Folks are wagging their tongues about a wisp of a girl who took off Mellor's arm. And no," he added with a grimace. "He wasn't fatally wounded, contrary to what many hoped."

Glancing inconspicuously around the room, he noted the drinking room was filling fast with regular evening patrons. The lute player had taken a break and was now sitting on the edge of the small stage nursing a foamy glass of ale. Raucous voices and boisterous laughter filtered through the tavern, which would make their conversation impossible to overhear, but he wasn't taking any chances. What they had to discuss was for their ears only.

"Might I have your name?" she asked, looking not the least bit concerned.

Sellie arrived at their table with a steaming bowl of spiced beef stew, accompanied by a heel of day old bread. "His name be Feran Lambert, and you best keep one good eye on him," she said with a friendly chuckle. "And Feran, I'll be keeping me *other* eye on you." Playfully, she scorned him with shakes of her stubby finger, Sellie paused long enough to wink before bustling away.

The woman across from him eyed him coolly from beneath the thickness of her lashes. "It seems Mellor isn't the only one with a reputation around here."

Shrugging, he looked away to study the faces of the crowd as she ate. When she finished, he noticed she'd cleaned the bowl of every drop of stew. Well, few people left any morsels on their plates when it came Sellie's cooking.

The realm of night had dropped its blanket over the city and still more people entered the inn. Even with all the noise, Feran refused to talk in a room of possible eavesdroppers. As if reading his mind, she rose. "Shall we take our walk now?"

Nodding with relief, he extended his arm out for her to take. As she threaded her hand into the crook of his arm, a strange swelling of air encompassed him. He stumbled and quickly righted himself. *What in damnation was that?* She seemed impervious to the odd occurrence.

Saying nothing for fear of sounding foolish, he placed several coppers on the table and started to lead her toward the door. Suna stopped. She scooped up the coins and dropped them back into his hand with a frown. Digging into a pocket of her dress, she pulled out a silver dellion and placed it on the table beside her empty bowl. He smirked with a sheepish roll of his shoulders.

Hoping they looked like any other ordinary couple, they headed out for an evening stroll, but he sensed heads turn to stare at the beauty on his arm. Keeping up the ruse, he took a moment to admire the fresh coat of whitewash Cam had recently applied to the exterior of the inn. "The Bailors always keep their place neat and tidy." He pointed to the myriad of thanias blooming in both bowed window wells. "Sellie's touch, of course," he added when he noticed her lingering stare. "It always feels like home when I stay here." He realized too late that he'd spoken the latter part out loud.

Without another word, he guided her north toward a garden park a short distance up the road. Several awkward minutes later, he stopped at a group of aesthetically placed boulders situated next to a gilded wrought iron bench.

"So, you are Feran Lambert. Well, Master Lambert, where do you hail from?" she asked once they were seated.

His past was his own business, and he'd had plenty of practice skirting around the subject. "Originally? South of here. Near Abbotsvale, but I call nowhere home, other than Cam and Sellie's."

"And what is it that you do, Feran Lambert?"

So, I'm not the only one trying to figure out why we've been paired together. First, he needed to know more about her. She was a mage. That much he knew. "A little bit of this. A little bit of that. You have my name. Can I have yours?"

"Suna."

"That's it? Just Suna?"

She emitted an exasperated sigh. "Just Suna."

"Well, *just* Suna, where do you hail from?"

"A small village several leagues from here. I was their wizen." She immediately stared down at her hands.

He heaved an inward sigh. *Okay. I can live with wizen mage'ic. The worst she can do is foretell a storm or fix a broken bone. That might come in handy.* "Was? Is there a reason you're not their healer anymore? Did they run you out of town for doing something wrong?"

She answered his joke with a hot glare. "Can we skip the dancing around the blackbirch and tell me what it is you're doing here?"

The thick edge of irritation in her voice was difficult to miss, so he offered her one of his infuriating smiles; the one that usually melted women's hearts. "I guess the same reason as you. Besides scaring the bejittles out of me, the dreams gave me a pounding headache for days." All amusement faded when he caught sight of a group of men moving in their direction. *Hellfire, not now.*

Putting aside all joviality, he leaned close. "I want you to do exactly what I tell you to do. Understand?" He slid his arm around the base of her back and drew her close. She stiffened like granite. He ignored the appalled look on her face and thought, *I'm going to get clubbed for doing this, but I'm sure there's worse punishments.*

Without warning, he bent and kissed those strawberry lips he'd been admiring all evening. She attempted to pull away, but he held her tight and mumbled, "Don't move."

The rumble of several heavy-footed men trotted by. When the sounds of their clinking armor faded, Feran took a quick glance over his shoulder before facing what he knew was coming. Unfortunately, anger didn't come close to describing Suna's expression. "Look, I meant no disrespect. Truly. I saw the guards coming and, well, it was the only thing I could think to do in order to hide that beautiful face of yours."

Suna's heated stare followed the retreating backs of the guards until they turned a corner and disappeared from sight. Despite the violation, her sigh sounded relieved.

Feran still felt the pressure of those delectable lips against his, and he wanted more than the mere taste he'd stolen. The stirring between his legs vanished when she swiped the back of her hand against her mouth with a grimace. His ego did a quick downward spiral. Never had a woman done that after he'd kissed them. In fact, he was usually complimented on that particular skill… amongst others.

She stood abruptly and stared down at her boots. "I think we should get back to the inn. Perhaps you're right. I need to stay out of sight for a while."

She sounded breathless, but he couldn't tell whether it was from fury or embarrassment. Either way, the blow to his self-esteem stung. *I'm getting too old for this nonsense.* "We'll at least make an appearance in the drinking room. That way, if questions are asked, they'll remember a beautiful woman instead of a wizen."

He suddenly felt awkward and unsure of himself, which was completely alien to him. With women, he considered himself quite skilled in the wooing department. Apparently not with this woman.

When she nodded, he took her arm—again that strange shifting of air surrounded them. When their eyes met, the same unspoken question lay mirrored in hers.

CHAPTER EIGHT

They hurried back to the inn to find the drinking room more crowded than before they'd left. Peals of laughter rang out, followed by a din of voices shouting for more ale or wine. Through the thick pipe smoke that now permeated the entire tavern, Suna saw two men and a serving wench now occupied their table. It was obvious the woman was serving up more than food and drink. The barmaid looked up and sent Feran a scathing scowl before turning her attention back to the guardsmen.

Ignoring the fake blatant displays of affection the woman made on the soldiers, Suna studied the throng instead. Her airways constricted at the mass of so many bodies crammed into one space. The once capacious drinking room now looked, and felt, like a closet. She wanted to discuss the strange occurrence they'd just shared when they'd touched, but not here. Suddenly, Feran's warm, calloused hand engulfed hers.

"Come on!" he shouted over the crowd. He pulled her towards the bar where she noticed Master Bailor frantically waving at them. The innkeeper tilted his head and shifted his eyes toward the back stairs. Feran tugged her behind him as he headed in that direction.

Men stared in open appreciation as she squeezed her way through their pressing bodies. An assortment of hands touched parts of her where none were privy to be. Trying to overlook the surreptitious trespassing upon her person, she concentrated on the planks of wood beneath her boots until they broke free of the rabble and were now standing by the stairs leading up to the rooms, waiting for Bailor.

The innkeeper soon joined them by politely pushing patrons out of his way. By the time he stood beside them, his face was red from exertion and beaded with sweat. His lungs bellowed as if he'd just run a distance. He maintained one eye on his customers and the other on her.

"Guards were here looking for you," he managed in between gulps of air.

Feran's gaze did an anxious sweep around the room. "What did they want?"

Bailor focused only on her. "You know what they wanted. Mellor's claiming you robbed him." His tone revealed he didn't believe a word he'd just said.

She drew back. "I—"

"I believe you, m'lady," he said with a kind smile. "But it matters not. I've had a few encounters with Mellor and his thugs myself and there's little love lost between us. I'm more than pleased you taught him a lesson. I just wish I'd been there to see it. The guards are looking for a woman dressed as a traveler carrying a rather vicious looking sword and sporting dark fiery hair. Several of my regulars saw you come in here today." He peered at the crown of hair adorning the top of her head. "It's only a matter of time before that information reaches the guards' ears." He half-turned toward the table occupied by the barmaid and her friends.

"My cloak was drawn, and—"

"Much as I'd hate to see you go," Bailor offered sadly.

Feran swore unceremoniously under his breath and grabbed her arm. "We understand, Bailor, but right now I see a bigger problem heading our way."

She peered over one of Bailor's meaty shoulders and saw four scruffy, ill-humored looking men stroll into the inn. They shoved people aside with barrel-sized arms and scowls that promised a swift beating to those who didn't comply fast enough.

"Get out of here. I got the missus to pack some provisions for you. Use the back stairs. You can pay me when we next see one another, and I'll expect that to be soon." Bailor directed the last statement at Feran.

The innkeeper turned and started toward the bar, his strides determined to rid his establishment of the disgusting vermin that had just walked in.

Feran tried to stop him. "Bailor, we need horses."

"They're waiting outside by the stable. Hurry. Go!" He didn't look back as he jostled his weight through the crowd toward the repulsive group of men.

Feran grabbed her hand and took the stairs two at a time. When they reached the hallway, he stopped. "Pack your things and meet me here. Leave the dress on. We'll need it if we're going to get out of Odarian."

With a nod, she entered her room, packed her scant belongings and stood ready and waiting in the hallway. Feran emerged from a room two doors down. With her scabbard in hand, Suna wrapped her sword within the folds of her cloak before he could see it, but she wasn't quick enough. He stumbled when he caught sight of the emblem engraved upon its hilt. She'd have some explaining to do, but he said nothing as he took her hand again and raced for the back stairs leading to the alley outside.

The cool, night air raised goosebumps across her exposed skin and she wished she'd had time to don her traveling garb.

True to Bailor's word, they found two roans saddled and waiting for them. The animals nickered heartfelt greetings. Suna paused long enough to brush her hand down the elongated nose of a spirited chestnut mare, who danced upon her hooves.

As she murmured to the animal, Feran hoisted himself up onto the saddle with an impatient glare. "Introductions can be made later."

She tried to mount, but the dress proved a hindrance. Shooting him a scathing scowl at the smirk plastered across his face, she gathered the material in front and hiked it high above her knees in a very unlady-like manner. After placing her left foot into the stirrup, she heaved herself up, dress and all. Feran's lingering stare at her exposed legs made her heart hammer inside her chest. She pursed her lips and pressed her heels into the roan's side, which sent the horse galloping, leaving Feran in a cloud of dust.

Soon unfamiliar streets widened into what looked to be the business section of Odarian.

He'd better catch up soon or there's no telling where I'll end up.

The smugness of her impetuous actions now leaned toward concern. She didn't know this city well and at this hour, few people were out. She couldn't very well stop and ask for directions.

Feran suddenly materialized beside her. "Slow her down!" he shouted over the mare's pounding hooves on the flagstones. "No attention, remember?"

She pulled in the reins. The roan lessened her strides to a more normal gait.

"Slide the dress down over your legs."

Her scowl went unnoticed as she pushed the material over her knees.

"When we reach the gates, let me do the talking."

She paused when she caught sight of his expression. Biting back her retort, she realized he wasn't being offensive nor contentious, just careful. And judging by that frown pinching every corner of his face, he wanted out of Odarian as much as she did.

As the horses ambled at a more leisurely walk, Suna took the opportunity to look around. In the square a short distance up the road stood a statue of a warrior, his sword raised high to the heavens. She didn't need to read the inscription or see the emblem engraved on the sword's hilt. It was Aires Bricken, the renowned Guardian who'd traveled with the legendary Divenean Di'Vennor. He'd been born and raised in Odarian.

Perhaps it was a trick of the night, but shadows seemed to slither over the monument as if trying to obscure it. It felt as if the city tried to hide from her. The lights that flickered on the streets looked dim, and the closer they approached the gates, there was not a soul around. Threads of fear filtered through the darkness around them. *The people here are scared. Why?*

When they rounded the next corner, the inner gate came into view. Several surly looking guards approached and immediately blocked their path.

"Hail, Feran," the largest soldier called out.

With relief, she noticed that at least one of them had smiled the greeting.

"Now where in goat's breath would you be heading at this hour? Have the pick'ins at ol' Bailor's gotten thin?" The guard's gaze lolled over her for mere seconds before returning to Feran.

The other guardsmen nodded and returned to their posts to leave the two men to talk.

Feran spurred his horse forward. "Hail, Ambert. How's the family keeping?"

Suna waited, wary and alert.

"Alissa's due any day now," the guard announced as he puffed out his massive chest.

Feran chuckled. "Well now, how many will that make? Six? Seven?"

She squirmed in her saddle. This was not the time to be sociable with one of the sentries, but when Feran glanced back her way, she realized it was all a ploy.

"Eight!"

"Where do you find the time?" Feran teased.

She fought the urge to roll her eyes.

Ambert moved closer to Feran's roan. "Now where might the two of you be going at this hour?" He dug in his ear with a sausage-size finger.

"Just searching for a little alone time, if you know what I mean."

Suna clenched her reins tighter and stiffened her back. *That man is incorrigible,* she fumed.

"Sorry, but I can't let you leave. We got an alert out for a woman who did away with Mellor's arm. If anybody asked me, we should be celebrating the loss." Ambert paused to spit a wad of phlegm onto the ground. "So who's your friend?" This time the guard stared hard at her.

Feran slid from his horse, placed his arm around the soldier's shoulder and led Ambert safely out of earshot. Suna heard the rumble of their voices, but couldn't decipher their words. She was about to grasp her mage'ic to eavesdrop when someone spoke behind her.

"If you would, my lady, please dismount."

She shifted around in her saddle. Three Elite Guards stood poised, swords drawn, waiting for her to do as they'd asked. She looked in Feran's direction, but he was too engrossed in his conversation with Ambert to notice what was happening behind him.

She dismounted and faced the group of men. The guard on her right reached for her saddle where her cloak had slipped down to reveal her scabbard and sword. Thankfully, the emblem remained hidden beneath the worn leather. But it wasn't the sword that had drawn their attention. It was the several thick strands of black copper-colored hair spilling down the length of her back that had escaped from her frantic ride.

"You will follow us," ordered the captain.

The other two guards took each of her arms and began to lead her away

"Hold right there," Feran yelled out, noticing her predicament at last.

"You should pick your entertainment better," Ambert called out with a raucous chortle. He returned to his post to leave matters in the capable hands of Odarian's Elite Guards.

When Feran caught up to her, his eyes pleaded for her not to say anything as he mouthed *trust me*. He turned to the Elite Guards. "Where are you taking her?"

Suna cringed at the challenging tone he used.

"To the Magistrate. She'll answer for her crime at the morning's tribunal," the captain said without breaking stride.

He moved ahead of the group and stopped, his eyes narrowing dangerously. "For what crime?"

"Theft and assault with the intent to kill," the man leading the procession said as he walked around him. "You know the laws."

Feran's voice rang through the street like a decree. "Then I insist on *impractu factual*. I demand that she sees Lord Mollster. Now."

Every man halted, their faces paling.

"We can't, and won't disturb the underlord with a matter such as this, Feran," the captain replied.

Suna cringed. This wasn't going well at all. If she hadn't wanted to appear like an ordinary citizen, she'd have stepped in and defended herself, but she had to remain as incognito as possible. Feran asked her to trust him. She believed trust was something earned, not given. She'd follow his lead. For now.

Feran straightened with a furious glare. "I believe the correct term to be used here is *general*."

She immediately looked to the ground. *General?*

The guard on her right spoke. "But Feran, you told us never to use—"

"You will address me as *General* Feran from here on out. Now take her to see Lord Mollster and no other. I'll meet you there."

The last order was for her benefit, but she was too preoccupied with the other name just mentioned. *Lord Mollster. So much for keeping my identity secret.*

* ~ * ~ *

As the guards led her down the complicated patterns of streets, not a word was spoken. She attempted to get her bearings, but soon gave up. She'd been to Odarian once before, and the coach she'd travelled in had taken her straight to the castle for Mollster's coronation.

So many years ago; so many memories she'd repressed.

By the time they reached the doors of a gray stone castle nestled on a small knoll overlooking Odarian, her escorts' tension and uncertainty coiled around her.

They pushed through the doors and stopped with her in the middle of the room. There they waited.

Suna studied the antiquated tapestries donning the stone walls amidst the various suits of armor and shields, some rusted and dented beyond further use. They hung about the capacious hall like forgotten trophies; hints of a past that no one believed in or cared about anymore. Nothing had changed in the least since her one and only visit to Odarian so many years ago..

An ornately carved throne of bleached snakewood, currently empty of its occupant, sat on a modest dais directly in front of her. She took several deep breaths and waited for the inevitable.

Long, tenuous minutes passed before the green velvet drapery hanging behind the dais drew back and a sinewy man stepped forward. Thinning, limp hair in varying hues of black-gray framed a time-beaten face. Tapered fingers grasped the front of his olive-colored silk robe. On the fabric above his heart was the crest of Odarian.

Mollster looked particularly unhappy. Roused from his bed at this time of night had put him in a foul mood. With his robe trailing after him, the Underlord of Odarian sat on his throne and motioned to the guards to bring her closer.

She approached, head down. Irritation oozed from him.

"Now what in the devil's lair is so important that I'm rustled from my bedchamber at this god-awful hour of the night?"

"We've captured Mr. Mellor's assailant, my lord," the captain explained, bending to one knee.

"And what, pray tell, is she doing before me instead of the Magistrate?" he asked with icy coldness.

Suna winced.

"I requested it."

She shifted around at the sound of Feran's voice. Standing beneath the majestic arched entrance, Feran looked, and acted, like a true general. Inwardly groaning, she turned back to Mollster and kept her head bowed.

The underlord's voice dripped with sarcasm. "General Feran. So nice to see you again. Is there a reasonable explanation as to why you'd order such a thing? And at this time of the night, or should I say morning? Weary bones like mine need all the rest they can get."

She listened to the approach of Feran's heavy footfalls until he stopped at her side.

"I do apologize, Lord Mollster, but I feel a great injustice has been done by arresting this woman. She did nothing but defend herself. Mellor has been before these tribunals enough times to know that you shouldn't doubt my…our…words."

"I believe that's a decision I make. Or at least the Magistrate."

Feran wasn't helping her situation at all.

"I mean no disrespect, my lord—"

She took over before it spiraled further out of control. She lifted her chin and looked the underlord square in the eye. "I bestow upon you a fair evening, my Lord Mollster. I assure you that it is a grave misunderstanding that I stand before you."

She sensed Feran gawking, but was thankfully quiet at last.

Mollster wagged his finger in her direction and squinted to peer more closely at her. "Come here, woman. Let me see you better."

She stepped closer. At the same time, she began removing the pins from her hair so that it fell down around her shoulders.

Mollster stiffened with a gasp. "Lady Suna!" Without hesitation, he turned to the three guards who'd escorted her in. "Take your leave. Matters will be dealt by me."

With rapid nods, the guardsmen bestowed their salutes and hurried out the Grand Hall, closing the doors quietly behind them.

Suna stole a sidelong glance at Feran. Confusion swam in his eyes, but he stayed quiet. She returned her attention back to Mollster. "I apologize for being a party to such an unfortunate set of circumstances, my lord," she began, bowing to one knee and staring at an invisible spot on the floor. She hoped he remembered her kindly. If not, there was the possibility she could end up in some forlorn dungeon comprised of power that rendered rogue mages useless. Childhood ghost stories of Komis'Na flashed through her mind. She shivered despite herself. And Feran's burning stare wasn't helping matters, either.

"It's been a long time since your face has graced these lands, my lady," Mollster said, his voice quivering slightly. "What brings you here to Odarian? And under what circumstances?"

She rose, unflinching. "I was accosted by this Mellor when I first arrived behind your city's gates. If you've collected recounts of the incident in question, you'll know that I didn't provoke him. He came at me first." Hurt that he could think such a thing of her, she knew rumors were like that—gossip always shrouded the truth.

The underlord rubbed his chin thoughtfully. "I see, but now a man must live his life without an arm. Is there justice in that, Lady Suna?"

"There's always justice when someone has to defend themselves against unsavories like Mellor. She's a woman, for goat's sake. How wrong is that?" Feran piped up in her defense.

She was grateful for his support, even though he hadn't been there to witness it firsthand.

"I will point out here that men like Mellor have no idea what manner of woman she is either. And how is it that you've been caught up in all this, *General*?"

Confusion flitted over his face as he stepped nearer to her. "My business is my own. And I would appreciate just *Feran*."

"Your business is mine when you walk within the walls of my kingdom," Mollster retaliated with more than a hint of anger. He grasped his robe tighter around him.

Feran bowed. "I meant no disrespect, my lord, but please, this is a travesty to everything you uphold."

Appealing to the honor and wise judgment of Mollster seemed to be the only way out of this quandary, and she sensed Feran grasped the same idea. Even though he had no idea who or what she was, he stood in staunch defense of her. *Indeed a gem.*

Mollster leaned into the cushions of his throne and steepled his fingers, scrutinizing both of them carefully. Too carefully.

She remembered the underlord as a young lad. In fact, Mollster had been about the same age as the King had been when she first began her service as the royal family's advisor and wizen, but those were memories she preferred left buried.

"Lady Suna, I demand that you speak of the events that have brought you before me," Mollster said at last.

As succinctly as possible, she recounted what had happened between Mellor and herself.

"And there was no other way in which to defend yourself?"

"At the moment, none that I could think of," she murmured before aiming a scowl in Feran's direction as he choked on a snicker.

"Why are you here? Now? In my kingdom?"

The gist of his question caused her to stare at the floor. In truth, she didn't know herself and she suspected neither did Feran. How could either of them adequately explain to Lord Mollster the real reason without it sounding like a lie or some embellished fairy tale?

Feran stepped forward. "May we ask your forbearance to speak in private?"

This time Suna gawked. Could Lord Mollster be trusted to know about this quest? Would he even believe them? Apparently it was a decision Feran felt more confident with than she did. Her memories of Lord Mollster were that of a young boy who had the proclivity of placing bell frogs down the dresses of little girls.

Mollster nodded. "First, let's do away with all this formal nonsense. And secondly, what's spoken here shall remain between us, unless I deem other ears should hear of it. Do we understand each other?"

"Thank you for your indulgence, Lord Mollster," she said, her thoughts a jumbled mess as to how to begin.

"Come. This room is too drafty for these old bones." The underlord's tone belied more weariness than he projected.

Feran climbed the steps of the dais and held out his arm for the lord to take.

Mollster took his help with a thankful nod. With his free hand, he swept back the velvet curtain and led them into a hidden room behind his throne.

Sporadically placed candles gave the chamber a welcoming glow. Better yet, the warmth coming from a blackened brazier filled to the brim with heated stones chased away the chill Suna had developed since leaving Bailor's Inn.

D. Thomas Jerlo

Absently waving at two of four chairs, the underlord motioned for them to sit. Try as she might, she couldn't draw Feran's attention. She sensed his angst as keenly as her own, but having had no time to concoct a believable story together, their only option was to speak the truth and trust in Mollster's judgment.

"I must say," he began as he slowly eased his bottom into a chair across from them. "I find myself somewhat surprised. My eyes are old and don't function as well as they used to, but Lady Suna, you're as young and as beautiful as I remember first seeing you. Is my eyesight deceiving me?" A small smile tugged at the corners of his lips.

Squirming under both men's unwavering attention, Suna dropped her head and said nothing.

"Then the rumors are true. Divenean blood runs through your veins."

She sensed Feran stiffen beside her. Suna closed her eyes and hung her head lower. *He was going to find out eventually,* she chided herself. *I would have preferred later, however. And without an audience.*

* ~ * ~ *

When Feran heard the word *Divenean*, he almost fell off his chair. *This is Lady Suna? The Lady Suna?* Shaken, he tried to collect himself, but it wasn't every day one found themselves paired on a quest with a legend.

CHAPTER NINE

Lord Mollster's thoughts turned to wayward days when Lady Suna had mentored every Dunkerk highborn child in ancient script and numbers. From those studies he'd learned that the Diveneans were entities born of the purest mage'ic, like the elves, when the world had just begun—before time had altered and bent such gifts to serve other purposes. The Elven race had preferred to stay to themselves in kingdoms entrenched with mage'ic and sequestered from the human race, while the Diveneans, who looked and acted more like the free folk, lived openly, although they hid their mage'ical abilities for reasons of their own. Few were ever certain about Suna's lineage, although many had speculated in secret— himself included.

Master mages and gifted with prolonged life, the Diveneans gave birth to the wizards and wizens of present day, although in later years they were few and far between born to them, for reasons unknown to him.

Ancient script referred to them as protectors of Etharia, as well as being the eyes and ears of the gods.

After the Elven race had disappeared over two thousand years ago, the Diveneans bound themselves to serve and protect these lands and its people. It would be more than a thousand lifetimes past when a Divenean king had ruled these lands.

Sadly, their stories had succumbed to legend, much like the elves, but tales were still told of them to this day. Karel Di'Vennor, perhaps the most recognized of the Divenean race, had many scripts dedicated to his deeds alone. When Mollster was a little boy, he'd dreamed of growing up to be just like him.

The memories made the underlord sigh. *Ah, the foolishness of youth.*

Suna's voice roused him from his reverie. "I beg you to keep my secret safe."

He studied Feran's ashen pallor and the way he fidgeted uncomfortably in his chair. *He didn't know?* Surprised, Mollster focused on her. "As you wish. We have other things to discuss first. What are we to do with your current situation?" He placed a hand over his mouth to stifle a yawn.

"Set her free, my lord," Feran cut in. "She was blatantly provoked."

He looked quickly away when Mollster turned to him. Suna had suddenly discovered something more interesting on her boot. Neither of them could look him in the eye. *As I suspected. There's something more going on here*, Mollster mused.

"Before reaching any decision, I must know this. What has brought your two paths together? I see a retired general and a Divenean, a race we haven't seen or heard from in many a year. I have to confess that I find this, um, friendship a little unorthodox."

Suna shifted toward Feran, but he refused to look her way.

Mollster waited. When neither of them spoke, he placed his elbows on his knees and sighed again. "I am underlord of Odarian, but it's nothing more than an insignificant title, as some of us have come to realize of late. We're lords bound under one great king who is no more. Our importance has whittled away to mean nothing. We reign. We collect the taxes. We rule justly… Well, some of us do. However, we make little difference anymore. We leave no honorable stamp to mark our passage."

He stopped. The truth of his words hurt more when saying them aloud. "There's little pride left in these lands since we've been left without king and queen. A lot has changed in that time. My eyes have seen much. The incessant in-house fighting for the throne. Ambushes along every border of our lands.

Greed. Intolerance. Now there's talk of shadowy creatures prowling the nights. I feel great unrest stirring, hmm? What is it that you're not telling me?"

When Suna and Feran straightened in their chairs, Mollster knew he'd struck a nerve.

Leaning forward like him, Suna began to tell her story of what had brought her to Odarian. When she spoke of the visitor in her dreams and what had been said to her, an icy dread settled in his soul.

"The visions revealed Etharia as a wasteland, its soil soaked in blood. The darkest of evils roamed freely through the lands killing at will. It is the end of our existence," she finished softly.

Rendered speechless, he turned to Feran, who recited pretty much the same as she had. In fact, both accounts were almost identical.

A quest. How did it come to this? Mollster worried.

As he pondered the ramifications, it felt like the quiet of the room became too thick to take a breath. "It's strange that the two of you would be destined together, true, but if I remember my lessons correctly, with my thanks to you," he directed to Suna, "ancient script purported that Di'Vennor had the aid of a null warrior. I find this partnering more than fortuitous, don't you think?"

Her blue eyes widened.

Feran's face paled.

It had the desired effect he'd hoped for. "So what exactly are you to do now?"

Suna's unwavering calm returned. "I believe we must find a key."

Feran shook his head. "No. It's a person. I think. Well, it's *something*."

Mollster frowned. "A key? A person? Which is it?"

"What's with a key?" Feran asked with a folded brow.

"Since the stranger of the message disappeared, I've been dreaming, visions actually, of a key. It floats above my head. Gold with simple cuttings along the spine. It's very small, delicate, and old. I sense significance in finding it," Suna explained.

"Interesting," Mollster murmured.

Feran scratched his head. "My dreams are haunted by something else. Something dark hides in the shadows of my mind. I don't know what it is, but every time I dream about it, it grows larger until? Until my dreams are utter blackness. And the cold?" He shuddered. "It's like black ice that won't melt. I don't know what kind of creature it is, but its touch is like nothing I've ever felt before. Cruel laughter fills my head, slicing bits of my brain away. Sometimes, I swear, I can smell it. It's death. A decomposing body left out in the sun too long, but worse than that. It fills my dreams. Everything inside me becomes dead. Then I see a fire. I run to it, but there's no heat. I can't wake. I try to hide, but..."

He stopped. A haunted glow illuminated in his eyes. "Then there's another. He's a small thing. I never see his face. Just a distorted image of something undersized and, well, crooked. There's something so wrong about him."

He stopped and ran a hand through his hair. "I don't know. I could be losing my mind."

"Does he stand about eight hands high? Small and gnarled, dragging his left leg behind? Big head, small body, with a very bad case of the sniffles?"

Feran eyes widened as he nodded. "I know he's connected to the shadow, but I don't know how. He doesn't scare me like the other one does." He looked relieved at getting that off his chest, as if he'd been hiding some horrid secret. "You've dreamed about him too?" he asked with a hopeful lilt.

She placed her head in her hands and groaned. Like a waterfall of fire, her hair fell forward to hide her face.

Mollster leaned closer. "Are you all right, Lady Suna?"

She straightened. Fury flashed in her eyes as she recited her encounter with Ilio. When she finished, Feran swore under his breath.

Mollster watched the two across from him battle their doubts and apprehensions. "Perhaps the key and this Ilio are connected? Find one and you find the other, yes?"

Feran jumped to his feet. "That's it. It's got to be. If I'm dreaming about him, and you're seeing a key, they have to be connected. His trail is what, a day old? If we go now, there's a chance we can catch the little bastard."

Suna rose with a small smile. "Thank you, Lord Mollster. Your insightful wisdom is what we needed to make sense of this situation. An outsider's view, so to speak. May we have your leave?"

With difficulty, he suppressed a grin at the adolescent memory of when she'd been his first pleasure dream. Such nonsense to think of at a time like this, but it just popped into his head. He was old, yes, but certainly not dead. And her beauty hadn't waned in the least.

However, before granting her request, he needed to learn one thing that had been bothering him for years. "Lady Suna, you and General Feran have my honored leave, and anything else I can provide, but I need to know something. It's troubled me for years."

She pursed her lips as if knowing what he was going to ask.

"I would very much like to know what happened the day you left Dunkerk and never returned."

With his hands grasped in front, Feran resumed his seat, looking as eager as he felt to hear her version of events.

"Do you remember the circumstances?" she asked quietly.

He nodded. He hadn't been a small child, but rather a boy on the verge of manhood.

"Then you'll remember that King Markes had gone hunting with several parties of the High Houses."

"He refused to take me. Told me I was too young for such things. Bah!" Even after all this time, he still nursed the hurt.

"When I arrived in the woods, his Guardians escorted me to the place where he lay, but by that time I was too late."

She stopped and swallowed hard. "King Markes had already passed from this realm. I was told he'd fallen from his horse and struck his head on a rock. The heir to his throne lay in Queen Saliste's womb. When she'd heard the news, she became hysterical. I wasn't there to give her comfort. In her distressed state the baby began to emerge. Too soon."

Mollster's heart ached as he watched the memories consume her. She carried the scars deep, and it was obvious that not one of them had ever healed. He cast a fleeting glance at Feran, who sat like an apt pupil listening to a history lesson. And in retrospect, he was.

"King Markes' body was returned to his chambers to be prepared for burial," Suna continued. "I was immediately summoned to the Queen's side. I found... I couldn't save either of them. I failed to protect them, as was my Divenean duty."

Her words stung like stagnant reminders of the losses his people continually suffered. "This is the reason you left Dunkerk without so much as a goodbye?" He couldn't fathom what she'd gone through. *And still is,* he thought sadly.

She nodded.

"To carry such unbridled guilt for something that wasn't your fault?"

She shrugged and didn't answer.

He could do nothing to alleviate her pain. Only she had the power to do so.

Mollster turned to Feran, knowing that he, too, fought inner failings. Accomplished in his own right, he knew the man's worth more than Feran did himself. Rising to the esteemed rank of General under King Markes' former army, he was the youngest ever decreed the title. The man had done quite well for himself and he felt it a shame that Feran didn't see it the same way.

He remembered the young man when he'd first joined the Elite Guards of Dunkerk. Feran had excelled at all forms of soldiery, including his talents as a strategic tactician. All the high lords of Dunkerk took interest in worthy men like him in the hope that one day they'd lead their own armies.

Mollster had kept his eye on Feran for himself, but before his twenty-first naming day, the young soldier rose to the rank as General of the Guardians. Not an easy feat, and certainly not for one so young. Men of the Elite Guards who showed promising soldiering skills were sometimes promoted to Guardian status. But to earn the title of "Guardian" was difficult. These men had to secure their place as a Sword Dancer first, which training is so intense that when some men failed, they left the service altogether. To become their general was more than extraordinary.

The Guardians specialized as personal bodyguards to the King and Queen. They were men of staunch honor and duty, but as no sovereignty sat upon the throne during Feran's tenure, they'd become nothing more than worthy titles shared by men who lacked monarchs to protect. He'd always suspected Feran had left the service because of those reasons, and why he held such high regard for the young man. In his own mind, Mollster would have done the same.

Being born after King Markes' death, Feran never knew an Etharia ruled by a sovereign. He'd become a man lost without a purpose or a rightful cause to serve.

Until now.

The throne remained unoccupied since King Markes' demise, but not for lack of continuous back-stabbing and assassination attempts from several of the High Houses. In recent years, augmented unrest, speculation and suspicion had begun devouring everything and everyone around them. Only an heir of King Markes would rule, if Mollster had anything to say about it. Unfortunately, that royal bloodline was dead and with it his hopes. Dunkerk and the rest of the kingdoms of Etharia were precariously balanced on an edge of anarchy.

These dark omens of Suna and Feran's couldn't have come at a worse time.

* ～ * ～ *

Mollster guided Suna and Feran through the cavernous back halls of his castle. He'd signed and sealed the Negation of Crime Order against her and was now leading them toward the exit via his castle's private gardens, which would give them the opportunity to leave Odarian unseen. "I'll provide you a small escort for your journey—"

"No!"

Their unified protest echoed through the gloom of his sleepy keep. The flickering flames contained in neatly placed wall sconces brightened and dulled as their voices carried hollowly down the stone tunnel.

"That would only draw attention to us," Feran said.

Suna nodded. "Thank you kindly for the offer, but we'll be faster and more inconspicuous on our own."

Mollster grasped the iron door handle and pulled. The rarely used hinges screeched in protest. "Then my falcon couriers are at your disposal." He gave a trill whistle of three short notes followed by one long one. Seconds later, a falcon landed on a tree branch a few yards in the distance. After he shooed the avian away, it spread its wings and gave a tetchy squawk before taking flight.

The night air greeted them with the robust scent of damp earth and a myriad of sweet, floral scents coalescing as one. In silence they walked the stone path.

"You two must be careful. There's been strange—"

"I know what you're about to say," Feran cut in. "And it's all codswallop. I mean no disrespect, Lord Mollster, but those stories running through the streets were invented to scare children. I've traveled as far north as Saingarth and even farther south past Fainsworth. I haven't seen anything remotely close to the yarns I've heard of late. Black ghosts draining people dry? Storms of fire instead of rain? Come on." He shook his head in disgust.

Just then a crescent moon peeked out from behind the cloud cover. Like a malevolent grin, it stared down upon the trio.

Suna stopped beside a gilded metal bench and sat. "What stories?" Her impromptu meeting with Ilio made her worry if others had suffered similar encounters.

When Feran *humphed* something under his breath, Mollster pointedly ignored him. Dropping his voice to a lower octave, he darted his gaze around the shadows of his well-groomed garden. "They say that Balthazar's favored minion, Isafel, is free."

At the mention of those two names, the air in the garden seemed to grow colder.

Feran rolled his eyes to the inky sky.

"Who are *they*?" she pressed.

"I don't take to the listening to gossip, but Odarian has had some very mysterious deaths of late."

"Any eyewitnesses?" Feran asked with a sarcastic lilt.

The underlord growled. "I'm privy to things you are not." He then softened his composure and moved to sit beside her. "In all my years, never have I seen deaths like those." He closed his eyes and shuddered.

Leveling Feran with a disparaging glare, Suna asked, "In what manner did they die?"

"Believe me, it's not because of age I look this way. It's a heavy burden I bear for the safety of my people."

Evil simmers beneath the bowels of Etharia, and if all comes to be as I have seen, no living creature shall ever live free.

That ominous message was becoming an obsession. But it was all beginning to make sense. Only a Divenean would be powerful enough to withstand the horror about to transpire.

Suna studied the preoccupied glow of Mollster's eyes as he swallowed several times.

"It was as if these people were killed from the inside out. By the seven shades of Hell, even the infant..." the underlord exclaimed. His hand did an angry swipe over his face to hide the tears suddenly welling in his eyes. "Every bone and organ crushed, yet not a mark found on them. Some bodies were beheaded, their wounds cauterized by fire and not by a blade."

She stared off into the distance. "I know what the key is for."

An eerie calm transcended over the gardens. Even the melodic drone of the insects fell silent as if waiting for her to finish.

"There are Divenean teachings known only to our Fold. What the people of Etharia consider myth were once derived from actual recounts of events, but the passage of time has clouded fact into fiction. There isn't enough time to explain it all, but I understand the words of warning given to Feran and I." She glanced up at the luminous rings of the half moon. "The Kruthos. It's been found."

Feran moved closer. "What's a Kruthos?"

"It's the lock that binds Balthazar within his prison. How could I have been so blind? If Isafel managed to escape his imprisonment, it means the wards that were holding him have weakened enough for him to do so. He's searching for the key to release his Master. Isafel is hunting the world of the living. Again."

Turning, she met Mollster's horror-struck expression with staunch resolve. "This is the key I've been dreaming about. And you?" She paused with an inquisitive stare at Feran. "Your stranger is Isafel himself. He needs you or he wouldn't be wasting his time invading your dreams. He must have been coming for you, but I reached you first."

Feran blanched. "Coming for me? Wait. Both those monsters are said to be locked in two impenetrable prisons for all eternity. Bound by mage'ic created by the Diveneans. Imprisoned by the strongest mages ever. You mean those things actually happened?"

His voice had taken on a shrill quality. There were few Etharians who didn't fear those demons, but they'd never been real. Only stories to frighten—until now. Unfortunately, Suna had nothing to offer in her Fold's defense. Far too many years had passed since she'd had dealings with her own kind—or the outside world, for that matter.

Mollster's shoulders slumped as he placed his head in his hands. "So time has brought us to this juncture. The strife consuming these lands? It's all been leading up to this, hasn't it?" He lifted his head and met her gaze.

"Nothing is ever what it seems, my lord," she replied.

The underlord's lips twisted into a condescending sneer. "I can only surmise the worse if a Divenean has been asked to carry out such a task."

"Why all the glum faces? We catch this little imp and get the key. It can't be too difficult." Feran's enthusiasm fell short.

She frowned. "That little imp, as you call him, possesses strong mage'ic. His prowess surprised even me. Someone gifted Ilio with black powers. I fear we're going to be hard-pressed in capturing that one."

Mollster took one of her hands within his own. She noticed it was soft and uncallused—a nobleman's hand. "If it's within my power to give, you only have to ask for it, Lady Suna."

She realized he understood the daunting importance of their quest. "Send messengers to alert the neighboring towns and villages. Keep your people inside after twilight. And you must assemble every underlord to council to share what you've learned this night. You have to make them believe that Isafel is free. And above all else, amass your armies."

His eyes rounded. "You don't think—?"

"Like you, I'm privy to information others are not. I know Balthazar is forming his own legion. Fiends of which you've never battled before. The war to end all wars is brewing… and this Ilio? He's but only one of those abominations. How Balthazar managed to bring such a thing to this plane of existence, I don't know. His final oath to the Diveneans who imprisoned him was that he'd return. As retribution for his bondage, he'd devour these lands into darkness and chaos. With Isafel's help, that oath may be fulfilled. First, he must escape. And for that he needs the key. If lowly creatures such as Ilio can be gifted with dark mage'ic, then there's no telling what that demon is garnering inside that dungeon of his. He's not the only monster imprisoned between our worlds."

Speechless, both men gaped at her.

She rose from the bench. "It's time to fulfill my Divenean obligations."

Mollster got to his feet and stared long and hard at her before turning to Feran. "This task is appointed to you, General Feran Lambert. And don't give me that look either. Once a general, always a general. Remember well that Di'Vennor's own warrior, Aires Bricken, an Odarian I might add, had no more special attributes than you. I must confess that I'm saddened that you two must carry this burden, but I can't think of anyone better appointed to such a task. The future of our lands appears to lay perilously balanced. I harbor no doubts that you will endure, but your vow to me, to an underlord of Etharia, is you will keep Lady Suna safe. Do you understand the gravity of my words?"

Feran straightened his carriage and nodded.

Suna realized that the mischievous boy she'd once scolded for pranks had listened well to the lessons she'd taught at Dunkerk. Mollster had grown into a good and just underlord. He should have known that her Divenean lineage held its own unique, ominous powers. Mollster's concern for her safety inched its way into her carefully shielded heart.

The underlord shifted around to her. "There's horses tethered out back. I always have a couple ready and waiting for when I want to escape the tedium of ruling and be alone with my thoughts. I'll ensure the guards will not hinder you at the gates."

Feran placed the first two fingers of his right hand to his forehead, lips, and then over his heart. An underlord had just ordered him to fulfill a sacred duty, and as a Guardian, he couldn't refute it.

Like Suna, duty bound him as well.

When Mollster snagged her into his embrace, she instantly stiffened, feeling awkward at the intimate gesture. It'd been many years since she'd had human contact. Tears came unbidden as buried emotions threatened to unleash. She yielded reluctantly in his arms. Then she stepped back.

Without a word, she and Feran followed the path Mollster had pointed out.

* ~ * ~ *

When the thorny brambles of his zenia bushes swallowed them from sight, only then did Mollster brush away a meandering tear. He smiled—a rather sad smile—but a smile nonetheless. For the first time in a long time, a kindling of vigor began to flow through him. "Godspeed you two. Until we meet again," he whispered to the night.

He turned and made his way inside.

CHAPTER TEN

The passing countryside lay unusually hushed. Suna kept extra vigilant. Neither of them spoke as the horses ran. It felt inappropriate to break the silence hanging like a wet coverlet over them.

No crickets chirped.

No birds flew.

No small creatures ran afoot.

Occasional slips of mist rose and slithered through the night air like ghostly phantoms off the cold ground. It felt as if the land attempted to hide behind an impenetrable shield.

A few leagues outside Odarian's walls, Suna pulled her mare to a stop.

Feran followed suit. His gaze encompassed the surroundings as only a trained Guardian could. "This isn't the time."

"Do you even know where we're going?"

Both animals stamped their hooves, eager to be on their way again.

In the gloom, she saw his brow furrow as he fidgeted with his reins. "I'm pretty sure you're going to enlighten me."

They were in the open with the cover of forest still some leagues away. This wasn't the place to stop and have a discussion, but Suna sensed they were heading in the wrong direction.

Just like a woman. Always wanting to talk about things.

She bristled at Feran's blaring thought. Without thinking, she retaliated. *I, unlike most women, can turn your brains to mash. If you don't want to discuss which direction we're to take, suit yourself.*

He jerked back as if she'd slapped him. "H-How did you do that?"

It was one thing to be rude, but quite another to label her as a typical woman. That, she was not. "Perhaps that'll curb any more of your judgmental comments, Master Feran. Now, do you want to discuss where we're heading or shall we continue following a false trail?" Placing her hands on the pommel of her saddle, she waited.

That condescending grin of his returned.

What in damnation does he find so amusing? His constant roguish attitude was exasperating.

"Is this how it's going to be? You read my mind. I follow your orders without question?" He actually looked eager for an answer.

"What do you mean?"

"You *know* exactly what I mean."

With a halfhearted shrug of her shoulders, she chose her next words carefully. "Well, no. To be honest, I can't read your mind all the time."

"Then how did you do that just now?"

No one had ever questioned her abilities before. How did she explain something that came as natural as breathing? "We're anxious. And wary. When emotions like that run high, they come to the surface and are revealed in a person's élan. Facial expressions? Body language? It brings a person's thoughts to my mind as if they've been spoken aloud. I see the way you're riding. The stiffness in your shoulders. The distant look in your eyes. Your emotions made it easy for me to concentrate on your thoughts. Sometimes they come as clear as if you'd spoken aloud, depending on the sentiments behind them."

His eyes rounded.

She'd struck a nerve. Possibly two. However, who was she to talk about how important emotions were, but he was the last person in this world or the next that she'd discuss her inadequacies with. "I promise not to go where I'm not welcome," she added begrudgingly.

She shifted in her saddle and surveyed the gloomy countryside. "When I left camp, Ilio's trail was heading south. Why are we heading east?"

"Very astute, *Lady* Suna. In order to cross the Carberra River, he'll have to make for one of the ferries. According to my estimation, that's currently the direction we're riding."

"Which ferry?"

"He was heading south, but not now. I picked up his tracks half a league back. He's heading for the main one. Carberra Ferry."

She nodded and grabbed her reins. "Good. The sooner we catch him, the sooner we'll find out more about the key. If you're through with this discussion, I suggest we be on our way."

She flew past him in a spray of dirt and pebbles.

Feran watched the vivid coppery-red of Suna's hair flailing out behind her as she rode off, never once looking back to see if he followed.

I'm riding with a Divenean. And no less Suna the Great herself. Moreover, she can read my bloody mind! Can this get any worse?

CHAPTER ELEVEN

Lord Mollster readied himself for bed for the second time that night. The damp night air of his gardens had created a deep chill that had settled deep into his bones. Exhausted and heavy of heart, he worried about the two he'd said farewell to.

"Will there be anything else, my lord?" the buxom chamber-maiden asked with an expectant gleam in her eye.

Mollster smiled, albeit sadly. He slept alone most nights. His wife, Sonie, had departed this world long ago in a manner identical to Queen Saliste. Lately, he found little pleasure in the occasional supple body that was eager to frequent his bed, preferring the extra room to stretch out his arthritic limbs. *Strange how things change and I can't remember when they had,* he mused cheerlessly.

He offered the servant a smile. "No thank you, Malenda, and thank you for the extra fire-stones beneath my sheets."

After the door closed behind her, he slid beneath his blankets relishing in the warmth emanating through the soft down of his coverlet, but it seemed that no matter how many heated stones lay beneath his bed, an indelible cold had permeated both his body and his soul.

* ~ * ~ *

Odarian woke to its usual bustle amidst the clamoring of roosters who crowed out their welcomes of another day. People went about their morning routines ignorant to the danger looming over them. Mollster's duty as underlord was to keep his people safe, and he took that charge seriously; however, he couldn't say the same for all of them.

When his Infers had returned, Mollster greeted them alone in the Grand Hall. The two men he'd chosen had traveled on his swiftest destriers and just returned road worn and mud splattered. He'd couriered not a request, but rather a summons to all four underlords of Etharia.

Both Infers stood before him with heads bowed, offering him the customary homage of the first two fingers to forehead, lips, and heart. Mollster tipped his head in acknowledgment and waited for one of them to speak.

Janek, the tall, handsome soldier, spoke first. "We've done as you've ordered, my lord. I have delivered your summons to Lords Ethbridge and Conac. I must confess," he added, his eyes glinting with puckish satisfaction. "He was none too pleased to be woken at that hour."

Mollster didn't need to be told who Janek spoke of. A glimpse of Ethbridge's sour scowl flashed in his mind.

"I have done the same to Lords Fenwick and Greth," the other Infer cut in. Laren was smaller in stature, wiry and of homely countenance due to the numerous spider-webbed scars on his face.

Mollster studied his two most reliable men. They had done well despite the lack of time and distances they had to cover. "I thank you both for your due diligence, and I commend you on your speed and stealth. Please see Treasurer Tomas for your bonuses. Be dismissed with my deepest thanks."

Although it exhausted him to use such staunch formality, these two deserved no less. It was not an easy job traveling in the dark of night and covering as many leagues as these two had done, but time was of the essence.

Mollster resisted the urge to wring his hands in restless anxiety. *Now I wait for their arrival and two particular shades of Hell to follow.*

* ~ * ~ *

Two days later, the first two underlords to arrive was Nyles Ethbridge, Underlord of Vansgaard, from the north and Tobas Greth, Underlord of Carberra from the east. Both traveled with a garrison of fifteen men each. A significant amount of arms, but not enough to insult or appear threatening.

Several hours later, the Underlord of Laspeth, Allory Conac, Ethbridge's southern neighbor, and Marken Fenwick, Underlord of Kravelle, arrived from the southeast, each bearing five men apiece. Placed in suitable quarters, Mollster refused all requests for an audience, even from his two dearest friends, Allory and Marken.

The next morning the four underlords and their retinues met at the entrance of the Grand Hall. As sure as rain, an argument erupted over the amount of men to be allowed inside. Bitter words and insults soon followed. Thankfully, no swords were drawn.

Mollster heard the uproar as he entered the Grand Hall through his secret room. Just before he had to intervene, he heard them agree that each company's escorts would wait outside to allow them to speak in private. Sound advice, and coming from Fenwick he wasn't surprised. The man was always the diplomat.

Mollster had his staff arrange five chairs in a semi-circle just below the dais of his throne. Above all else he wanted to ensure there was the least amount of formality as possible and that everyone attending would feel on equal ground. He was already seated in one of the chairs when the underlords pushed their way through the ornate doors.

After Conac and Fenwick entered, Mollster refused to look either of them in the eye for fear of giving anything away. He sensed their confusion, but more importantly, their concern at the calling of such a council.

The men took their seats in silence.

As usual, Greth took center stage. "What's the meaning of this, Mollster?" he demanded. As wide as he was tall, the Lord of Carberra displayed his arrogance every time he opened his mouth. Heavy jowls hung from an angled face that stretched bloodless lips into a permanent scowl. Brown beady eyes outlined in black kohl stared about his kinsmen in contempt. Greth's reputation for ruling with swift, fair justice was renowned, but in recent years it'd become more swift than impartial. Mollster held little regard for this brute of a man, and even far less respect for his bullying ways.

Seething at the underlord's brazen disregard for his sovereignty, Mollster gritted his teeth and began. "News has reached my ears. Dire news. I've called this council to ask you to ready your regiments for battle." Not surprisingly, snorts of disbelief followed.

Allory Conac's gravelly voice cut through the ruckus. With his thick stomach and tree trunk sized legs, the Lord of Laspeth stood. "Why should we be readying for war?" Standing a full head taller than Greth, and almost as wide, with cropped blond hair and sparkling amber eyes that gave his large face an almost innocent, child-like quality, this particular underlord could be as ruthless as Greth, but always fair and levelheaded. His pointed question silenced the others. All of them waited for an answer.

"I can't divulge the source of my information, but believe me when I say that these rumors we've been hearing about Isafel being free are indeed true. He's managed to break free of his prison and is killing at will. These deaths in my kingdom and yours? He's to blame. The stories we read as children are true."

Conac's hard stare laid Mollster bare. "And you know this how?"

He refused to divulge Suna's secret, but how was he going to get these men to believe him? "I was occasioned by a visit from a Divenean."

Ethbridge jumped to his feet. "You lie!" His black hair shone with oil and hung in its usual stringy strands about his sunken cheeks, adding to the elongation of his prominently pointed face.

Mollster stood and faced the scoundrel of Vansgaard. "You dare insult me in my own house, Nyles?" He enunciated each word slowly in an effort to quash the urge to run him through.

"Damnation, men. Sit down. We're not going to find out anything foaming at the mouth like rabid animals. Now sit!" Greth growled.

Ethbridge glared back and did what he was told, all the while grumbling under his breath.

Mollster resumed his seat and studied the Lord of Vansgaard. *That man has become a dangerous foe to defy respect in my presence. And I see he's grown another set of balls. Greth's to be precise.*

He returned his attention back to the matters at hand. "I swear upon my honor and upon the memory of King Markes and Queen Saliste. A Divenean attended my court with this news. We're to prepare for war and send messages of warning throughout the lands. Isafel is attempting to free Balthazar. The Kruthos has been found."

The four men stared at one another in disbelief. Long, drawn out minutes followed. Mollster sensed them sorting through their history lessons and the implications this could have. "Well?" he asked when no one spoke.

Ethbridge sneered down his hooked nose. "Been hitting your private wine stock a little hard? The Diveneans have all disappeared. We've heard nothing from their race since...?"

No one spoke Suna's name.

"So there's one left. Imagine that." One of Conac's meaty hands ran nervously over the top of his spiky hair before he fell silent.

They knew all too well that the deaths of King Markes and Queen Saliste had forever marked a change in Etharian history. And a sad, irreparable one at that. No one had seen or even heard from a Divenean since that unfortunate turn of events, so why now?

The Lord of Odarian turned to the one man who'd remained quiet. He'd been studying his friend's ill countenance since the start of the council and wondered what Fenwick's thoughts were on the subject.

As the youngest ruling lord here, Marken Fenwick suffered the most ridicule. At fifteen, King Markes had appointed Fenwick as ruling underlord of Karvelle. Many thought him too young and dimwitted to rule, but Mollster and Conac knew better, as did the king. Fenwick had a weakness for finely bred horses, and women, and not particularly in that order, but he also possessed a proclivity of recreating famous battles that had taken place over history. If anyone here could shed some light on the situation, it would be him.

Karvelle's library was like no other. It even included a massive collection of various tacticians' diaries of diplomats that had done nothing during their piteous lives except record every minute detail of battles lost and won. Only the kingdom of Dunkerk could boast of a larger collection of histories.

A quiet man of easy disposition, Fenwick's baby-blue eyes and prominent high cheekbones gave a seductive quality to an otherwise devilishly handsome face. Long, pale lashes contrasted against the ginger hue of his feathered hair that brushed against his shoulders. With his long legs stretched out in front of him, he stared thoughtfully around the group before speaking.

"I can't say I disbelieve you, Lord Mollster," he said carefully. "But I find it rather difficult to grasp. No one has seen a Divenean since, well, since Lady Suna, and no one really knew for sure about her."

Mollster averted his gaze, hoping Fenwick didn't see the effect her name had on him.

"She was a remarkable woman, Lady Suna," the Lord of Karvelle murmured. "If one of their race has indeed survived, then with this news, there's still hope left for us."

Greth gave a dismissive wave of his hand. "Phaa! Hope is for weaklings. Swords make better statements."

Ethbridge's eyes glinted with dangerous intent. "I agree with Greth. Let's hunt Isafel down and put an end to him once and for all."

Mollster tried to keep his contempt from showing, but failed. Those two idiots preferred to fight a force they couldn't win against, not without mage'ic. *How can these men be so inane? And they call themselves underlords?* He shook his head. "If the Diveneans couldn't accomplish the demise of Isafel, what makes you so sure that you'll be able to achieve such a thing?" He posed the question not just at Ethbridge, but to everyone. "One must remember that if Isafel takes human form—"

Conac's brow creased into a multitude of lines as he leaned his large frame forward in his chair. "What do you mean?"

"You didn't listen too well to your studies, did you?"

Conac gave a sheepish shrug.

"I know that he can take human form and thereby be unrecognizable, but I've been advised his plan to do so has been thwarted. Isafel could become the High Regent, even a general leading one of your armies."

Ethbridge gave an indignant sniff. "You know this how?"

"Did none of you study during your youth?"

Fenwick opened his mouth, but Mollster was quicker. "This information has been verified. I've promised to keep their identities safe. The two who visited me are on their own quest."

The sting of Fenwick's inquisitive stare drilled through Mollster. Little passed by the Lord of Karvelle, contrary to what others thought, but even with his two closest friends he'd keep Suna and Feran's secret safe for as long as possible.

Greth crossed his arms across his barrel chest. "You expect us to amass our armies and do what? Sit around and wait? Wait for what, Mollster?"

"I can offer no more than what I've just told you. Balthazar is creating an army such as we've never seen before. This news? Does it not explain the happenstances that have been occurring all over our lands? He'd vowed to destroy our world."

Ethbridge stood and mimicked Greth's stance. "He's imprisoned, man! How in damnation is he building an army?"

"If there's enough will, evil will find a way. Balthazar is contained in a prison similar to that which held Isafel, but with one difference. Balthazar's has a lock called the Kruthos, which needs a key. If Isafel managed to escape, how much time do we have before Balthazar can do the same? Key or no key. How he could create an army is beyond my scope of understanding, but I believe the person who told me this. Is there a theory you'd like to share with the rest of us, Lord Ethbridge? I eagerly await your wisdom on these issues as you seem to know so much more than I do." He nearly choked on the formality, but he couldn't lose control now. If Ethbridge or Greth saw any weakness they'd pounce on him like a timbercat on prey.

Ethbridge's face turned pink, then crimson before finally settling on a deep shade of violet.

Greth lowered his black eyes with deliberate slowness, silently motioning for Ethbridge to take his seat.

Mollster watched with quiet amusement. *So Ethbridge has been promoted to lapdog status. Interesting.*

"There are..." Fenwick stopped when all eyes turned to him.

"Get on with it, man. We don't have all day," Greth snipped.

"Now see here. I don't appreciate—"

"Enough of this childish bickering. I didn't want to bring formality into this, but if need be I will. This Hall sees Fenwick," Mollster cut in. Emotions and common sense were like duck oil and vinegar. The two didn't mix, and in this room there were far too many equal portions of both. They had to maintain civility if they were to get anywhere.

"Thank you, Lord Mollster." Fenwick's eyebrows knit downward as he began to explain. "From what I know, Isafel can take human form only when he's strong enough to achieve this. Which means his diet of blood and bones would have had to be for some time. If this is indeed the case, the demon has been free for...?" He hesitated. "... Some time. From what I've read, he'll attempt to find someone who'd best serve his purpose, be it either a man or woman of power.

Someone whose personality and strength would benefit him the most. You say you know who this person might have been?"

Mollster looked away, despising how easily the underlord could read him. "Yes, but he now accompanies the Divenean. He's safe. Although this means little. Etharia is filled with a multitude of suitable hosts that could do a great service for that evil entity." It was difficult, but he refrained from looking in Ethbridge or Greth's direction.

Greth snorted. "Is there anything else in that brain of yours that might add something useful to this discussion?"

Fenwick sneered back, not the least ruffled. "Perhaps this discussion should be better left to men who know so much more than I do. I'm sure your substantial wisdom on the subject would serve this council well. The floor's yours, *Lord* Greth."

It was rare for the young underlord to allow Greth to bait to him, but Mollster knew Fenwick's unpretentious disposition infuriated the large man even more. The Lord of Carberra bristled with rage, but kept silent.

"Be that as it may, we still don't have a clue as to what's going on here," Conac piped in.

"I think we have more important things to discuss than *rumors* of Isafel being free. The Barbs are increasing their attacks at every border of our lands. Even though I've requested more men from Dunkerk, those louts there know nothing about what we're dealing with," Ethbridge said with his usual sneer.

Conac jeered at the northern lord. "That's more important than Isafel? Your priorities need some reevaluating, Nyles." Ethbridge attempted to retort, but Conac was quicker. "I find it strange that we've had no such uprisings in Laspeth. Why's that?"

"Because you offer them free hands to pilfer your stocks and run amuck through your lands. And you have the audacity to call yourself an underlord?" Ethbridge threw back.

"You forget that these Barbs are people of Etharia as well," Conac retaliated.

Mollster inwardly groaned. This was an ongoing argument that raised ire in both men—nay, in all of them.

"The mountains have grown harsher with each passing season, and contrary to what you think, crimes are met with just punishments, Ethbridge. Not an iron fist," Conac said wearily.

"Men. Please. We're dismissing important issues—"

"There's a way of identifying Isafel, if he takes human form."

Fenwick's statement silenced the feuding men. "There will be odd symbols that will show on his or her wrists, neck and ankles like Menjio tattoos. They're the markings of the underworld, as well as the insignia of an unwilling soul."

Mollster heart hammered inside his chest. "And if the human's willing?"

Fenwick stared pointedly at Greth. "I can't say, but I would think there are few who'd willingly cross over into eternal damnation, but I could be wrong."

Greth rumbled. "You dare?"

"Enough!" Mollster's voice resonated so loud that it carried outside the Hall. Several sentry retinues pushed open the door to ensure all was right inside. He dismissed them with a nonchalant flick of his hand before continuing. When the door closed, he lowered his voice to a more tempered tone. "The future of our lands is in jeopardy and you men squabble like disparaging children."

The insult drew outbursts of indignant denials from Ethbridge and Greth. Fenwick and Conac hung their heads.

"The answer to my summons is quite simple, men. Will you amass your armies?"

Mollster didn't relish the thought of the repercussions if he received negative responses back. If indeed it was war they were about to face, may the gods help them if that battle began on their own doorsteps.

CHAPTER TWELVE

Feran ran the horses as hard as he dared to the edge of the Sa'Dimmen Woods. The area consisted of a small coppice of bulky oaks enmeshed within a few sporadically spaced gangling pines some sixteen leagues west of Carberra Ferry. It would provide adequate shelter from any prying eyes and give them a few hours of rest.

The sun had just reached the midday mark and he felt more exhausted than the horses sounded. He'd have to remember to thank Bailor for giving them two of his finest animals.

The pounding between his eyes and the relentless heat of the sun had set him in an ill-tempered mood. He dismounted and continued the silence he'd maintained throughout the balance of their ride. Even now he refused to look in Suna's direction, finding it far safer than having to suffer the consequences. When he heard her fumbling off her horse, he couldn't stop from giving one last jab. "Not used to riding?"

He kept his back to her as he tethered his mount to a gnarled oak, so he didn't see her eyes roll back into her head or her knees buckle as she fell in a helpless heap to the ground. However, his finely honed instincts made him turn just in time to see her slip beneath the roan's forelegs. He reached her a second before her head smacked onto the ground. Her eyes were half-open and glazed over.

Hellfire! I'm an inconsiderate fool. He hadn't stopped to think how exhausted she was. Succumbing to only a few hours' sleep the night of Ilio's uninvited appearance at her camp, to her adventures in Odarian, and now leading her on this dogged pursuit knowing full well he pushed himself to the limits, he hadn't given any regard to her state of being. Guilt wrapped around him like a vise.

He drew up a makeshift bed with blankets from their packs and made Suna as comfortable as possible before starting a small fire. He began boiling water, although he had no idea why. In stressful situations women always wanted hot water. *Perhaps for tea?* Bailor had packed several varieties of herbs, but he couldn't distinguish which were which. *She's a wizen. When she wakes, she'll figure it out.*

With Suna resting, he attended to the horses. When he lifted her dust-covered cloak, there in plain view was her scabbard and sword. He cast a sidelong glance over his shoulder as he pulled out the weapon. Burnished metal and sharpened to a razor's edge, the blade radiated from the noonday sun. The weathered handle drew his attention to the emblem emblazoned on the hilt, just as it had when he first saw it in the hallway at the inn. He'd thought then he'd been mistaken. Not now.

How in damnation did that woman get a Sword Dancer's blade?

He replaced the sword where he'd found it and tucked her cloak back into place. More puzzled than ever, he studied the tiny woman wrapped in the protective confines of the blankets. Anxiety and uneasiness stirred in him.

He returned to the fire after brushing, feeding and securing the two roans. Using his cloak as a pillow, he settled on the ground and faced her. Suna's hair caught the sunlight and glinted as if fireflies danced within its thick locks. He saw she kept her hands clenched into fists and curled tightly beneath her chin as she slept. The gentle rise and fall of her chest stirred his loins as he watched the swells of her breasts contract and expand under the thin fabric of her dress.

Beautiful. Untouchable. Completely unemotional. And volatile. That woman is fire.

Merely thinking such thoughts about a Divenean could have him trussed and hung by his toenails, but he couldn't help himself. There was something broken inside her, and for the strangest reason he felt an undeniable need to fix it.

He stared at her for the longest time before sleep claimed him.

* ~ * ~ *

When Feran woke, Suna was crouched by the fire brewing herbs into two steaming cups of boiled water. "Would you like some?" she asked without looking his way.

"Depends on what it is."

She half-turned and held his stare. "It's malezia. Master Bailor was kind enough to provide us some."

His brow folded.

"Malezia is a natural herb," she explained. "When it's steeped in hot water, it releases certain healing properties."

His shoulders rolled. "Sounds like wizen talk to me."

"Being an Elite Guard, and a Guardian no less, I would have thought you'd know what it was." She hadn't meant it to sound harsh, but that's exactly how it came out of her mouth. What was it about this man that made her lose all sense of civility? True, she was thankful for what he'd done for her. Waking to find a bed beneath her was more than she deserved, especially after the way she'd treated him, but why couldn't she just say thank you and be done with it? *Because I've lived far too long on my own, that's why.*

"Well, Lady Suna, do tell. What would a lowly soldier like me know about herbs?"

Her sigh rustled through the camp as she stood while balancing the two cups in her hands. She approached and knelt beside him. She was in no mood for their usual derogatory banter, and, apparently, neither was he. She studied the intensity in his verdant eyes. The familiarity she saw within them continued to elude her. With a shake of her head, she said, "I want to..."

She stopped, cleared her throat and began again. "I want to thank you for what you did for me. It was very kind." She thrust the cup out to him. A few drops sloshed onto her hand. It burned, but she didn't say anything. No one would get that satisfaction, and certainly not this boy-general. She continued to hold the cup until he took it, then she returned to her own blankets and sipped the hot, buttery liquid, keeping her eyes fixated on the dancing flames of their small fire. Stifling silence fell between them. "It replenishes strength, giving the body a boost when it's been drained of energy," she mumbled into her cup.

Feran sniffed the steam rising from his cup. "What does?"

"The malezia."

"It smells a little like my pipe tobac, but there's an undercurrent of fruitiness to it. So it's like koffea?" He took a careful sip.

"Koffea's a drug. Its purpose is addicting. This is naturalistic."

Shrugging again, he swallowed a mouthful. "Hey, this is good."

"I added a little honey. There's some salted pork and dried spiced fruits in the saddlebags."

The sour mood between them seemed to have turned. *All it takes is a little effort on your part. So why does he invoke these emotions in me? Have I changed that much?*

"Thanks, but I had some while you slept. You go ahead."

Awkward silence followed again. Then both their voices rang out in unison.

"Look..."

He gave her that lopsided grin of his—the one that created the odd fluttering in the base of her stomach.

"You first. Beauty before brawn, I always say."

"I know this is a strange situation, and you may be used to being in charge, but I take no leadership role here. We're both chasing the same thing. For me, I sense things differently. Thus, my reasoning and actions will differ from yours even though our goals may be the same."

One if his eyebrows arched and his tone held a thorny edge. "Explain *sense*, if you will."

She shook her head. *Definitely sensitive.* "I'm a Divenean. Nothing more. Nothing less. My senses and emotions are tied to these lands and its people. There's things I feel differently than you. And more intuitively." She looked away before mumbling, "And far too long have I ignored them."

"I'm a Guardian. No more. No less."

She met his gaze and held it. "You're more than a Guardian, General Feran. I don't profess to know how or why this quest has set our paths together, but be that as it may, I feel it's a meritorious one."

"Can I ask you a question, Lady Suna?"

"Please, just Suna."

He nodded at the subtle agreement reached between them. "Where did you get a hold of that sword of yours?"

She scowled toward the saddles lying on the ground beside the roans.

"Yes, I saw it," he confessed with a shrug. *Damn, I've offended her again. How is it that I cause her blistering nettles every time I open my mouth?*

Suna heard the words he didn't speak. They cut through her as a constant reminder of how much she'd changed. "I've been on my own for a long time, Feran. I find it difficult to communicate with people. I mean no disrespect or animosity, it's just—"

"There's no need to apologize."

"I wasn't apologizing. I'm explaining."

It was his turn to emit a frustrated sigh. "It seems that no matter what I say you take offense."

"Then stop acting like I am something of an anomaly. I am who I am, just like you. If we're going to get anywhere, I'd appreciate it if you would treat me as such."

He dipped his head. "I'll try, but it's a little intimidating, you know? If I tend to be a little awestruck and treat you differently, it's because it seems that every hour I'm with you I tend to learn something new, and it's usually something bizarre like you can fly. So, where did you get that sword?"

Placing her now empty cup on the ground, Suna draped her dusty dress over her knees and clasped her hands together. It was inevitable. Feran's questions needed answers. If they were to do this together, he deserved to know a little about her.

"As a Divenean, my task in life was decided by an Elder, as was the way with all in our Fold."

"I don't understand."

"A Fold is what one might call an extended family. Each Divenean served a specific purpose to these lands. Some could grow plant-life from parched soil. Others were memory holders of Etharia's histories. Some were even soldiers, like you. We all possessed mage'ic. It was inbred in us.

"You speak in past tense."

She shifted uncomfortably. "Mine was to fulfill one of the greatest of all needs. To protect and guide King Markes and his Queen."

"And what do you do when your tasks are finished?"

She looked to the flames and stretched her hands out toward its heat, wishing she could crawl straight into its fiery depths and disappear. Did she dare tell him that her mage'ic was inexplicitly tied to her emotions? "We return to our Fold and live out our days in peace and isolation."

"Then there's still more of you?"

"I haven't seen another of my kind, nor can I sense them anymore. After I left Dunkerk, I went into isolation of my own volition."

For a moment, sadness crossed over his face. "How did you get that sword?"

"I had to learn many different forms of self-defense, including the ancient sword dance of the Qaissa."

From the angle where she sat, she saw Feran's eyes widen. Without a word, he rose to his feet and pulled out his sword from the scabbard lying beside him. Upon the steel below the leather wrapped hilt lay the same emblem that adorned her blade. A lightning bolt surrounded by a circle of flames.

She wasn't the least bit surprised. The Qaissa training was so intense that only the strongest, finest swordsmen achieved the rank of Sword Dancer, and those men served as Guardians. She looked up, speaking before he had a chance to say what she knew he was about to. She didn't need to read his mind this time to know it was there. "I'm quite aware that women aren't taught this art of defense, but as I told you before, I'm no ordinary woman."

She tried to concentrate on the flames and convince herself that it was the fire, and not his expression, that was causing the heat inside her.

"See? That's what I'm talking about!"

"Excuse me?" The potency in his stare felt hotter than the fire.

"Never mind." He ran the fingers of his hand through the tangles in his hair.

"Would you care to practice? It's been some time since I sparred with a real person."

He shook his head and chuckled. "I'm definitely going to take you up on that offer, Suna, but right now we have to get moving. We may be able reach that imp before he crosses the Carberra River."

Disappointed at the lost opportunity to practice with a fellow master, she gathered up the blankets and strode to their horses. She began saddling the animals while Feran kicked dirt over the dying embers of their campfire and packed away their supplies.

They rode at a steady pace until twilight's gloom darkened the skies to midnight black. Like the night before, the land cloaked itself in ominous silence.

"This is Ilio's wake," Suna shouted over the horses' pounding hooves.

Feran moved closer, matching her stride for stride. "What do you mean?"

"It's the evil emanating from him. His presence silences the land. He creates a darker night. The living hide. Balthazar will bring this and much more horror if he's freed."

"You're just trying to cheer me up, aren't you?"

In the distance, strange flares of light suddenly lit over the eastern skies. They reined in their mounts and stared up at the erratic bursts of colors slicing through the sky like lightning. Then it stopped.

Feran shifted uneasily in his saddle. "What in damnation was that?"

"Ilio has reached the ferry." With a snap of her reins, Suna's roan took off at full speed.

~~*

As Ethbridge waited in the dusty cubbyhole, he stared at the round beveled glass window that hadn't seen a washrag in years. It was quite by accident that he'd found this secret place, and he chortled quietly at the sweet memory.

The previous year he'd found himself seated at one of the high lords' table at Harvest Festival, one of many lavish affairs Mollster hosted. Having become quite proficient at making up excuses to explain his usual absences, he'd reluctantly accepted that particular invitation on Greth's insistence. Much to his chagrin, the Lord of Carberra hadn't shown his face, which left Ethbridge surrounded by an array of buffoons and misfits who had the audacity to call themselves proper lords and ladies.

He'd passed over the many succulent dishes and settled on a bottle of Mollster's most expensive wines, all the while admiring Odarian's tantalizing serving wenches. One in particular, an amber-haired maiden with cherry lips and a come-hither haze in her doe-like eyes caught his attention. He'd winked at her all evening. When she'd finally reciprocated, he decided to enjoy himself at Mollster's expense. After she returned to his table to replace the bottle he'd just finished, he leaned over and whispered promises he never intended to keep. The delightful vixen had giggled and nodded in return.

They'd left the party arm in arm, him staggering and her leading the way. The delicious strumpet guided him down a passage of Mollster's castle that he'd been unfamiliar with. She'd stopped at an aged tapestry hanging on the wall and drew it aside to reveal a cellar-like door built into the concealed alcove. "Only a few of the long-time servants knows this is here," she'd confided.

His blood had boiled with desire when her hot breath swirled in his ear. He'd quickly sobered up at the thought of what was to come next.

Once inside, he'd found some rope and tied her to a rusted metal headboard. Her chirpy laughter and naïveté had urged him to better ideas. Her chuckles were soon short-lived when he brought out his new riding crop. After he'd ripped her bodice from her shoulders, their delightful tryst began. His cries of pleasure, and hers of pain, rang out down the empty corridor. He knew the scars he'd left on her backside would mend in time, but he sensed the others he'd rendered would never heal.

Once he'd had his fill of her, he kicked the young girl from the room, where she stumbled to her knees on the floor, a broken mess, bleeding and sobbing. He'd sneered at her weakness as he passed her to return to the dining hall, peeling off his bloodied leather gloves as he went.

He'd looked for her during his visit here today, but found her gone from Mollster's employ.

His attention returned to the present as footsteps sounded outside in the hallway. Ethbridge drew himself further into the shadows as the door creaked open and a large shadow filled the entranceway.

"Nyles?"

He hissed. "Close the damn door."

Greth fumbled his way inside. There was a resounding *thud* followed by a string of profanity. "Damn you to the three Hells, man. Couldn't you have found a more lighted place to meet?"

He watched in amusement as Greth rubbed his shin, his eyes having adjusted to the gloom long ago. "No one knows we're here, so stop complaining. This part of the castle has been closed off for years. Mollster and his two lackeys are meeting in his private bedchambers anyway. I saw them heading there when I left my room. Believe me, this is the safest place to talk."

Greth snorted an inaudible retort.

Ethbridge hoisted himself up on an abandoned crate in the far corner and dangled his thin legs over the edge, smirking as the large man ambled his way toward him, this time carefully maneuvering a path through the obstacles.

The large underlord growled again as he sidestepped an array of discarded boxes and forgotten furnishings. "How did you ever find such a rat's nest?"

"Mollster may be an idiot, but he does employ some of the most superb serving bitches."

"I don't need the details of your sordid affairs," Greth replied with a growl. "We're here to discuss business."

His mood soured. "What's this about a Divenean? And Isafel?" He despised the way his voice quivered. Even saying the name brought chills to ice his spine.

Greth's eyes slit dangerously. "He's a fool. Been listening to rumors. No one's seen a Divenean in years. It's just a ploy of Mollster's, but it won't affect our plans."

"Well, he certainly isn't going to sit around doing nothing while he waits for our answer. It's damn inconvenient for this to happen now. Do you think he knows?"

Greth leaned against a pile of bric-a-brac. "Mollster is as dimwitted as he is old. First we return home and deliver our responses to him after we've thought about it further. We're amassing our armies, Nyles, but for different reasons. Nothing will deter us from the original plan. Do you hear me?"

"What makes you so confident?"

Greth offered him a condescending jeer. "You seem to forget that I have a little inside help."

"And you seem to forget that your nephew thinks with the wrong head," he snipped back.

"He'll do as he's told. What Wendel lacks upstairs, he makes up for with that cock of his. Women will do anything for something hard and thick between their legs,"

Ethbridge chortled like a fool. Greth soon joined in.

"In fact," the Lord of Carberra added. His eyes glinted dangerously in the gloom. "Kingdoms have been won and lost for far less than that insignificant little hole."

CHAPTER THIRTEEN

The ferry guardsmen were apprehensive when Karel approached the first outpost, and rightly so. These days, everyone harbored a wariness of any man, woman or child who journeyed at night, but they soon came to realize there was little to fear from the stranger, especially after Karel weaved them a tale of his life as a traveling bard. Believing his every word, they begged him to stay and play for them.

Pulling out an ebony grezadil from his double-wrap belt, Karel placed the flute to his lips and began to play. The other two guards who'd been resting inside the second outpost soon joined the musical festivities. He played several songs, much to their delight. Soon they were clapping and tapping their feet to the bouncy tunes that flowed effortlessly from his musical instrument.

As Karel entertained the men, his élan honed in on the approach of another entity. He immediately stopped playing. With a flourishing bow, he put away his instrument and smiled heartfelt apologies at the insistent urgings of the ferrymen to play on. He paid them little attention as he focused on the small, contorted figure limping his way closer toward them. It wasn't the oddity of the individual, but the corruption and evil preceding it.

So the soldier of ill will shows himself, Karel mused with a laden heart.

Bidding the guardsmen a fair evening and a promise to return, he strode along the shore of Carberra's waters just as Balthazar's child reached the first outpost. With a touch of his mage'ic he listened to their exchange of words.

"The ferry isn't running this night. You'll have to find other means of travel or come back in the morning," the first guard called out.

"I have silver to pay. You will take me," the imp replied.

Karel stopped and shrouded himself within a spell of shadow to watch unseen. He'd vowed to take no action, but he worried whether his conscience would allow it.

Realizing the stranger was nothing more than a deformed dwarf, the other two sentries returned to resume their slumber.

"State your business," the second soldier said.

"I need passage to the Gates. You will take me." It wasn't a request, but a demand.

In his mind's eye, Karel saw the first guard raise his brow in disbelief, but his features soon turned to loathing when the imp stepped further into the firelight.

"There's no passage for you this night. Go and find other means."

The creature sneered back and wiped a crusty sleeve under his runny nose. "Could passage be bought if I was perhaps taller and not so uncomely?"

When raucous laughter erupted from the men, Karel cringed.

"No ferry will be traveling these here waters tonight, so be off with you," the first soldier said, his face twisting into a repulsive sneer.

The creature moved closer and grinned. Karel's blood turned to ice when he saw the decaying teeth and disfigured face, which was more recognizable now with the firelight reflecting off the water.

The second guard took a defensive stance and gripped his sword. The imp waved one of his crooked arms in his direction, which sent the soldier hurling through the air to land with bone crushing force against the far wall of the main outpost. He dropped like a boulder to the ground. While the injured guardsman drowned in the blood filling his chest, sickening gurgling noises sliced through the shocked silence.

The other guard gawked at the imp in disbelief. Then the fool rushed forward with his sword drawn.

The two other sentries, now roused from their beds, stumbled out in time to see their brother-in-arms levitating several feet above their heads.

The guard in the air shrieked as a loud ripping sound tore through the night. The men watched helplessly as the suspended soldier's body split from the base of his crotch up to his neck. Then the man's head fell to the left, dangling from the shoulder by strings of stretched, mutilated flesh. His eyes were wide and his mouth still open in a scream that had been instantly silenced. He hung in the air as two separate halves.

The imp released his mage'ic and the lifeless body dropped at the feet of the other two horrified ferrymen. Blood and guts suspended by the spell sprayed out like an afternoon shower, drenching the two who stood transfixed in horror.

Still standing at the water's edge, Karel watched the scene unfold in his mind. He clenched his sword, uncertain what to do.

The imp narrowed his eyes into slits. "Now which one of you will live to ferry me across?" When neither guard answered, he captured them within snaking bands of dark, indigo mage'ic.

Karel couldn't allow the loss of more innocent lives. He hurried back to the outposts, careful to keep the hood of his cloak over his face. "This seems to be an unfair fight. If you release those men you have my word I'll ferry you across myself."

He kept one eye on the imp and the other on the two men whose expressions of terror tore at his heart. He had to be cautious in discharging his mage'ic for fear of alerting the two he knew were following, but his choices were looking slim.

Ilio sneered and ran his sleeve under his runny nose again. "Do you care for these men's lives over your own?"

"My life could be deemed as unimportant as yours, Ilio. Or just as important."

A flash of fury, and surprise, passed over the creature's face. With a twist of his hand, he crushed the life out of one of the ferrymen he held before releasing another spell. This time directly at Karel.

As Karel had hoped, the imp wasn't strong enough to separate the flows of his powers. The other guard dropped like a stone to the ground.

Karel moved fast as a surge of black energy charged at him. The power emanating from this vile creature staggered the Divenean. A ferocious *whoosh* of vile alchemy missed him by mere finger lengths. This close to such unnatural elements made him recoil.

Karel turned and ran from the water's edge to the front of the far outpost. It was inevitable. He'd have to use his powers.

He retaliated with a blinding blast of his own mage'ic as Ilio raced to the left. Dirt exploded several feet in the air behind him. Once it cleared, the creature had vanished. He threw his next spell with both hands out. The outpost on the left exploded. Thick splinters of wood shot through the air like toothsticks.

Ilio proved cunning. He'd waded through the water from behind and attacked Karel from the right. The noise that followed deafened him.

Even though the blast of the imp's mage'ic landed a few hairs short of its mark, Karel hadn't been quick enough. Agony flared down the side of his ribcage as the creature's spell stripped a layer of skin off his body. He wiped at the ashes burning his eyes, sensing a trap about to be unleashed. Desperate to find the little demon through the dense smoke, he spotted him at last—trying to untie the ferry's docking ropes. The creature turned at the last moment. Unprepared, he threw a wild blast in Karel's direction just as Karel released his own spell.

Both grey and white energies hit simultaneously. The violent concussion of conflicting powers meeting head on ricocheted both of them several feet into the air. The remaining outpost on the right exploded into towering flames. Karel landed hard on the pathway leading to the water. He heard rather than felt his head connect with the flat of a rock.

He woke to find the imp and the guardsman gone, as well as the ferry. Karel now knew without a doubt the task Balthazar had appointed to the creature.

He's found the scent of the Kruthos' key.

He'd have liked nothing better than to have killed the imp outright, but Karel couldn't interfere. He needed the vile beast. Like Isafel. The paragon he'd created had to remain unaltered. Certain events needed to happen without intervention.

On shaky legs, Karel rose and gathered his wits. Billows of black smoke rose from the one outpost still engulfed in flames. The other structure was now unrecognizable.

With an unrelenting throbbing in his head, he hurried westward toward the nearest copse of trees. When safely out of sight, he chewed a handful of zelato leaves and picked out the bits of dried blood matted in his gray-streaked hair from the cut on his forehead. Then he washed his face and the wound with water from his waterskin.

After wrapping himself within the confines of a concealment spell, he closed his eyes and muttered an incantation to accelerate his healing.

He felt the world shudder then. A rippling concussion that carried like an ominous warning throughout Etharia. The paragon he'd worked so hard to create had begun. He smiled as he fell into the abyss of healing sleep.

His protégé and null warrior had reached Carberry Ferry.

CHAPTER FOURTEEN

The currents of the Carberra River flowed less swiftly here on the ferry side, and under the night sky, it glittered like pieces of broken glass scattered across its surface until the waterway disappeared into infinite blackness around a northern bend that extended several leagues from the main flow of the river. There the shores grew narrower with fast, dangerous currents and a muddy bottom. Tributaries from the Carberra fed every kingdom and village in its vicinity with fresh water.

On the northeastern shores was Lord Greth's lands—and directly across both sides of the Carberra River, Valhallen Gates. From there, Kingshead Road, which led to Dunkerk.

Suna and Feran halted at what was left of the two outposts that had once stood as the docks of Carberra's crossing. The devastation ripped the air from her lungs. One building was nothing more than a pile of embers. The other consisted of scattered bits of charred wood that clogged the water's edge. Three male bodies, possibly four, lay strewn across the area like torn apart, waterlogged rag dolls. The insignia on the left forearm of one uniform drew her attention. A three mast Trireme adorned by three gold stars encircling the bowsprit.

"These men belonged to Lord Tobas Greth, Underlord of Carberra," Suna said.

She discovered the docking lines of the one ferry cut and found floating among the debris, while the other had been destroyed beyond use. Her hope vanished. Behind her a guttural growl erupted from Feran.

"What kind of *thing* is this Ilio?" Feran snarled between gritted teeth.

"What Ilio touches, he destroys. It's his nature. He's an abomination birthed from the fires of perdition. And he obeys and follows one master. He's but a paltry soldier intent on fulfilling his orders."

She glanced over her shoulder to give him a moment to let her words sink in before turning to study the chaos around her. *Ilio could have killed these men without such unwarranted damage.* She closed her eyes and brought her quickening to life. Her élan moved forward, searching for those unique threads of mage'ic inevitably left behind. She staggered. *Another mage!*

Her viewings of late had been nothing short of extraordinary, and this time was no different. Thick, twisting ribbons of blinding white light moved in fluid formations like sensuous dancers caught in a waltz she couldn't hear. She ventured a timid touch, a mere speck of her consciousness to discover the residual pattern inherent in all mages, but Ilio's distorted imprint, which consisted of masses of sinuous gray vileness, kept her at bay and made her wince. It continued to battle in between the patterns of brilliant light to diminish its brightness. There was something familiar about those dancing white bands. Something that tugged at her.

Just before she could touch on the elusive memory, Feran strode by and wavered her concentration. Suna released the quickening to watch him approach the two skittish roans. He whispered words to ease their obvious anxiety. They didn't like the sulfuric smoke burning their eyes, or the stench of freshly spilled blood.

Feran mounted his horse. With a haunted gaze, he stared out across the water, all the while fidgeting with his reins. "We won't be crossing here. It's more than half a day of hard riding if we're going to reach Jorja Ferry. Maybe longer. Worse, the horses are almost spent." He stopped and squeezed the bridge of his nose.

She turned her attention to the water because the defeat on Feran's face almost broke her resolve. He had a habit of hiding his emotions behind some form of mockery. However, in this instance she knew he couldn't find one. "There's another way."

"How? You're going to mage'ically build us another ferry?"

"It's a means of traveling. A spell. A conjuring called *Manifestis*."

His brow crinkled. "Out of the pot and into the fire?"

And there it was. The jester had returned. She'd wager half the gold in her belt that mage'ic was one of his least favorite things—next to her. "It's a powerful spell," she said. "I'd invoked the same the day King Markes passed from this world. I had to reach him quickly."

Feran slid down from his saddle. "How dangerous is it?"

She struggled with the fact she'd even suggested it. If they journeyed south to Jorja Ferry, which was an additional three to four hours of hard riding, they'd have no choice but to dock at Merkanna as that was as far as the ferry went up river. From there they'd have an hour, maybe more, of riding before getting to Valhallen's Gates. If they crossed east into the kingdom of Carberra, there was a good possibility of hiring one of Lord Greth's swiftest ships that would take them directly to Kinghead's Road.

Either way, it would be days before they reached Dunkerk. By that time Ilio would be lost within its walls. In a kingdom that size it would take weeks before they found a scent of him—if at all.

"What about the horses?"

"I've never used this spell on more than one person," she confessed with a grimace. "I think it's best we leave them behind and continue on foot."

"How far can we travel using this Mana-festa spell?"

She focused on the glassy water. "It's called *Manifestis*. How many leagues is it to the other side? Then to Carberra?"

"At this point of the river? An hour by ferry to cross, and then we'd need horses. At least a day. Probably more."

"The horses stay." Just as the words left her mouth something unusual brushed like damp cobwebs across her consciousness. Concentrating on a small copse of trees dotting the horizon less than a half league north, the sensation vanished as quickly as she'd felt it. Whatever it was, she didn't have time to dwell on it.

In good conscience, Suna had to tell Feran what she'd seen here. Their partnership hadn't started out great and keeping something like this from him felt wrong. Even dangerous.

She drew a deep breath and began. "This is a battle scene, Feran."

"Tell me something I don't know."

"Someone else tried to stop Ilio from crossing. That's why there's all this destruction. The creature is maniacal, true, but this would have been a waste of his time and energy. All mage'ic leaves a residual imprint.

A mage's inscription, so to speak. What I see here is white light battling with depravity. Namely, Ilio."

The sound of Feran's laughter ricocheted around them.

In the midst of all this death that was the last thing she expected to hear. *Honestly, he's as infuriating as Mollster was in his youth.* "What's so funny?"

As he continued chortling, Feran managed to spit out, "We're not alone, Suna. Don't you get it? We're not alone."

The cryptic message: *You will never be alone again, Suna Di'Viao. This I promise.* A reminder that all wasn't lost. Hope that was forever trying to fade flared to life.

Feran's laughter faded as he squinted into the distance. "What's stopping Ilio from using the same spell?"

"I think if he knew of such an incantation he'd have used it. But…"

"But what?"

"It's a powerful form of mage'ic and one that can't be expelled at leisure, but I want to discuss—"

"How dangerous?"

His constant interruptions were exasperating. She inhaled and counted to three before letting her breath out. "All conjuring's can be dangerous. If Ilio had used it, I'd be able to see telltale signs of the spell. As I said, mage'ic leaves a residual mark. The more powerful the spell the deeper the imprint. There's nothing here." She hesitated.

"Will you just come out with it already?"

"There's other mage'ics at play here. Not just the imp's." She moved in front of her roan and ran her fingers down its elongated nose. The animal nickered in response.

"You still haven't answered my question. How dangerous is it to me?"

"It's... Well... Mage'ic reacts differently to a null's body."

"How much time will we save to cross the Carberra and make it to the other side using this Mana-whatever? Alive, that is."

"Less than an hour, give or take a few minutes. I haven't traveled this particular route, so I have no mental picture of landmarks."

She saw a moment of confusion cross his face before she turned away. "I'll have to envision the other side in order to maintain a strategic course. There is the possibility..." She stopped and looked over her shoulder at him, but Feran's attention was focused on the water. "We could end up in the middle of the river. That's why I asked how far we are. If I can visualize the distance, then I can place us safely on the other side." *I hope.*

"Are you serious?"

Do I tell him everything or let him experience it?

By expending that amount of energy, she'd be rendered weak. Very weak. Although she'd fare better than Feran would, at least in the beginning. His reaction to mage'ic would be almost instantaneous. It would take at least half a day for symptoms of the depletion of energy to manifest in her. However, if she had to choose between his ill-effects and hers, she'd choose her's in a heartbeat.

The stronger the emotion, the more resilient the spell. Her mage'ic was tied to her emotions. However, she'd been alone so long, she worried whether she had the ability to do this. The last time had been for King Markes, and the need then had been great, indeed.

Do I risk this with Feran being caught in the middle? Unfortunately, they'd been left with little choice.

Conjuring a spell of this magnitude would take every emotion she could muster—and maintain control. It was a risk she had to take. "Feran, this isn't easy to conjure. Because of its potency, there's going to be some after-effects."

"Like what?"

"Because your body's chemistry has no protection against the infusion of spells into a system that is resistant to any forms of intrusion, be it a germ, or in this case, mage'ic, there's going to be some adverse effects. Mages wield mage'ic. Thus, we're impervious to its effects. At least some of them."

Suspicion pinched the corners of his eyes. "How unpleasant is this going to be?"

"The spell places extreme stress on the natural balance of a null's body."

"You make null sound like it's a bad thing."

Just tell him. She turned and stared him straight in the eyes. "You'll be on your knees heaving the insides of your stomach out and praying to the gods to take you."

His mouth dropped open, but not a word came out.

"It's not a pleasant thing for nulls. Not pleasant at all," she murmured. *So why do I feel bad for telling him the truth?*

Without hesitation, he began unsaddling his horse.

Suna unbuckled the straps holding her saddle in place and slid it to the ground before slinging her travel bag across her back. Rising up on her toes, she whispered into the roan's velvety ears, "Thank you for our safe journey."

When both horses stood stripped of their fetters, Feran slapped them on their rumps and sent them running west toward Odarian. Her vision blurred with tears. As if reading her mind, both spirited roans looked back with goodbye nickers. They continued to run, eager to return home.

"Here's hoping they make it back. If they don't, my debt to Bailor will take years to pay off," Feran grumbled. "Not to mention having to leave two perfectly good saddles for anyone to take."

"They told me they'd behave and return straight home."

The corners of his eyes crinkled as he grinned. "Did they now?"

"Yes. By the way, don't kick their sides so hard with your boots. Your roan complained about a bruise you'd given him."

Without waiting for the wisecrack comment she knew was to follow, she proceeded to the water's edge to make preparation for the spell.

The success of invoking something this powerful lay in splitting her élan, which meant separating two halves of herself, including her emotions, into equal portions. As well, there were two of them to transport. One half of her élan to shield and transport Feran, and the other to do the same for herself. Double the endurance to maintain. Was she strong enough? *He's going to despise me more after this, if that's at all possible.*

Suna took a deep breath and exhaled slowly. "Feran, please come and stand by me."

* ~ * ~ *

Feran's enthusiasm evaporated into uncertainty. He'd never had direct contact with mage'ic other than the odd mages' kiosks he'd visit during festivals in Dunkerk. Harmless sideshow varieties of slight-of-hand tricks and disappearing acts didn't come close to what Suna had suggested. However, their need to get to Valhallen's Gates before that imp far outweighed his misgivings.

Before he approached the water's edge, he whistled for one of Mollster's falcon couriers. It wasn't long before the avian swooped low and landed on the ground beside his feet. Feran wrote a hasty note to the underlord and sent the falcon flying to Odarian. Then he went to stand beside Suna, all the while wishing his guts would unknot.

The lapping waves that hit the tips of his boots sounded almost musical. Intertwined with Suna's murmuring in a strange language, her voice and the sound of the water meshed in perfect harmony. From the corner of his eye, he saw luminescent light surround her. With every beat of his heart, it grew brighter, larger. When she faced him and opened her eyes, therein was the true nature of her gifts. Pervaded in a rapture he'd never know, a power he could never touch, she radiated with the life of mage'ic within her. He stared, awestruck. She was beautiful before, but now? There were no words to describe her.

"Take my hands."

Her voice sounded as if she travelled through a cave. The tone hummed not only in his ears, but throughout his entire body.

He did as she asked and took her hand. The instant their fingers touched that irregular shift in the air occurred again, just as it had in Odarian, but this time it was far more intimate—like touching her soul. Fire and ice raced down his spine. He cried out, but there was no sound.

The light around Suna somewhat faded, and she stumbled slightly, but her lips continued to move in silent oration. The glow around her strengthened and engulfed him.

Those odd mini-explosions whenever they touched was one thing, but what happened next was unbelievable. It was as if the very water rose up and submerged them, though it was neither wet nor cold. It filled the small space between them, pushing them closer like lovers. He'd be enjoying this in any other scenario, but when he realized he couldn't breathe, panic ensued. He closed his eyes and tried not to scream. His head pounded as he struggled to hold his breath.

"Relax, Feran. I'm with you. Don't be afraid to breathe."

The melodic drone of her tone wrapped him in a sense of security he hadn't felt since before the passing of his mother. Then came a sudden rush of exhilaration.

He cracked open an eye and realized they were inside an oblong sphere made up of what looked to be thousands of tiny mirror images of themselves. It felt as if they were standing still, but the images didn't. Each moved in blurring sequences. His stomach flipped. He squeezed his eyes shut again, hoping he wouldn't get sick. As strange energy sizzled across his body, radiating warmth followed.

"Not much longer."

The sound of her voice penetrated through his fear and delved deep into the nonexistent water that had and had not drowned him. He relaxed and dared to take a breath.

The next thing he knew he was on his knees spewing out everything he'd ever eaten. His head swam like no amount of mead had ever done. He tried to move, but he retched worse than before.

Suna was suddenly beside him trying to pry his mouth open and feed him some kind of dried, leafy substance that sent him into another violent fit of regurgitation.

"Feran, chew on a few of these leaves. It'll help settle your stomach. Please try."

"I'm—not—moving," he managed in between a round of dry heaving.

Spittle ran down his chin, but he didn't care. Finally, she managed to force a few sprigs in between his teeth. It took everything not to bring them back up. He forced himself to swallow the grass-like mixture as he wallowed in a fog of agony that refused to end. Several long minutes passed before he tried moving his head. Thankfully, he found the world tilting a little less sadistically.

"Have a few more leaves." She hand-fed him. This time he discovered the substance easier to swallow.

"You'll feel more like yourself soon. Now rest."

He turned in her direction. Suna knelt on the ground beside him looking worse than he felt. Dark circles hollowed her eyes and the pallor of her skin was like that of twenty-year-old whitewash. There were obvious side-effects to her that she hadn't bothered to mention.

"Move slowly. It'll lessen the head-spins." She lay supine on the ground and stared up at the smattering of evening stars.

"Where are we?" he whispered, too afraid to speak louder for fear of bringing on another round of spewing.

"I don't know. Thankfully, we're not in the river. We'll rest for an hour or so. Just know that we've saved ourselves days of travel." Her voice was laden with weariness.

He moved beside her wondering if it'd been worth it. In order to catch that little demon? Yes, it was.

Every inch he gained was a victory against the nausea threatening to take him ten feet under. By the time he made it next to her, she'd fallen asleep. Too weak to care, Feran closed his eyes and joined her.

* ~ * ~ *

Mollster stormed into his bedchambers and petrified the poor chamber-maiden who'd had the unfortunate luck to be turning down his bed at that precise time. "Leave me!"

Malenda completed a half curtsy before running from the room like a frightened burrow-rabbit. He knew it wasn't fair to take his frustration out on her, but he was past livid. *I'll apologize later. When I simmer down.*

Once the door closed behind the fleeing woman, he erupted like a spoiled child in the throes of a tantrum. "Think about it?" he fumed as he cut a path across the carpet. "What in the devil's lair is there to think about? We're at a major crux and those two fool-headed ignoramuses have the audacity to suggest sleeping on it? Oh, and let's not make any hasty decisions?"

As he stormed about the room, he picked up one figurine after another to throw, but thinking better of it, he slammed them down only to continue his furious back-and-forth pacing.

With the Kruthos found how much time is left for us? Can we even fight a war against demons and expect to win with no Diveneans to aid us?

When a faint knock sounded outside his door, he bellowed like thunder. "I don't want to be disturbed!"

"My lordship?" a timid Malenda squeaked. "Lords Fenwick and Conac are here to speak with you. They're insistent, my lord. I apologize, but..."

Mollster lulled his anger beneath folds of resignation. It was inevitable that he'd have to face those two men, but he would have preferred later.

He poured himself a large goblet of mulled wine from a festooned flagon Malenda had placed on his bedside table and gulped down the entire contents. Fire scorched his throat and warmed his belly, but it also dulled his fury. He grabbed the decanter, two extra glasses and carried them to the area of the bedchamber Sonie used to call the sitting room. He missed her so much, especially at moments like this. She would have been quick to calm his anger with just a touch of her hand.

"Show them in," he said, sounding calmer than he felt. He settled into his favorite chair just as the door opened.

"Malenda?" he called out before the maid had an opportunity to scamper away.

The door opened again, although she remained hidden from view. "Yes, my lord?" Her meek voice trembled.

"There was no reason for me to speak so rudely to you before. Please accept my apology. And see to it that I'm not disturbed for the rest of the afternoon."

The words rushed from her mouth. "Yes, my lord. Of course, my lord. Will you take your evening dinner in your chambers?"

"No. I have things I need to attend to. Thank you again," he said, eyeing the two underlords who were helping themselves to his wine before sitting in two flanking overstuffed chairs.

Malenda added a hasty, "Yes, my lord," before closing the door behind her. The rustlings of her petticoats and slippered footfalls faded down the corridor.

Before taking a sip, Fenwick raised his glass in Mollster's direction, his thoughtful stare boring into him. "It's nice to see you in more relaxed circumstances, my friend."

"I as well," Conac added with a tip of his glass.

The three men sat in comfortable silence, each drinking and waiting for the other to begin.

When enough time had passed, Mollster shrugged. "I can't tell you any more than I have."

Conac's rumbling sigh filled the quiet of the room. "We know, but there's other issues we need to discuss nonetheless."

He didn't like the sound of that one bit, but then again, nothing these days seemed to be of happy news. Shifting beneath their inquisitive stares, he waited.

"Ethbridge is up to something, and I don't like the feel of it." Conac stopped and took a deep swallow of his wine. "The Barbs have been talking. They've noticed that Vansgaard's troops haven't been out on regular patrols."

Fenwick's eyes narrowed suspiciously. "That's odd. He seems to take great pleasure in capturing as many of them as he can. Then executing them."

"But not lately, and that has me concerned. He's learned quite a bit from Greth."

When Conac stretched out his thick legs, Mollster noticed the sheen of his polished boots and concentrated there, not wanting to look at either of them. "Do you have substantive proof of this?" he asked. He knew it was common practice for each of them to employ their own network of spies that worked the kingdoms. Extra ears and eyes came in handy when keeping a watch on those two particular underlords, but information like this needed verification.

"She's a woman who occasions Ethbridge's bed. Although not one of his favorites…" Conac hesitated with a grimace. "She's been a fount of information to me for several years now. She advises that their pillow talk of late has consisted of some rather closed mouth innuendoes."

"Innuendoes? That's of little use to us without proof. What makes you think he's up to something?" Mollster took a sip of his now lukewarm wine.

"Because, and this is what I've been told, his lovemaking, if that's what you want to call it, hasn't been as, well, violent."

Fenwick stiffened. "Violent?"

Conac gave a repugnant sneer. "His sexual tastes? They aren't exactly what you and I might call ordinary. Ethbridge likes pain, or rather giving it as pleasure. My girl has a strange taste for it. That's why I sent her to Vansgaard."

Fenwick's eyes glittered with mischievous teasing. "And how does one find an *experienced* woman such as that, my dear friend?"

Conac grinned. "Quite by accident, I must say."

Fenwick looked to be enjoying this far too much. "Does your sweet Lady Venna know of your, um, peculiar tastes?"

Mollster leaned closer. This levity was well needed.

"This was before Lady Venna, I'll have you know." The underlord gave an indignant toss of his head, though a roaring chuckle followed. "Whether you believe it or not, our meeting was quite by accident. When she asked that I do, well, certain things to her, it got my mind working."

Fenwick opened his mouth, but Mollster held up his hand. "And she just agreed to prostitute herself out for you?" He tried not to smirk.

Conac's cheeks flushed as bright as the primroses in Odarian's gardens, which contrasted the whiteness of his hair. "We've strayed a bit off the topic here, don't you think?"

"Yes, yes, of course, but one does need some amusement on solemn occasions such as this. Do tell, man." Mollster's frustrations and anger dwindled. He could always count on his two fondest friends to make him feel better.

Conac threw up his hands in surrender. "Look, I performed my *duty* and then I asked if she would like to perform another for her lord. With appropriate pay, mind you." Giving them a patronizing glare, he took a mouthful of wine, pursed his lips and swallowed hard.

Refusing to say more, he stared over Mollster's shoulder at the silver armor on the wall. Armor that had yet to see battle.

"That's just the cut and dried version," Fenwick whined. "Details would help the matter out so much more, don't you think, Mollster?"

He rolled his eyes and returned to the subject at hand. "What do you think Ethbridge is conniving, Conac?"

"His borders have been unmanned for several months. The Barbs have always tried to stay out of his clutches, but they tell me it's worse now."

Mollster felt as confused as Fenwick looked. "How can it be worse if there's fewer of his border patrols?"

"When you become accustomed to something and it's abruptly taken away, would you not be wary?"

Mollster nodded as he stroked his chin. "I see your point. My personal opinion? I think he *and* Greth are up to something."

"That pompous swine Greth always has something up one of those fagel sleeves of his. I'm sure you've heard the rumor that he's placed his dimwitted nephew, what in damnation is his name, Wendel something or other, in contention for the throne?" Fenwick scowled and took a long swallow of wine.

"They're rumors. I don't place any truth in such things." Mollster leaned back and rubbed his temples. "There's far too many of those stories to contend with these days."

"Tittle-tattles concerning Greth usually turn out to be true," Fenwick spat.

Mollster knew Fenwick endured the most from Greth's umbrageous nature because of their neighboring lands. The young man spoke from personal experience.

"I have to agree with Mollster," Conac added carefully. "With the news that you've just placed on our laps and these deaths occurring in every kingdom, I've become quite interested in listening to such tales of late. Beneath all the embellishment is some form of truth." He paused. "Personally, I think Greth's going for the throne."

Stunned silence filled the bedchamber as they stared at one another. Mollster realized he hadn't been the only one nursing the same concern.

"This could be the reason why they're both so adamant about *sleeping on it*," Fenwick added, stirring the amber liquid in his goblet with a finger. "They're working in cahoots, but what could Ethbridge possibly gain?"

Mollster reached a similar conclusion at the same time as Conac.

"I'll kill him!" the giant underlord bellowed as he jumped to his feet and slammed his glass down on the table. His chest heaved, his face redder than ever.

"Let's not be hasty here, Conac. We have no proof Ethbridge is going to try to take control of Laspeth from you."

Fenwick pushed forward in his chair and continued to swish the wine around in his glass. "If Greth gains the throne by nomination, then what's stopping him from offering Ethbridge power over not just Laspeth, but Karvelle? Or even Odarian? He'd be king and have the authority to replace us all with other High House members without lifting a sword."

Conac slumped back into his chair. "He'd have control over every Elite Guard and Guardian of Dunkerk. He'd rule absolute and usurp us all." His paw-sized hand ran over the shorn bristles of his hair.

Fenwick's baby-blues glazed with anger. "And if Greth gains the throne, I'm sure he'd do just that. This Divenean?"

Mollster looked away. "I cannot say who it is or what their quest entails, but believe me, Isafel is free. With everything else we have to deal with, we have to concentrate our attention on the most urgent."

"We believe you, Mollster," Fenwick cut in. "These deaths that not only your people are suffering, but mine, and Conac's as well, aren't right. At least it's something we know about and can at least fight against."

The man's sigh that followed sounded as laden as Mollster's heart. "Let's deal with the most important issue that we can, shall we? First, Greth and his lapdog Ethbridge. There're only two of them and three of us. You know the saying. Strength in numbers? You two will amass your armies and await further word from me. As we speak, the Divenean and warrior are heading toward Dunkerk." He ignored their shocked expressions. "We'll wait and see what response we receive back from Greth. Ethbridge won't move a snail's inch without his authorization, that interminable pile of goat dung," he spat under his breath. "We shall keep this bit of information between us for now, but be wary, men. Be very wary."

Conac and Fenwick nodded. Like Mollster, the tribulations that were now before them were more than any Etharia had ever faced.

CHAPTER FIFTEEN

Suna was the first to rouse. The night's heavy dew had created an uncomfortable heaviness in her bladder, which brought a hurried need to relieve herself. Her tongue felt thick, like a fat, fuzzy caterpillar had made its home in her mouth. The back of her eyes ached from the sun's intense glare and it was only early morn.

She stood and stretched muscles that had grown stiff from lying stationary so long. Right now, she had to contend with her full bladder. A fever would begin to kindle—an after-effect caused by the consumption of such an exorbitant amount of mage'ic. Her mage'ical skills had weakened. As a wizen, she hadn't used them to their full potential, but she knew the more she wielded, the stronger she'd become. The residual effect that was coming would dissipate in a day, but judging by the height of the sun and the heavy humidity already in the air, she'd be suffering in short time.

At least she'd feel better than Feran. For a little while.

After searching through the one pack Feran still had strapped across his back, she pulled out her rumpled traveling clothes and hid behind some thick brush to relieve herself. Once properly attired, she ripped apart the hem of her dress and fashioned a scarf to wrap around her forehead to prevent the sweat already beading on her skin from running into her eyes. By the time she finished, her jerkin was stuck to her skin soaked through and through with perspiration. She then began the tedious job of combing out her hair with her fingers and braiding it into a thick fishtail.

She peered at him as he lay cushioned on the soft grass. Sleeping soundly on his side with one arm draped across the other, he seemed to have endured the lingering after-effects better than most. She barely remembered what had happened after the invoking the spell, but seeing him suffer like she did was ingrained in her memory.

Feran mumbled and rolled over. One of his eyes opened, then the other. When he moaned, she moved closer.

"How do you feel?" she asked as she knelt beside him.

He smacked his lips and scrunched up his face. "Like a timbercat just crapped in my mouth." When he struggled to sit, he fell with a strangled whimper.

"Try not to move too quickly. Your body's still weak. It'll pass, I promise," she said, using her most soothing wizen tone.

He mewled and placed a hand over his eyes to shield the sun's glare. "So you say, if I survive that long." He peeked through his fingers and looked her up and down. Worry creased his forehead as he moved up onto his elbows to get a better look at her. "I should be asking if you're all right."

"I'll be fine. Soon. Like you, I experience certain after-effects, too. A fever to be more precise. Combined with this heat?" She stopped. With this dense humidity, her increasing body temperature would begin taking a toll on her. Without a doubt, the distance between them and Ilio would continue to grow if they didn't get moving.

Snarling out a gasp of pain, Feran stood and swayed like a blade of grass caught in a breeze. He shifted northward. "I hear water. Where are we?" His gaze swept over the trees that canopied them. The air here was laden with the thick scent of pine, and every once in a while a light caress of a cool breeze blew in from the water.

Suna turned her face toward a tantalizing gust. "On the other side of Carberra. Maybe a few hundred yards or so from shore."

When Feran teetered on his feet, she moved to help him, but he waved her away. "Just give me a moment to get my sea legs back. I'll be fine." His eyes narrowed. "You don't look too good. Come on. There's a few ways I know of to bring down a fever."

"I'll be fine," she protested, but the thought of cool water running over her skin was almost as overwhelming as pushing back that lock of hair hanging over his eye. Now why would she notice something like that?

"No arguments. Besides..." He stopped to sniff at his underarms and wrinkled his nose. "I could do with a bath." His face lit with that usual boyish charm of his. When she refused to take the arm he held out, his grin disappeared.

She was beginning to know this soldier and judging by the firm set of his jaw and her own desire to cut down the heat coursing through her body, she gave in. When her fingers brushed against his arm that strange shuddering of air surrounded them again, although not as potent as before. She immediately pulled away.

"Why does that keep happening whenever we touch?" he asked with a furrowed brow. He swayed again and quickly righted himself. "I mean, you almost lost yourself in that spell when you took my hand. What's going on?"

"If I knew, I'd most assuredly tell you. I thought it was just me."

Without another word, or touch, Feran pushed his way through the mass of billowing bullweeds growing in wild abandon along the shore. She followed in silence.

Here the currents of the river moved far faster than on the western side of the Carberra, but they were still not half as dangerous as its main body of water at the mouth of Valhallen's Gates.

Suna headed straight to the water's edge. With her clothes and boots still on, she walked into the frigid spray and closed her eyes. Bone numbing cold lapped around her calves, thighs, and hips as she moved deeper in the water. She then submerged completely. The rushing currents roared in her ears. Thankfully, the fire coursing through her eased some as well. When she emerged, she had difficulty catching her breath. Feran rushed to her side before she could rub the water out of her eyes.

"Are you okay?"

His quickness, and stealth, surprised her. She stepped back too hastily, which caused her boot to slip on the moss-covered rock bed.

He reached out and grabbed her to keep her from falling. This time there was no dishevelment of air. He pulled her toward him. Their bodies pressed together as sculpted stones cut to precision. Chiseled muscles beneath Feran's clothes rubbed against her. His arms felt strong and warm. Nerves ignited. The cleft between her legs pulsed in a way she'd never felt before. She sensed the racing of his heart in conjunction with her own. He inhaled when she looked up at him through her sodden eyelashes. His verdant gaze held her fast, as if seeing her for the first time. But his expression? She couldn't describe it even if she tried, nor could she explain the sensations flaring inside her. She shoved him away, her face burning, but not from the fever.

Feran opened his mouth to say something, but clamped it shut.

Dripping wet and standing thigh-high in water, she tried to look away, but she couldn't help but notice his shirt she'd soaked when she'd pressed against him. The material clung to rippled grooves cut deep into his abdomen.

She focused across the river instead toward the two destroyed outposts she couldn't see. The distance revealed no smoke or flames. Turning north, she followed the shoreline. The imprint of her mage'ic was easy to see, but there was nothing of Ilio's putrid taint. He hadn't come this way which meant he travelled further north.

"We should be moving soon," Feran muttered. "We have a lot of daylight left, and I don't want to waste it."

The sound of his voice broke through her reverie. "Yes. We can be at the Gates by twilight, if we move fast." *I hope.* Her response sounded forced, but at least it disguised the disappointment at not being able to find Ilio's trail.

She sloshed her way out of the water and passed Feran, but sensed his leer following the clinging leather of her pants that she knew accentuated every dimple, curve, and sway of her hips. A deep sigh and his one brazen thought rumbled through her as he dived head first into the icy waters.

Thank the gods for cold water.

She didn't know why, but her frustration flared. There was a time when such trivial emotions never affected her. Why now? Feran infuriated and fascinated her. And it confused her to no end.

She stomped to where he'd left their pack and snatched it off the ground. She swung it over a shoulder with a clenched fist, seething inside. *Cold water indeed!*

As she waited, she emptied the water from her boots and squeezed out her braid. The realization that she shouldn't have been trespassing in his thoughts in the first place brought her irritation to a bare minimum. It was increasingly difficult to figure the man out. More agitating was the fact that she was uncertain whether his attention was unwanted or not. They had plenty in their buckets already without adding more slop to it, and this was certainly no time for tomfoolery. Still, she found it difficult to slow the racing of her heart.

The bullweeds soon parted and Feran emerged soaking wet, sporting that infamous grin of his. "Well, that was refreshing." He looked anywhere but at her. During his dip, he'd removed his shirt, but had left the vest on unlaced. He pulled his shoulder length hair to the side and squeezed out the excess water. From a pocket in his pants, he pulled out a thin strip of black leather, gathered his sodden mane into a neat ponytail and wrapped the leather several times so that his hair lay flat against the nape of his neck.

She watched, mildly amused. His clothes clung to him as provocatively as hers had done. With deliberate slowness, her line of vision moved from his face and travelled languidly downward, stopping for a moment at the open vest and his russet-tanned skin and muscles she ached to run her hands over. Proceeding further down, her eyes lingered for the longest time on his powerful hips, muscular legs, and finally his groin. "We have Ilio's trail to find." She turned on her heels and followed the shoreline north.

His chuckle followed in her wake. Much to her surprise, she discovered herself grinning as well.

* ~ * ~ *

Less than a league from where they'd landed, Suna stopped. "He was near here." Off she ran.

In a small area of sandy beach devoid of bullweeds and brush they found the ferry—a listless waste of wood rising and falling in the current, its broken prow purposely sunk into the shore. Ilio made sure that any future use of it would be futile.

A few feet away they found the guardsman with his neck snapped. The insignia on his uniform was identical to the one they'd found at Carberra Ferry.

She pivoted north and closed her eyes.

Feran sensed subtle vibrations in the air and knew it was her mage'ic.

She shuddered and faced him. "How much farther is it to the Gates?"

"From this side of Carberra Ferry?" He squinted and scanned the horizon. "Maybe two, three leagues, give or take, but from where we are now? I can't really tell. It depends how far north we've landed. Why?"

When she looked up, he stepped back, shocked by the amount of anger in her eyes.

"We're not going to reach him in time. He's going to get to the Gates before us. Hellfire!"

The profanity that slipped so easily from her lips didn't sound natural. In fact, any show of emotion was unlike her.

She flung down their pack and grimaced in pain. "We're not going to reach him in time," she repeated beneath a resigned whisper. She slipped the drenched scarf off her head and sank to the ground. "He'll be over the Carberra and on his way to Dunkerk before we're even within a league of Valhallen."

He'd reached the same conclusion, but was feeling a bit more optimistic. Even if Ilio made it to Dunkerk, Feran still held sway with many of the spies working within the royal network. Several were close friends, including Viktor Bossa, who commanded the entire net. They might not be able to catch Ilio now, but there were other ways.

At this moment, he was more concerned with the pale hue of her face, the way her shoulders slumped with exhaustion, and how bruised and swollen the veins beneath her eyes looked. The spots of color on her ashen cheeks didn't look natural. He'd pushed her too far once before. He wasn't about to do it again. His oath to Mollster would be adhered to at all cost.

He plopped on the ground beside her and took hold of the waterskin he'd filled earlier and passed it to her first. "This heat is draining," he muttered. He wanted to give her a reprieve from the chase, but if he'd told her to rest he knew an argument would surely ensue. He'd be subtle with his intentions. She'd taught him that much. "Can I ask you a question?"

"Yes."

"If you resided in Dunkerk for, well, I don't know how many years." He hesitated, fumbling to find words that wouldn't offend her. "I mean, this is a major gateway into Dunkerk. Didn't you travel this way before?"

Suna fidgeted with the strap of the pack before answering. "When I left Dunkerk, I traveled to Carberra and then the Jorja Ferry route before heading west. I kept my identity hidden. I wanted no one to see me. No one to know of me. There I made my home on the outskirts of a small village called Kanora."

She turned away as she always did when she spoke about her past. "I wanted seclusion. Where no one knew me. The few villagers who weren't afraid to see me came for my wizen skills. Other than that, I never left the sanctity of my glen. Not since their deaths. Not until now."

He watched the familiar sadness darken her delicate features. "Weren't you lonely?" he asked without thinking. The rawness of her pain flowed through him as if it was his own.

She stiffened. "Loneliness is not an option for a Divenean, Feran. Our purpose in life is to fulfill our task. For those reasons, we're always alone. I was raised within our Fold, so I wasn't really alone. When our task is completed, we return to the Fold to live out the rest of our days."

He opened his mouth, but she was quicker.

"The entire Fold was my family, caring for me as I did them. When I reached a certain age, I was assigned a mentor. My Elder taught and guided me in the ways of Divenean mage'ic in order to fulfill my purpose, just like any other Divenean. It was then I learned the ancient sword dance of Qaissa."

Feran choked on a mouthful of water and coughed until tears ran down his cheeks. Full grown men had failed the Qaissa, yet this tiny woman achieved the title when she was but a child?

"When all our lessons are completed and our Elder decides that his or her Divenean charge is ready to serve their purpose, only then do we leave the Fold. When I was ready to fulfill mine, my Elder invoked a *Manifestis* spell. I traveled to Dunkerk in this manner. I never saw him again. In fact, I don't even remember his face."

Her brow crumpled. "King Markes was just a boy when we first met. He never traveled far from his kingdom as his every move was shadowed by the constant threat of assassination. When my purpose was done..." She faltered and the timbre in her voice quivered. "When my services were no longer needed, I left Dunkerk. We should be moving on."

Her cheeks flushed more, whether from embarrassment or fever he couldn't tell, but he wasn't about to ask. This was a subject she wasn't comfortable discussing. So why did she do so now? What made her lower her defenses? *That wall she keeps around herself is like her prison,* he thought sadly. *And this guilt she carries? She's nurtured and fostered it into a living, breathing thing that sucks away every ounce of joy in her life. No wonder she never smiles.*

Suna stood and picked up the pack.

"I believe it's my turn to carry that now." He took the satchel from her. Thankfully, no argument followed. Strange as it was, she was the first woman his charms didn't work on.

* ~ * ~ *

Thinking that making polite conversation as they traveled was safe, he began to explain the lay of the land. "The currents from here to Valhallen flow faster than anywhere else. Travel depends largely on the weather and winds. People journeying from Jorja way end up docking at a small village called Merkanna. There's a trail there that meets with the main roadway to the Gates."

She nodded as she listened.

"Carberra Ferry is the most direct route as it takes you straight to Valhallen's Gates, which is at least four to six hours faster than the Jorja route. Again, it depends on the weather." He stopped. Ferry or not, it would have taken a day or more to reach Dunkerk if they went by Jorja. Then, contingent on the availability of ships, there was no guarantee they'd be there in a day. But even now that hope withered for them.

Suna kept her silence as they followed a forgotten path obscured by overgrown shrubs and wild grass. It wasn't long before she began tripping on the odd scattered stone or protruding tree root that sometimes crossed their path. Sweat soaked her hair and clothes.

Feran's worry grew.

No more than an hour passed before she stumbled to her knees. When he placed an arm around her shoulders, half-carrying, half-leading, she didn't protest. Now he knew for sure she was in trouble.

This far east he couldn't recall any village situated close to Carberra, and having never traveled this route before, he was at a loss as to which way to head. It helped that he knew the imp was heading straight for the Gates, so he kept northward, keeping to the shoreline and searching for telltale signs of Ilio's trail.

Gigantic pines and goldenwoods towered overhead, their leaves wilting in the humid, scented air. Thankfully, they offered some well needed shade from the unrelenting sun. He stopped to rest with Suna leaning heavily against him. When he saw her eyes roll back, he knew they needed help. And soon.

As if in answer, he looked up to see a few wisps of gray smoke billowing upward from the tree line.

It wasn't long before he came upon the thatched roof of a farm sitting in the middle of a small cleared piece of land adjacent to a garden. On its left, he saw part of a road which he knew led to the Gates. Feran steered directly toward the farmhouse, with Suna battling to put one foot in front of the other.

A scruffy looking farmer stood on the other side of a rather dilapidated picket fence, greeting them with a suspicious glare. Several years older than Feran, the man's face was weather-beaten from long hours in the sun. His faded blue eyes had a tired look that seemed forever encased in sadness. Gripping his rusted pitchfork tightly in his hand, the man's critical stare roved over Suna. "Can I help you folks?" he asked.

"Our horses were stolen by bandits near Carberra Ferry. We've been walking for hours, but my wife isn't well. I have silver to pay for a room, if you would be so kind?"

As the farmer took in the rich cut of his clothes, Feran noticed the man's worn gingham patched pants and dirty vest that had seen better days. The worn-out sandals and crowned straw hat that kept the sun's wrath at bay made him look more like a vagabond than a farmer, but something in the man's demeanor pulled at him. Something familiar.

A timid female voice sounded from inside the ramshackle farmhouse behind him. "Harrod?"

"It's all right, Tana. They're travelers who have met ill fortune," the man called out over his shoulder.

An emaciated woman emerged, her hands protectively covering the protrusion of her stomach. Clutching tight at the bottom of her threadbare skirt was a white-haired little girl, her silken locks curled tight against her scalp. Wide, cerulean-blue eyes peeked anxiously from behind her mama's dress, fearful but intrigued by the strangers.

Feran's heart melted at the sight of the child. "Hello there, little one. What's your name?"

She hid further into her mama's shadow. "Matilda," she whispered shyly.

"Well, you are the most beautiful thing I ever did see. This is a gift for your beauty." He flourished a silver dellion from the pocket of his vest and held the coin out for her to take. The girl's eyes widened like moons as she clutched tighter to her mother's dress. Harrod's eyes rounded as well.

He turned to the farmer. "I'll give you two more if you'll provide us shelter until my wife is feeling well enough to travel, but I need a private room. I don't care if it's in that shed there, but it must be private."

Harrod nodded. "Of course."

"You're welcome to our room. A cloth covers the entrance, so you'll have all the privacy you need. Thank you, kind sir. Thank you," Tana added.

He fumbled inside his pocket for two more silver dellions and handed the coins to Harrod. Feran knew this amount of money was more than these people had seen in a long time. "I have to draw this fever from her, so privacy is of the utmost importance."

Suna suddenly fell limp. He swept her into his arms. She weighed a stone more than a feather. "Take me to the room. Now."

Harrod opened the creaking gate. "Tana, show him."

The woman led Feran into the sparsely decorated farmhouse. He held Suna protectively against his chest while sidestepping a small table with four unbalanced chairs. Intermittent drafts of air coming down the flue stirred the ashes beneath a soup pot that hung above a fire-filled hearth cut into the girth of the far left wall. The delicious scent of simmering chicken and vegetables filled the stuffy air. The house was tiny, but cozy and clean. Two small rooms were nestled on the right with faded red cloth dividing each area. He offered a small smile to Tana as he flipped aside the material. On the floor lay several down-filled sacks sewn together to create a bed. He positioned Suna on the edge of it, knelt in front her and placed his hand under her chin, forcing her to look at him. His fingers burned by the heat radiating off her face.

"Suna, this fever's bad. You're on fire. I have to draw it out of you. If I don't?" *She's a wizen. She knows the dangers.* "Do you understand what I have to do?" He rested his palm against her right cheek and drew back with a startled hiss.

The more he thought about what he was about to do, the sicker he felt. This would definitely change their relationship. Then again, what kind of bond did they have now?

Suna mumbled something vague and ran her tongue over her parched lips. She gave a bare minimum of a nod.

"Lie down and undress. Then put the blanket over you. I'll come back in a few minutes."

Feran found Tana waiting beside the rickety table. "I need more blankets."

The woman scurried away without a word.

When he thought sufficient time had passed, he reentered the room. Suna hadn't moved. He was in a predicament for sure. He didn't relish the thought of having to undress her, but there was no other way.

Easing her head down onto the feather mattress, he removed her boots and stockings first, which he noticed were still damp from her swim. He spied the laces on her pants and stopped. The leather was stuck to her thighs like a second skin, soaked through and through. Tana entered the room like a waif, holding out several woolen blankets. He took them with a grateful nod. He was about to dismiss her when a better idea popped into his head.

"Would you please help my wife undress?" he asked, trying to make it sound like it was the most natural thing in the world. When the woman moved toward the bed, Feran quickly exited and paced outside the entrance like an expectant father.

Tana reappeared and gave him an odd look before asking, "Is there anything else you need, my lord?"

"No, Tana. Thank you. And your family. I'm no lord either. My name's Feran Lambert. And my wife? She's... Sena." He offered her one of his infamous smiles and was delighted to see the woman blush like a maiden. She gave a small curtsy and exited the farmhouse.

When Feran pushed aside the cloth, his stomach coiled into knots, which made him wince. Those muscles still hadn't had a chance to recover from his retching episode. Peering toward the bed, he realized how tiny Suna looked beneath the mound of blankets. With a deep breath, he undressed and slipped beneath the woolen layers. She mumbled something incoherently, lost in the throes of her fever to make sense. The heat emanating from her was like licking flames of a bonfire. Drawing her body close to the curves of his own, her back and legs brushed against the bareness of his skin. Moisture leaked from her every pore. Then came violent convulsions. In the midst of that was the strange shifting of air. Thankfully, it happened just once, and not as strong as before. Strange though they were, they seemed to be getting weaker.

He wrapped his arms around her and held her against his chest, speaking softly in her ear. In short time she calmed. Now he was as soaked as she was.

In any other circumstance Feran would have been enjoying himself quite well, but this was no dalliance with some common woman. This was *the* Lady Suna.

The amount of heat radiating from her body was staggering. He marveled at how she'd been able to walk the distance she had. A sweet, honeysuckle scent permeated from her sweat. She moved closer, her bare buttocks brushing against parts that shouldn't be touched, at least not without a reaction. Grimacing, he forced his thoughts away from the seductive curves of her body and the petal softness of her skin, but he couldn't stop his lips from brushing across her shoulder. The desire to kiss her became irresistible. When he pressed his lips to her shoulder, she pushed against him. He held her close and stroked her hair.

He didn't realize when he started, but he found himself humming a lullaby his mother used to sing to him whenever he fell ill. Suna emitted a docile sigh and snuggled close before falling into a deep sleep.

As Feran lay there, he wished more than ever for a bath. Preferably one filled with mountain glacier water.

CHAPTER SIXTEEN

Feran opened his eyes to gloomy silence and the uncomfortable itchiness of damp wool against his naked flesh. The mound of blankets insulating them were sodden from the breaking of Suna's fever. Thankfully, the heat he'd felt emanating from her had lessened at last. *She'll be fine by morning.*

He extracted himself from the bed and tipped the covers upside down so the dryer ones were next to her skin. When she stirred, he stood stone still, not wanting to wake her. Goosebumps raced across his naked flesh as he waited. When she didn't rouse, he scrambled for his clothes and dressed before tiptoeing out of the room.

A single candle burned in a lantern on the table beside the hearth. Harrod sat by the fire smoking a worn cob pipe, staring at the hypnotic glow of the flames. When he heard Feran, he turned. "How's your wife feeling?" he whispered as he tapped out the burnt remains of the tobac against the blackened stone of the fireplace.

"She'll be fine. Now," Feran replied. "Thank you for your kindness."

"Think nothing of it. You both looked like you needed some help. Plus, your silver is worth more than our meager kindness. These days one can't be too careful who they befriend. Too many liars, thieves and worse out there for my liking." His lips curled into a distasteful frown.

Feran glanced absently around the small hovel, wondering if he should go back to bed, but the thought fluttered the insides of his guts. Suna needed to rest. And he didn't need the temptation.

Harrod rose and limped toward him. With a gracious nod, he extended his hand. "I don't believe I properly introduced myself. My name is Harrod Kinkaid. And you've met Tana, and little Mattie, of course."

He grasped the man's calloused hand. "Pleased to make your acquaintance, Harrod. I'm—"

"I know who you are, *General* Feran," he said with a ghost of a smile crinkling the corners of his mouth. "You probably don't remember me, but some years back I served under your command as a sentry guard. How long has it been since you left?"

Feran grinned. "Apparently not long enough. You don't serve anymore?"

"Naw. I took a nasty fall from my stead and shattered my knee. I'm just thankful I can still walk. I have trouble sleeping of late, though. The ache in my leg worsens when there's fog, like tonight. I retired from service and saved a little money to buy this farm." The firelight picked up the impish mirth in his eyes. "You should have seen the place before I fixed it up."

Feran laughed along with him.

Harrod placed another rickety chair beside his own in front of the hearth and motioned for him to sit. "On your way to Dunkerk's Corn and Apple Festival, are ya?"

Feran took a seat and pulled out his pipe from the bag hanging off his hip. "Not really. I mean, my wife and I are looking for an old friend." He concentrated on filling the bowl and lighting it, despising the bitter bite of the lie. He'd forgotten about the festival.

"Well, I hope you find him. Or her."

"So do I, Harrod. So do I," he murmured. Together they smacked their lips around their respective pipes and stared into the fire, smoking in amicable silence.

Some time passed before Harrod's soft-spoken voice broke through the quiet. "It's difficult when someone you love is ill and there's nothing you can do about it."

Peering at him from the corner of his eye, Feran watched the shadows dance across Harrod's face, sensing the man's need to talk.

"Tana isn't carrying this child well. Mattie was difficult for her, but this one?" He sighed. "She barely eats these days." His shoulders slumped forward.

Tana's skeletal face floated through his memory. "Have you taken her to see a wizen?"

"I haven't any extra money to pay for such services. I barely manage to feed ourselves, now that taxes have almost doubled over the last four seasons. Lord Greth is dogged in collecting what he considers his, so whatever extra I grow, I try to keep for ourselves instead of selling." He tapped out the contents of his pipe one last time and placed it on a worn spot on the mantle. "I should be heading back to bed. Sleep well." He turned and placed his first two fingers to his forehead, lips, and then over his heart.

Feran jumped to his feet. "That's not—"

"You should know that after you left, everything turned tail-ass backwards." Harrod limped toward the room next to where Suna slept and pulled back the cloth, but he stopped before entering, his face creased in sadness. "Loss of good leadership does that, I suppose." Without another word, he disappeared behind the curtain.

Feran stayed by the hearth long after Harrod fell asleep. He returned to his room only when the fire had burned itself out and dawn had begun to kiss the eastern skies.

* ~ * ~ *

Suna woke to the shrill shriek of a child's laughter. Disorientated, it took a moment to realize someone lay next to her. She stiffened. From the itchiness of the blankets, she knew she was as naked as the day she'd entered this world. Peering over her shoulder, she saw Feran fully dressed, his eyes closed, with a hint of that incorrigible grin pulling at the corners of his mouth.

His right eye cracked open. "How're you feeling?" That smirk of his curled upward even more.

Heat rushed into her cheeks. It was a reaction she wasn't used to in the least. "Like I want to crawl in a creek and drown. I'll survive. Um?" She pulled the blankets up to her chin and searched the room for her clothes.

Feran got up and placed a neatly folded pile beside her. "Tana was kind enough to wash them."

Suna clutched the blankets tighter. When he refused to leave, she glared at him. "A little privacy isn't too much to ask, is it?"

Feran's smile stretched from ear to ear. "Good to see you're back to your old self." He started to leave the room, but stopped at the ragged curtain, his eyes twinkling. "By the way, there's nothing there I haven't already seen." His laughter followed him out.

A multitude of indignant outbursts ran through her head, but they failed to reach her lips in time. She was relieved to find herself alive, no matter how it was achieved. The fever could have killed her if it wasn't for what he'd done, no matter the cost to her dignity.

I should have known I wasn't strong enough for a spell of that magnitude, but I had to try. The infusion of that amount of mage'ic had almost killed her. However, the more she used, the stronger she'd become.

She dressed, fumbling with fingers that were stiff and sore, like the rest of her body. The unique properties of her Divenean blood would mend the aches soon enough.

Another string of girlish giggles rang out at intervals, followed by Feran's deep-chested laugh. It sounded a lot like Tuck and Tail, a favorite game she'd once taught to the children of Dunkerk.

As Suna laced up her vest, her stomach growled, which was another good sign she was on the road to recovery. She'd make a point of thanking...? What was her name? Tana. Yes, that was it, for the clean clothes. Events of the past day were still a little hazy, but they were coming back in snagging bits and pieces.

When she stepped outside the cloth-covered room, she spotted a plate of pale cheese, several cut up shriveled apples and a glass of milk sitting on a lopsided table. She snuck a piece of cheese into her mouth and swallowed, savoring the tangy salt. A piece of apple caused sweet juice to burst across her palate.

The air of the cottage lingered with the taint of Feran's tobac. She breathed deep and closed her eyes. She reached for the plate again just as a woman's soft voice sounded at the open door.

"I'm so glad to see you're up. Feran said you were feeling better."

Suna jumped with a piece of cheese poised at her mouth. Trying not to look guilty, she placed it back on the plate.

"No, please. That's for you. It's not much, but you need to get some of your strength back." Tana moved slowly into one of the chairs and sat. The short distance seemed to exhaust her.

As Suna chewed, she took in the greenish hue of the other woman's pallor. "You're not well."

The woman grimaced with a nod. "It's just the baby. No matter. I survived Mattie. I'll survive this one. I'm Tana. You're Sena, right?"

"Um, yes. And your little girl is Matilda." She didn't remember a lot after she'd arrived, but a fuzzy image of a little girl came to mind.

"Yes, our little Mattie. She's a handful, but most children her age usually are. I just wish I had the energy to enjoy her." Tana offered a sad smile.

"Yes. I remember the children at the castle." She stopped and quickly changed the subject, but an odd look passed over the woman's face. "Thank you for helping me."

"You're most welcome. It's not often we get visitors. These days one can't be too careful." Tana stood and immediately grasped the table, her face pale and beaded with sweat. She almost fell if it hadn't been for Suna helping her back down into her chair.

She knelt in front of the frail woman and took her hands. Before she could bring forth her mage'ic, the woman tried to pull away. Suna refused to let go. "It's okay. I'm a wizen. I can help you."

Tana's eyes widened, whether in fear or disbelief, she couldn't tell.

"Truly, I'm fine," Tana protested as she tried to stand again.

From the momentary touch of Tana's hands, she'd learned that there was indeed something wrong. "Listen to me, Tana," she said as soothingly as possible. "The baby isn't positioned right inside you. It's pushing up into your stomach sideways. That's why you're feeling so ill. If it's not turned, your delivery? And the baby?" Memories of Queen Saliste crashed through her mind.

Tears brimmed in the woman's eyes. "We haven't any money."

"Shush, now. How can you say such a thing after all you've done for me? Come. We need some privacy."

Taking her by the hand, she led Tana into the room the woman had graciously given to her and Feran. She instructed her to lie on top of the blankets before crawling beside her. Placing both her hands on Tana's firm, round belly, Suna closed her eyes and concentrated. Her fingers followed the outline of the tiny body. Just below a protruding rib cage, she found its tiny head. Somehow the poor thing had lodged itself in between the ribs. With a touch of her mind, she used gentle gusts of mage'ic. An ice-blue glow emanated from the bottom of her palms as she gingerly guided the baby's head downward.

Tana gasped and cried out.

Suna leaned back on her heels. "Would you like to know what you're having?"

The woman gawked in amazement. The intense pressure she knew Tana had been feeling was gone. She could breathe easier. And the horrid, burning bile that had made her nauseous had also disappeared.

"Harrod? Oh my. Harrod is so hoping for a son. Is it? Is it a boy?"

Before Suna's eyes that special aura that usually surrounds every expectant mother encased Tana at last, and the greenish hue faded from her face.

For the first time in a long time joy filled Suna's heart. "Harrod's wish has come true," she whispered.

Tana squealed in delight and hugged her so hard, several bones in her back cracked. "Thank you. Thank you," she gushed.

Suna shooed the woman away. "Go share the wonderful news."

After Tana left, she returned to the table and devoured several more pieces of cheese and apples, and drank the glass of goat's milk empty before following the woman's elated footsteps outside the farmhouse. She stopped to bask in the warm sunshine, feeling better than she had in a long time. The heat of the sun's rays caressed her skin. She peered up to see the blue sky feathered with sheets of fluffy, white clouds, a painter's palette for the entire world to admire. She looked at the crooked fence, and the gate that stood partially open. Strange, she had no memory of this place. The wooden stable was large enough to house four or five horses, but its foundation leaned much too far to the right. Both doors were pulled open. She spied three brown and white spotted goats and two sheep tethered inside. The pungent smell of freshly strewn hay and manure wafted in the faint breeze.

On her right stood a field of towering corn stalks, several rows of potatoes, and a patch of sweet peas, if she wasn't mistaken. The smell of freshly tilled earth intermixed with the manure smell. She breathed deep, drowning her senses in the splendor of the land around her. Toward the back of the rickety fence, several apple trees stood like wilted sentinels. Even from this distance, she saw the blooms this season had been scarce. A few overripe apples drooped from their spine-like branches as an open invitation to the assorted birds that had made their homes in the scattered leaves. Their melodic songs filled her with comforting peace. Suna reeled in a tranquility she hadn't felt in a long time.

Feel the shifting of the soil and sands. Follow the subtle hints it leaves behind. The knowledge it reveals...

Worry and fear eased. Fortitude saturated through her in calming waves of acceptance of who and what she was. She would not forget her duty. And she would not turn her back on her responsibilities to Etharia.

The echoes of a child's laughter drifted like music across the field. Behind the gangly line of apple trees, Feran ran in circles around a little girl as she squealed in delight.

As if sensing her gaze, they stopped and looked in her direction. Feran grinned and waved before sweeping the white-haired angel into his arms and jogging toward her.

She marveled at the beauty of this adorable child, who had her mother's eyes and delicate bone structure. "Hello there, little one," she said, giving the girl's nose a playful pinch. Suna took note that Feran looked quite comfortable with a child in his arms.

The girl giggled louder, then her face became a mask of seriousness. "I'm Mattie. I sure do hope you're feelin' better. I was really sick once. Mama and papa were scared, just like Feran. He was sad, but now he's happy again." The girl's scrawny arms hugged his neck tight before she pulled away.

Feran grinned. Then he rolled and crossed his eyes, making Mattie burst into another fit of giggles.

At that moment, Harrod and Tana strolled out of the stable hand-in-hand. Feran looked at them once. Then twice. There was no mistaking the glow surrounding Tana. He snuck a knowing glance at Suna and winked.

She ignored him, her ego still smarting over the last remark he'd thrown at her.

When Mattie saw her mother, she wriggled free from Feran's arms. "Mama! Mama! You're all better too!" she cried and ran full tilt toward them.

Harrod stopped and patted his little angel's snow-white curls before approaching Suna. "I don't know how we can ever thank you." His lips trembled and tears shimmered in his eyes.

"It's the least I could do. But we can't intrude on you and your family any longer, not if we're going to find passage to Dunkerk. Thank you for your kindness, and hospitality, but we must be on our way."

"Wait a minute." Harrod limped as fast as he could back into the stable and returned with a haggard dun in tow. "She isn't much, but at least you can ride her 'til you get some of your strength back. When you get to the Gates, leave her with a fellow called Lennox. He sells cured fruits and wines about three stalls on your left from the entrance. You'll know him when you see him. He's tall and skinny. Dark hair and skin. Most merchants don't carry a sword, but he does. He's ex-sentry like me. And a friend. He'll make sure ol' Beddy gets back home. Here. Please take her. It's the least we can do." He held out the rope for them to take.

Suna could have kissed him, but instead she hugged him. Then she turned to Tana and Mattie and did the same. At first it felt awkward, but when her embraces were reciprocated with even more fervor, it was then she realized how much she'd missed human contact.

Feran took the rope from Harrod and held out his hand, but the farmer dismissed it. Instead, he saluted.

Suna watched the display of honor from the corner of her eye. Feran straightened, his military-like carriage returning as he paid homage with a salute of his own.

Harrod walked with them to the end of the road, while Tana and Mattie stayed behind the rickety fence waving their final goodbyes. Suna and Feran had turned down their insistent offers of food, knowing the family had little to spare. She hoped Tana found the two silver dellions she'd left under the blankets. It was a small fortune when added to the three she knew

Feran had secretly placed on the mantle beneath Harrod's pipe. The family would fare well for some time.

They stopped at a small dip in the road several yards from the farmhouse. Harrod helped Suna up onto the blanket he'd draped across the dun's back. Then he stumbled back. Startled by his reaction, she looked down and discovered her scabbard and sword in open view, the emblem glinting in the afternoon sun.

Wide-eyed, he turned to Feran, who shrugged indifferently.

"Tana told me what you did inside. You're not just a wizen. I remember seeing you on the castle steps when I was but a boy, but I thought I was mistaken. Your beauty. Your hair. The soldiers gossiped about you being a Sword Dancer. I never believed the tales. Now I see your sword?" He stood there in revered awe.

She reached down and placed her hand upon the man's shoulder. "I hope to return one day and visit with your family again, Harrod, especially your newest addition, but until that time I beg of you to tell no one about our visit here."

She glanced back at Tana and little Mattie. "I implore you to keep my secret. It will keep you all safe."

He stiffened and placed his fingers to forehead, lips and heart and bowed lower than he had for Feran. "There is no favor I would deny you, Lady Suna." He dipped his head and stood back.

With rope in hand, Feran began leading the dun down the dusty road that led to Valhallen's Gates.

Suna gave a final glance over her shoulder and waved before the rise in the road took the farmer from sight.

* ~ * ~ *

It took some time before she mustered her courage and said, "Thank you for what you did last night, but I don't want it to be mentioned again. Ever. Understand?"

Without stopping, he shifted around with a grin. "A simple thank you would have sufficed."

"Is nothing ever serious with you?"

"If life was nothing but seriousness, duty and prudishness, what a sad state of affairs it would be, don't you think? When was the last time you had fun, Suna? Just plain fun. Or laughed until your sides hurt?" He turned away and concentrated on the road. *Well, I've gone and done it this time. She'll be steaming mad at me now.*

Waiting for the backlash he knew was coming, she remained oddly quiet. He braved a quick peek over his shoulder and saw her staring off into the distance, her eyes filled with that haunting sadness he'd come to recognize.

"I was born into a life of duty. Even as a wizen, I undertook the responsibility of keeping the village of Kanora safe and healthy. Everything I know and everything I do is for these lands and its people. I know nothing else. And my prudishness is none of your concern," she added with a scathing glare.

"A Divenean is still a person! They breathe. Piss. And laugh. Just like everybody else. True, you had duty. We all had duty. Hellfire, we still do. Have you stopped to think that perhaps it was your destiny that maybe, just maybe, King Markes' death was an ebbing of tides? Or perhaps that Divenean duty you cling to like a security blanket ended when he died? Is it even possible for you to fathom that it was his time to pass and your *duty*, as you call it, finished then? Or how about this? It's beginning now? You've floundered so long in your guilt that you've condemned yourself to a life of misery because you think that's what you deserve."

"This guilt is mine. I bear it because I must. It's penance for my failure. King Markes and Queen Saliste should both be alive, along with their child. I must live with it. No one else. And because of it, I do not share it. How do I find happiness in life when such emotions are gone from me?"

Taking a deep breath, he spoke slower, extracting more calm from within. "But there is, Suna. You found it in Mattie. You found it in Harrod, Tana and their unborn child. You found peace in their small corner of paradise. And there's no way in Seven Hells you're going to tell me differently. I find it heartbreaking that you don't realize that, especially now, knowing what we know. If we don't find that key, how much joy will there be left in this world? Whatever time we have, shouldn't we make the best of it? Otherwise, life has no meaning. And for me, life's worth living for now. Whether you're a Divenean or not, you're still human."

His outburst wounded her, evidenced by the redness staining her face. He also knew no one had ever said such things to her, or with such frankness, but he had to make her see herself with different eyes. Piece by little piece, he was determined to hit upon those severed nerves and try to ignite them back to life. The deep-rooted inner failings she'd nurtured for so long had to be fixed. And damn the gods, he was going to try to do just that.

She unnerved in ways he found disturbing, like her ability to read his mind, but she excited him far beyond the realm of any other woman he'd known. Never in a lifetime would he meet another like her. Why he felt this need to fix her was beyond his scope of comprehension, and to be perfectly honest, he'd passed the point of trying to understand days ago.

Her steely stare held him long and hard until a deeper flush spread over her cheeks. Surprisingly, a delicate smile curved the fullness of her lips.

Stunned, Feran shook his head and focused on the road ahead. For a second there, he could have sworn the smile had reached her eyes.

"This has been a great testament to my strength," she said after several minutes of stilted silence had passed.

If she was trying to bait him for another round, he was pretty sure he wouldn't get away unscathed. "What do you mean?"

"Since starting this quest, I've been arrested once and have fallen ill twice. It certainly doesn't say a lot for me, does it?"

He couldn't hold back a snicker. *Well, it's a start.* "Things like that just make you more human." He cast a sidelong glance and heaved a sigh of relief when he saw her nod.

Several hours later, the air filled with the sounds and smells of Valhallen's Gates. Feran looked to the dun and saw Suna shadowed within the red hood of her cloak.

They rounded a bend in the road and soon joined other carts and horses headed in the same direction. Travelers nodded cordial hellos. Traffic continued to build the closer they got to the Gates until they were elbow-to-elbow, many of them complaining about having to take the Jorja Ferry route. When they crested the next hill, the sun-bleached wooden spires of Valhallen's Gates came into view.

Cacophonies of screeching water gulls and a din of voices carried easily across the glittering waters of the Carberra River. A plethora of ships adorned with brightly colored masts sprinkled the horizon like an artist's palette. Several vessels were nothing more than inconspicuous dots in the distance. From their vantage, everything appeared normal. If Ilio had crossed here, he'd done so without force. When Feran looked back at Suna, he saw her lips purse into that severe line he now knew all too well.

CHAPTER SEVENTEEN

Wendel strode through the castle hallways as if he owned the place. And he would soon enough. Glaring down the bridge of his flattened nose, he sneered at the passing servants as if they were nothing more than squashed insects beneath his boots.

Like his uncle, Lord Tobas Greth, Wendel was a large man, but that's where the resemblance ended. Instead of heavy jowls, Wendel's youthful face was imprinted by pockmarks of adolescence. A stock of thick, blond hair crowned his head covering ears much too large for his face. A tad heavy-set for a man so young, his girth was as large as his ego, just like his uncle's.

The supple leather of his new boots squeaked like warring rats as he continued down the corridor, and the scabbard encrusted with emerald-cut rhinestones of every color bounced at his hip from beneath the short poplin jacket he wore. Like the boots, the weapon had been a gift from Lady Allena. It was a little garish, but such exquisite taste needed flaunting. And Wendel had most certainly earned it.

He couldn't help but shudder whenever he thought of that woman. Older and rotund, Allena currently held the power in Dunkerk. At least for now. Her insatiable sexual desires were sometimes so bizarre, he'd often wondered at his ability to perform for her. He'd made a habit of providing them both with blindfolds during their bouts of unsavory bed frolicking, learning early that keeping his eyes closed for such long periods took far too much work to do on his own.

As he made his way toward her bedchambers, he pondered the message he'd received from his uncle earlier that morning. Matters had to be expedited. *And not a moment too soon.*

Once his uncle took the throne, Wendel would have his choice of any high born lady in Dunkerk, and the licentious Allena was nowhere on his list of favorites

Several days prior, he'd been quite successful in his manipulations of the royal whore. She'd received an urgent supplication from Lord Ethbridge, demanding additional Elite Guards for his forces, and, of course, forging certain lies about Lord Conac. With Wendel's persuasive urgings, Allena acquiesced to the demands without checking the validity of the request. He couldn't believe how dense the woman could be, believing anything he said so long as he kept her satisfied. He was on his way to service her now. The thought instantly darkened his jubilant mood.

When he halted in front her private chambers, he took several deep breaths before rapping his knuckles against the wood. Plastering a feigned look of a doting caller on his face, he couldn't stop another shudder of disgust from running through him.

Allena's voice quivered with expectant glee from the other side of the wood. "Enter."

Wendel walked in and shut the door behind him. Thankfully, she'd drawn the velvet drapes across the windows overlooking the courtyard below. His suggestion, of course. Numerous candles burned throughout the room—her way of attempting an ambiance of eroticism. *Still too much light for my liking*.

"Come to me, Wendel," she said from the center of the bed, her tone fluctuating between a female cat lost in the throes of heat and an aged hag. "Make me scream your name again and again."

From the distance between them, he saw her eyes glow. Trying not to emit a nauseating groan, he concentrated on rehearsing the words he'd so carefully prepared for this particular rendezvous.

"It grieves me to tell you this, my sweet Allena," he began, choking down the urge to chortle hysterically. "My uncle needs me back in Carberra posthaste, so I must take my leave this afternoon." He turned away, waiting for the effect he knew this would have on her.

Allena jumped from beneath the bedcovers and ran to him, stifling on a sob. Standing there naked with the folds of her skin hanging about her like congealed jelly, he almost lost his breakfast. Although he tried not to look, he had little choice. This was one of the most difficult tasks—seeing her naked. Such scenes were hard to erase from the mind. More than once he thanked the gods for his short attention span and wild imagination.

"This cannot be, my love. What will I do without you?" She mewled like a spoiled child.

Greth had fathered no children of his own. Wendel was his only blood-birthed by a sister long since departed from this world, which proved quite effective in fabricating this portion of the tale he was about to tell.

"My uncle's rule in Carberra has been harrowing of late. His responsibilities are many, but he has no one else to rely on but me. If he were here, I wouldn't have to leave." His sigh sounded authentic, even to his ears.

Wendel flopped down into one of the chairs beside the bed and removed a thick, oblong object from beneath the cushion. He threw it to the floor, careful to hide his loathing. He'd rather not think about those toys of hers, especially the black marble one. He hadn't been able to sit for days after that experience.

The deep wrinkles around Allena's eyes caught her falling tears. "You must stay here with me, Wendel. What can I do to change this?"

The shrill timbre in her voice revealed exactly what he wanted to hear. He hid a satisfied smirk behind his hand. "You know the greatness of my uncle. He feels the lands are in danger of destroying themselves without a competent ruler. He spends all of his time worrying and ensuring that the other four incompetent underlords carry out their duties. He's only one man. Of late, much has been left to fate."

He stopped and wondered how much emphasis he should put into the last part of his speech. "Uncle Greth's love for Etharia holds no bounds. It's for this reason he's called me back to help with his rule. You know how I feel about him, Allena." With the lie still on his lips, he held her gaze.

Allena stroked his cheek with her lacquered nails, her eyes overflowing with tears. "Tell me what to do, my sweet boy, and I will do it, if it means you'll stay by my side."

"Convene the Council of Regents and place your vote for my uncle. I know you've been thinking about it. It's the only way I can stay with you. Then I can oversee all preparations of the coronation in his absence here in Dunkerk. I wouldn't have to leave your side."

She brushed away a stray tear with a pudgy knuckle. "I will do this for you, my love. Yes, of course." Her garishly painted lips puckered with despair. "Tomorrow I'll decree to the council to meet and place my nomination for your uncle. The majority of the High Houses will follow my lead." She smiled and brushed away the tears that had not yet fallen. "Then you and I shall marry," she added breathlessly. "We'll unite the two most powerful houses."

"A royal wedding, I think," he murmured, tapping a thick finger against his lips. "The noble nephew of the King of Dunkerk to wed the beautiful, High Regent, Lady Allena." He turned to her, keeping his eyes focused on her adoring face. "Then nothing shall ever separate us. Except death." He smiled, but not for the reasons she most likely thought. "Now, my love, let me show you proper thanks." Rising to his feet, Wendel began unbuttoning his jacket while frantically searching the room for his blindfold.

* ~ * ~ *

Suna and Feran stopped long enough to deliver Harrod's dun to Lennox and ask a few vague questions about whether he'd seen a small, crooked man in the area. The ex-soldier had advised he'd seen no such thing, but he did mention an odd fellow who'd shuffled through the area shortly before the break of dawn.

"I was busy setting up my merchant's table and didn't see his face." The ex-soldier's dark face puckered. "But when he passed, the stench that followed was like a disease. It wasn't only sickening, but disturbing. By the time I'd turned, he was gone. Did you hear what happened at Carberra Ferry?"

They feigned surprise and listened as Lennox told them his version, which, surprisingly, was the closest to the truth that they'd heard so far. They'd heard rumors on the road about dark horsemen wielding mage'ic, and even that Balthazar himself had destroyed the ferry. There were even some whispers that Lord Greth's men had set the fires themselves to cause dissention between the underlords.

"If ya ask me," Lennox added. "Something wicked is afoot."

* ~ * ~ *

Feran had managed to buy passage on one of Lord Greth's fluyts called *The Cavern Aplenty*. They were fortunate enough to find the ship docked and ready to sail to Dunkerk in an hour's time. He'd heard *The Cavern* boasted to be one of the underlord's fastest ships. The Captain had advised them that he anticipated a four to five hour journey, depending on the winds, before they docked at Kinghead's Road which would lead them directly into Dunkerk. Thereafter, one of the many coaches stationed there would take them the rest of the way, but it would be well past nightfall before they arrived behind the city's walls.

The array of gossip they'd heard about Carberra Ferry had been mixed with complaints about people having to be rerouted to Jorja. It was why the road they'd traveled had been so clogged with travelers as the majority of people would have arrived directly at the Gates using the western shores had Carberra Ferry been running.

The closet-like cabin of the ship was confining, but the long planks of meticulously cut greenwood pine that paneled the walls in a tongue and groove pattern added spaciousness to an otherwise sparsely decorated room. This was one of the most expensive berths, but only a few feet separated him from Suna. Sitting on opposite sides of the room on benches bolted into the walls, the only other furnishing was a wall table nailed to the floor beneath the oval portal window.

Since they'd boarded, Suna hadn't said a word. Feran was learning that her brooding silence meant to leave her alone. So he waited.

"I need you to tell me who currently holds power in the Council of Regents."

"The Lembarts."

"Who held power when you retired?"

"Again, House of Lembart, but their attempts for the throne were thwarted. That's one of the reasons why I left. I would rather be spitted and hung by my test...um...toes than see that house take the throne. After I left, I'd heard someone had poisoned Roree Lembart, the last male in that line. There's one left in the House. His widow, Lady Ellena Lembart, who currently sits as Regent."

He sneered. Just thinking about that detestable banshee left a bitter taste on his tongue. "I'd bet you a stable full of destriers and a chestful of gold dellions that she orchestrated the poisoning of her husband."

Suna didn't look surprised. "Who's next in line after the Lembarts?"

"Well, the rungs of power lie in the males of the High Houses. A queen can rule only after the death of her king and husband, but only as Regent. With a queen's demise, only the males are then eligible for the throne."

"I know the classifications of hierarchy, Feran," she said with a laden sigh.

Frowning, he sensed the wheels in her head spinning. He'd also come to recognize that her forehead always creased with thin lines whenever she was deep in thought. *Now, why would I notice something like that?* He shook the notion away. "According to the Doctrine of Rule, it would be Mollster, but—"

"I also know of the covenant that was signed between the reigning underlords. They cannot rule as king. No underlord shall have a monopoly of power. So that would leave who? The House of Reese, correct?"

Shifting uncomfortably on the bench, he wondered about her line of questioning. "That's right, but Lord Magnus Reese is old. Some say feeble-minded."

She was quiet for the longest time again. "Something is about to happen, Feran. I can feel it. We may have more on our hands than just finding Ilio."

It was a solemn statement and, unfortunately, nothing in her expression revealed what it was.

He'd felt the same wariness festering inside, but assumed it was because he didn't want to return to Dunkerk. Now here he was sailing straight into her waiting bosom. *Besides Ilio, what more can go wrong?*

"I don't know." Suna focused out the window on the white caps rolling in lazy sweeps across the water.

"You said you'd stop doing that."

"Doing what?

"Reading my mind."

"I was doing what?"

She doesn't realize she's even doing it. He'd have to remember to be more circumspect with his thoughts.

She offered an apologetic dip of her head before turning back to the portal window. "Sometimes things just pop into my head. Even though you may not have said it aloud, my mind assumes you have. Remember, it's the intensity of your thoughts."

Silence hummed through their cabin.

He waited, wondering what was going through her mind, but when she refused to say any more he asked a question that had been bothering him. "How did Ilio pass through the Gates unseen?"

Her frown deepened those delicate lines on her forehead. "He must have glamored."

"He what?"

"Ilio changed his appearance using a glamor spell. One can only invoke a spell like that for short periods of time because of the intense concentration needed to keep your appearance altered. I noticed a variation in his mage'ic just before we reached Valhallen, but I didn't know for sure until Lennox confirmed my suspicions. That's why no one paid attention to him."

"And to board a ship?"

"Invisibility. Again, he can only maintain that kind of mage'ic for for short intervals. A useful spell for stowaway purposes in order to board a ship."

She turned and faced him. "He's following the key, Feran."

Her statement was one he'd entertained as well. "How?"

"Mage'ic. I had suspected, but I know for certain now that Balthazar created Ilio for one purpose. To find the key. He's following its scent. Perhaps a vibration in the air. I don't know. The only good thing is that he's also guiding us to it."

Damn mage'ic. He concentrated on the diamond glints of sunshine dancing across the rising surf outside the portal.

More awkward minutes passed before she spoke again. "What have you been doing since you left the employ of Dunkerk?"

Startled, he rolled his shoulders and relaxed against the wall. "Tracking here and there. Mainly Barbs in the north. For some reason the town of Saingarth was having a particularly difficult time. Their raids of the villages were increasing, so they hired my services and a few retired Elite Guards from Vansgaard to help eliminate the problem."

She stiffened. "Eliminate?"

"If you're asking me if I hunted them down and killed them, the answer is no. The Barbs I captured were arrested and taken to Laspeth for appropriate punishment."

"Why not Vansgaard?"

"If I'd done that I would have signed each of their death warrants. Ethbridge pays little attention to the Severity of Crime laws. He just gets rid of them."

"I didn't know that."

He saw her filing that tidbit of information away. Then he turned the questioning table her way. "Tell me about your time in Dunkerk."

She immediately downcast her eyes. "There's nothing to tell."

He wasn't giving up that easy. "You were a teacher of children, from what Lord Mollster said."

"I was also King Markes and Queen Saliste's personal Guardian, but most of my time—"

He pushed forward off the bench. *Now I wonder if she really can fly.* This woman was a Guardian. And a Sword Dancer. *And* a Divenean. When he stopped to think about it, it made sense. *Will a day come when she doesn't surprise me?*

She stared back with resolute calm. "Few knew I was a Divenean to begin with, Feran. And even fewer about my status as a Sword Dancer. There were rumors, true. I'm sure my sword was seen at times, but my main duty was to protect the king and queen. With my mage'ic. My sword. Or with my life, if need be. Is this not a Guardian's duty as well?

"Yes, but—"

"Is this the part where you tell me it's not my fault?" she murmured.

The diminutive shadows inside the cabin highlighted the wretchedness that always washed over her face whenever she spoke of the subject.

"No. That's your responsibility now. If you need any help, let me know." His wink seemed to ease some of her tension, but not her sorrow. That was part and parcel of who she was. He regretted bringing the subject up, but he wanted to know more about the *real* Suna, and not the great lady the stories purported her out to be. Sadly, she kept herself locked up tight. *Untouchable. Just like fire.* "Perhaps you should get some sleep," he offered.

She brushed aside a stray wisp of her hair. "I'm about as rested as I can be. You've taken care of me enough. Here." She tossed him a blanket that was folded beside her on the bench.

He had to admit that the consistent rocking of the ship had produced a weariness he didn't know he possessed. It washed through him, lulling him to numbness. Content in knowing that he had time to catch a few winks before the ship docked at Dunkerk's Harbor, he stretched his body out across the bench. Unfortunately, his legs hung over the edge and blocked the entrance.

Suna stood and arranged the blanket over him.

When she returned to her side of the cabin, he lifted his head. "What? No bedtime story?" His grin vanished into a gaping yawn.

"I'll do one better." She took a deep breath and began to sing softly. The sweet highs and lows in the melody pulled him down into the blueness of her eyes. He began to float in languid tranquility. As he listened, he swore he'd heard it before, just not so beautifully. It took a moment to realize that he'd hummed that very song to her at Harrod's farmhouse.

* ~ * ~ *

As Feran slept, Suna's gaze followed the rugged line of his jaw and lips, which were slightly apart. She found herself fantasizing what they would taste like. Her cheeks flushed at the memory of the fleeting kiss they'd shared in Odarian, but the circumstances behind it had marred the moment.

She forced the memory from her mind and concentrated on the rise and fall of his chest. The urge to curl next to him and leave this world behind, if only for a few hours, became an ache that squeezed the blood from her heart. For her, there would always be duty. Love was for fools.

She leaned her head against the wall and closed her eyes. For the first time in her life loneliness wrapped around her—and for the first time in a long time, she cried.

* ~ * ~ *

The sounds of riggings banging against metal locks alongside the docks and the boisterous voice of the ship's captain bellowing out orders to his crew roused Feran. Well-wishers greeting old friends and others shouting for coaches rang through the air. Yawning, he sat up and ruffled his hair.

"Did you sleep well?" Suna asked.

He swung his legs over the bunk and stretched until his palms touched the ceiling. "Yes, I did. Thanks." He lowered his arms, his face lined with confusion. "Come to think of it, I haven't had that *other* dream for a while. Not since we got together, in fact."

Suna said nothing as she stood and picked up their pack.

He moved beside her, took the leather satchel from her hands and helped her don her road-worn riding cloak to ensure the hood was in place to conceal her face and hair.

"You might be recognized too, Feran."

All other thoughts vanished when she realized the close proximity of their bodies in this small space. Worse was that infamous grin he sported. This close up it was more than a little unsettling, especially with his teeth blazing bright beneath the dark, rugged stubble covering his chin.

As his body pushed against her, she tried to shift toward the door. In the process, her nipples brushed across the hard pecs of his chest. Her body instantly responded. She gasped and attempted to move away, but there wasn't enough space. Pleasure swept through her. Goosebumps the size of boysenberries raced across her skin.

Feran appeared oblivious to what he was doing to her.

"I've been gone long enough for memories of my face to fade. People rarely pay attention to a soldier anyway. If we stay away from the castle and barracks, we'll be okay. But seriously, that's the least of our worries."

Her heart raced faster when he looked at her. "What's the least of our worries?"

"My presence won't cause people to fall to their knees." He pushed himself out through the cabin door, chuckling under his breath.

Now alone, Suna drew several deep breaths to quell the wild beating of her heart. She followed him, more confused than ever at the range of emotions he continually ignited.

Emotions she had no idea she possessed or knew how to control.

CHAPTER EIGHTEEN

Dunkerk's three day Corn and Apple Festival had the docks teeming with an array of travelers. Lords and ladies brushed elbows with serfs and soldiers, and no one seemed to mind. The upcoming celebration appealed to every level of citizen—a reprieve from their mundane lives.

Suna and Feran strode across the busy docks toward the waiting coaches. After some haggling with one of the drivers, and the exchange of an exorbitant amount of silver, Feran obtained passage on a coach shared by a High House member and her eldest daughter.

Suna entered the carriage and sat on the bench across from the women. She pulled herself deeper within the confines of her cloak. It didn't take long to realize that the older woman was a nonstop chatter-cat, but it was the daughter that caught her attention.

She was a pretty thing, in a plain sort of way, with mousy brown hair draped fashionably over her left shoulder in three thick ringlets, who thought herself more beautiful than what she really was. *Royal bloodlines*, she mused, surprised by the stinging bite of jealously that followed.

The young girl ran sneering glances up and down Suna, her loathing at having to share their mode of transportation with what looked like a commoner readily apparent on her face. The girl was quick to assess the woman dressed like a man wasn't worth her time, so she pointedly ignored Suna and pretended to smooth out imaginary creases on her expensive gown before staring down her nose at her.

When the girl's gaze met with Suna's, the startled young woman inched closer to her mother, but she brightened like a dawning sun when Feran entered the coach.

With a resigned sigh, Suna pulled her cloak further over her head and closed her eyes.

Feran slid inside next to Suna. When he looked toward the opposite bench where the other two women sat, his thoughts blared through her mind.

By the darkest realms of Hell, help me now. Not one, but two spoiled harpies?

Suna winced.

It didn't take long to regret their decision about boarding this particular carriage. After introductions were made, Lady Moira's constant chatter with Feran, who couldn't interject a word in even if he tried, was one of the most annoying experiences of Suna's long life. From the shadow of her hood, she watched the daughter, Carin, sneak unadulterated looks of sultry invitation toward Feran. This girl grated on her nerves like no one had ever done before.

This journey would be so much more interesting if mother and that hag in the corner weren't here.

Carin's brazen thought blistered Suna.

"And to think we arrived at Lord Clairdon's late," Moira exclaimed, her high-pitched voice like the jagged edges of glass scraping over a rock. When she rolled her eyes to the ceiling with a forced chuckle, Suna shuddered at the pretenses some High Houses made of themselves. She'd learned long ago that the more pompous they appeared the less important they were.

Without stopping to take a breath, Lady Moira rambled on about some other dignitary dinner she'd attended, describing each dish in vivid detail and giving a list of every lord and lady who attended. She even described the color of the napkins.

Feran looked as if he wanted to curl under a rock and die, and Suna wanted nothing more than to join him. Lady Moira proved to be the epitome of everything she detested about the High Houses. The woman was annoying; her voice shrill and demanding; and she spoke so full of herself that there was barely enough room for all of them in the coach. The more she listened to the woman's droning, the more her head ached. And it was obvious Moira was having the same effect on poor Feran, who was stuck listening to the gabble.

More unsettling was her focus on Carin's unabashed behavior. Stunned by the degree of jealousy she felt, Suna grappled with this newfound emotion. *He's not my property. Nor have I placed any claim on him. So why is it that I want to throttle the life out of this girl?*

Throughout the centuries, Diveneans sometimes married nulls, although it wasn't a common occurrence. She'd often reflected on whether the lack of inter-mage'ical marriages might have caused the decline of the Divenean race.

Children born within her Fold were rare. As far as she knew, Suna had been the last infant. Her Fold had been small, consisting of eight family members. As a child she had assumed there were more of them scattered throughout the lands. Unfortunately, she'd been wrong.

As she continued studying Carin, she knew this raw emotion burning inside her was ill-founded. Still, the fact that she felt anything whatsoever was even more baffling. Diveneans were supposed to be immune to petty human sentiments like jealously. Either the world had changed—or she had.

Feran? She knew the timbre of her voice resonated through his mind, adding to the headache she felt pounding between her eyes, and his. She sat with her head against the corner of the carriage, looking every bit asleep. *Just sit and pretend you're listening.* His dislike of her trespassing inside his head was evident, but what she was about to do next might make him change his mind on the matter. *I have to stop this incessant woman's blabbering.*

You're not the one who's being tortured by it.

His retort dripped with sarcasm, but he kept his attention focused on Lady Moira as he continued to nod like a fool.

Move closer to me. His surprise rippled through her. Being inside his head was a little unnerving. Between her unfounded anger at Carin, which she sensed confused him, and the pounding headaches they shared, their sensations coalesced together rather uniquely.

Feran did as she asked and inconspicuously inched his way closer, stopping when their thighs touched. In the next breath, blissful quiet filled the coach. It was an inconsequential use of her mage'ic, and well warranted.

Lady Moira's mouth hung open in mid-sentence. Carin's not so innocent brown eyes stared vacantly ahead.

Suna slipped the hood of her cloak off and shook out the braid of her hair. "I swear, if I had to listen for one moment more, I was going to strangle the woman."

"That makes two of us." As he leaned forward in his seat to study the two women, he waved his hand in front of their faces. Not an eyelash moved. "What did you do to them?"

"I've suspended them in time."

One of his eyebrows lifted.

"They know nothing of what's transpiring now, nor will they." She concentrated on making herself more comfortable on the coach's wooden bench and pushed aside the longing for the softness of a down-filled cushion to ease the constant jarring of the wheels over the rutted roads. "I'll release them when we get closer to Dunkerk. Maybe."

Feran smirked. "If I didn't know better I'd swear you're developing a sense of humor."

"I didn't do this for a joke. It was for sanity purposes only." *The girl is indeed pretty,* she admitted begrudgingly. *Is it only Carin's interest in Feran that has me so unsettled? I have no claim on him. Where do these emotions come from? Perhaps it's because I'm returning to Dunkerk that has me irritable.*

He waved his hand again, but the women continued to sit like frozen fish bait. "So they'll wake up and think their trip was shorter than expected?"

"Yes."

He fell quiet. As the familiar countryside of Dunkerk rolled past, she became absorbed in her own memories.

When the circular outer walls of Dunkerk came into view, a sense of homesickness tightened around her heart. In the muted darkness of night, the city loomed like an icon of wealth and power. Flickering oil lamps glimmered along its many streets, some sputtering and dimming before flaring back to life. Even from the distance, the kingdom shone like a star.

Fortified by two towering stone turrets, Dunkerk had withstood time itself. And never had an army breached its walls. An expansive gatehouse attached to an iron portcullis materialized the closer they approached the massive main gate. Trunks of timber covered with iron slantings created the sliding doors that protected the first entrance into Dunkerk. Situated directly above to provide adequate protection for the defenders of the city in case of attack was a walkway with a half-wall. Hoardings attached to the outside of the crenellation made a breach of the first set of gates near impossible.

The second line of defense they passed through was just as impressive. Like the first entrance, the second gate was similarly built, but instead of a crenellation design on the top wall, a wide allure ran the length of the city that could accommodate hundreds of archers. Loopholes lined both sets of walls, staring outward like hungry, empty eyes. If an enemy ever gained the first wall, Dunkerk's defenders could trap them between the first and second gates, using the cover of the loopholes to attack from above.

Directly on the other side of the city was a steep cliff that dropped dangerously to a water inlet leading out to the Kasprian Sea, which made Dunkerk unreachable even by ship.

Numerous buildings, large and small, gleamed like iridescent structures in the gloom of night. But nothing shone as bright or as capacious as the main castle... and beside it, the Palace of Kings.

Nestled like a gem upon a small hill next to Dunkerk's castle, the palace connected directly to the Regents Gallery by a glass ceiling wall-walk. As far as she knew, no one had entered the palace since King

Markes' demise. As doctrine dictated, every door should have remained sealed. No one was allowed entry but the next King of Dunkerk.

By far, the palace was the tallest and most beautiful of all the structures in the lands. The doors, stepped window frames, and all the outside flutings and fixtures, including the balconies, shone in gilded silver that caught the reflections of a blazing sun during the day or the many lights of the city at night. No matter what time or season, the Palace of Kings shone as a beacon across Etharia.

The tallest turret of the palace rose several hundred feet higher than the spires of the castle beside it, dwarfing it in comparison. On an oriel just below the pinnacle, five large banners blew in the breeze, each depicting the major realms of the lands.

On the east side, Lord Greth's gold, three mast, three star trireme waved like elegant silk in the wind.

Situated next to it was Lord Conac's ocher banner embroidered with three stars crowning three mountains.

To the east, Karvelle's banner symbolized a large potter's wheel in a circle of white waves framed in royal blue with bright orange thread that ran through it in a checkerboard pattern.

Lord Ethbridge's crimson shield and war hammer on an ebony background stood parallel with Karvelle's banner.

Directly in the middle of these four and raised slighter higher than the rest was Lord Mollster's emerald hands wrapped with thorns.

On the very tip of the highest turret flew the standard of Dunkerk, its pristine background symbolizing that no enemy had ever taken the kingdom. Framed by a crimson border of small flames, a gold crown adorned its center with five stars arranged in a semi-circle above it, each portraying the colors of the five banners that unfurled below it.

These standards were symbols of hope and freedom to the people of Etharia, but right now, they did little to inspire Suna. She would never admit it, but ghosts waited for her behind those walls.

"I have to release them now," she said softly.

"Can't you wait until we're at least stopped inside?"

She sent him a stern frown.

"Okay, okay. Wishful thinking, is all."

The silence instantly shattered with the shrill, monotonous voice of Lady Moira's ramblings as she picked up right where she'd left off. Suna was certain it was more annoying than before.

Carin's eyes swam with confusion as she peered out the window.

"That's very interesting," Feran replied with a polite nod in Lady Moira's direction. "Don't you think so, *Sena*, my dear?" He turned, realizing too late that Suna had resumed her deceptive sleep pose, which left him to fend for himself against the torturous chatterbox.

You little witch," he mused.

Name calling is rather childish, don't you think? With a sigh, Suna opened her eyes and daintily stretched. "My goodness, we're here already?"

She sensed Feran stiffen beside her.

Suna turned her attention to Carin. "You know, my *husband* and I were just visiting Odarian. That gown you're wearing is all the rage there, too."

The young girl's pouty disposition became indignant ire. Dunkerk professed the latest fashions, far above Odarian or any other kingdom. Suna had provided just enough sting to insult. The young girl swung her head so that her curls bounced against her cheeks and gawked at her mother.

Lady Moira looked as if she'd choked on her tongue.

At least they're quiet again.

Ripples of Feran's silent laughter bubbled inside her. Suna slid closer to him and took his calloused hand within her own, playing up the role as his dutiful wife. *I didn't think this would be so much fun.*

Her heart beat faster at his touch, and she was thankful that was the only sensation she felt. For some reason the strange shifting of air that had sometimes occurred between them seemed to have disappeared.

A hand so small that can wield such power.

Feran's thought touched upon her soul. She immediately removed herself from his mind. With effort, she masked the pounding in her chest and addressed Carin. "My husband and I were just on a hunting expedition. It's been a rather long and tiring journey. I'm looking forward to returning home. You and your mother must come and visit us. For tea and sweet cakes, perhaps? I could see if any of Mistress Maven's novices can fit you into their schedules. As you know, her shop is very busy." She tilted her head to eye the younger woman up and down in the same appalling manner as she'd done to her earlier. The insult was blatant, and definitely unforgivable in this circle of society. And Suna knew it.

Mistress Maven had owned an exclusive dress shop affordable only by members of the High Houses. She'd taken a chance on mentioning the name, hoping it still existed. Judging from the shocked expressions on both women's faces, it did. Mistress Maven was most likely dead and gone, but when Suna knew her, she'd been apprenticing several young studies to take over the business. It was nice to know some things hadn't changed.

Carin's mouth opened, but then she snapped it shut. Her mother sat in stunned silence, desperately trying to see inside the hood, no doubt for ammunition to gossip about later.

Play with fire and I'll scorch you. It was nice to know her diverse people skills were still useful.

Narrowing her eyes as thin as her lips, Lady Moira directed her question to Feran while glaring at Suna. "What did you say your name was?"

He slumped forward and mumbled politely, "Feran. This is my lovely wife, the Lady Sena. We're related to the House of Lembart."

As the older woman's eyes slitted even more, Suna realized the copper-wheels in her head were working overtime in an effort to remember where they placed on the rungs of society. "You *do* look familiar. Have we met before?" Moira snipped.

Plying for information to no doubt share with her high circle of friends, Suna mused ruefully.

Feran dipped his head. "No, my lady, for I would have remembered such a delightful introduction."

The coach slowed before coming to a complete stop inside the inner bailey of the second gate. Even at this hour of night, the city bustled with activity. Several coaches were arriving or leaving, following some obscure schedule. Crowds of people milled about either shopping for wares from the kiosks still open or waiting to pick up friends or family. Thick clouds of dust from the wheels of the many carriages clogged the air and stung the eyes.

Feran opened the door of the coach and waited for the two women to make their hasty exits. Once they stepped down and passed by him, Suna let out a chuckle.

One of the drivers of their coach held out their only piece of luggage. Feran took their pack and placed it over his shoulder. Holding out his hand like a lord in waiting, Suna grasped it and stepped down onto the wooden platform, demonstrating more grace and style than both those highborn women combined.

The Lady Moira and her daughter vanished quickly into the crowds, apparently wanting nothing more to do with their ill breeding. Suna wasn't the least bit sad to see them go. She'd picked up on a few of Carin's thoughts. For a high bred lady her dirty mind could have rivaled a foot soldier's. *That girl is no innocent maiden.*

The coach pulled away and sped through the gates to begin its journey back to Dunkerk's harbor, leaving them amidst the throngs of people rushing to and fro.

Oil lamps glowed like shimmering fireflies from wooden standards erected alongside wide flagstone streets. Suna slid the hood of her cloak back a bit and stared toward the Palace of Kings. It had been far too long since she last stood on this soil. Memories came and went with startling clarity. With considerable effort, she pushed them from her mind.

Feran leaned close. "Where to now?"

She closed her eyes and grasped her quickening in an effort to find Ilio's imprint in this mayhem of activity. Assaulted by so many auras and colors, it was impossible to pinpoint the imp's trail. His foul presence was here for a certainty, as her sensitive nose picked up his unique stench, but there was no way she could identify which direction he'd taken. With a submissive sigh, she released her mage'ic and turned to him, knowing he was not going to agree with her proposal. "I suggest we head to the main castle."

His mouth dropped open, but he was quick to recover. He moved even closer and whispered, "Then we risk being recognized."

She gave a grim nod. "I know, but finding Ilio by traditional means is not going to work. It's like finding a herring bone in a sea of water. This was my greatest fear," she added with a laden sigh. "We're going to have to draw him out to us."

"And how in the Seven Hells do you propose doing that?"

"Either I make an appearance or General Feran will have to." It was a shrewd suggestion, and one she didn't want to entertain, at least not yet, but she was fresh out of ideas.

"Look," he began. "I have a plan that might work. The city seems the same since last time I was here, so this should make things a little easier in our search. There's a tavern, but not suited for you. Your upbringing, I mean."

She opened her mouth, but Feran rushed on.

"A complex network of spies work the intricacies of Dunkerk's underground. There's a man I know. He frequents this particular tavern. The sooner we can get information about Ilio out to the network the sooner we'll be able to find that hellion. Stay here. I'll be back shortly."

Mellor flashed through her mind. "You're not leaving me here alone."

"I'm just going to see whether the network's still operating. Things may have changed in my absence, but I think not. If I send out a description of Ilio, someone will come forward about his whereabouts. A creature like that can't hide for long. Not without being noticed." His scrupulous gaze studied the streets.

"I'm coming with you. I have no desire to stay here by myself. People might begin to ask questions I can't answer." Without waiting for a reply, she pulled her hood tighter around her head, a habit she was developing, and rather despising.

He shifted awkwardly from foot to foot. "This tavern is no place for you."

She arched an eyebrow and crossed her arms over her chest. Seconds later, she began tapping the heel of her boot.

He groaned and slapped his forehead. "Here we go again. Just once, I'm going to win an argument."

Suna muttered, "Not likely, but lead the way, *General*."

He turned right and headed toward the west side, a part of Dunkerk she'd never occasioned when she'd lived here. She walked beside him, surveying the sights through the cowl of her hood. It wasn't long before she began to understand his apprehension.

CHAPTER NINETEEN

In any kingdom large or small, distinctive levels of society exist, and Dunkerk was no different. Even in its apparent cleanliness, certain sections of the city were far less 'civilized' than others. It didn't take long for Suna to realize that Feran was leading them straight to the seediest side.

Populated by low-income scullery maids and mards, first year guards, and trades people, it also played host to the majority of thieves and cutthroats. People who ventured into this section either lived here or were in search of fulfilling some form of illegal activity. Even the Elite Guards preferred to stay clear unless a slaying took place. Unfortunately, those instances weren't a rare occurrence. The buildings here lacked proper upkeep. Bawdy taverns lined streets lit by sporadically lit lanterns which created a hovel for undesirables.

Suna was thankful for the concealment of her hood. However, her modest vest and skintight breeches did little to stop the leering looks and jests called out by the occasional drunkard or a few brave men willing to withstand Feran's furious glares.

When they passed several pleasure houses, a cacophony of feminine voices called out asking if she was for hire.

Do I look that cheap? she wondered.

Feran walked with an air of authority coupled by a fiery expression forged like iron on his face. He'd pulled aside his cloak so his sword was readily visible. It acted as a deterrent, more so when the Sword Dancer's emblem on his blade caught certain eyes. Only a fool would want to dance with a master swordsman.

Suna had the misfortune of having to hide her's inside her cloak, hoping to draw the least amount of attention. Several times she brushed her fingers across the pommel for a sense of security.

At last they stopped in front of one of the most squalid-looking places yet. Inside, dim candlelight flickered against cracked windows that had never been washed. Blotches of black stained the outer walls. From where she stood, it was difficult to discern whether it was excrement or blood. In retrospect, she hoped for the latter.

A weathered sign that could have read Ratty's Grin, or better yet, Rats Inn, which gave better validity to the establishment. The sign hung above the weathered door with a rusty chain. Just below it, a vagrant lay sprawled across the uneven steps in a pool of congealed blood glistening beneath his head. Suna rushed to him. He was bloody and beaten, but was sleeping off the koffea.

She heaved a sigh of relief and turned slowly to Feran, staring in disbelief. "You aren't serious?" she hissed.

"You said you wanted to come with me, so here we are. We'll keep up the ruse of us being husband and wife. That should keep you somewhat out of scrutiny. I hope." He lowered his gaze, but she sensed he didn't believe a word he'd just said.

"Who are we looking for exactly?" She scanned the littered streets and made mental notes of the numerous alleyways shrouded in shadow. One had to be aware of all escape routes, just in case, and two sets of eyes were better than one, especially in a place like this.

His face sobered. "You don't have to do this, Suna. You can wait here."

She narrowed her eyes.

Throwing up his hands in frustration, he glowered at her. "Don't say I didn't warn you. Let's go."

They stepped over the vagrant's body and entered a dingy, smoke imbued room with wooden benches and tables scattered about in frivolous patterns, so unlike the orderly drinking room of Bailor's Inn. The floor consisted of rotting rushes that reeked of vomit, sour sweat, and blood. A few patrons occupied the tavern, each sitting alone in a different darkened corner.

A buxom woman with a face pancaked with makeup, frowned at them from behind the bar. Suna caught sight of the woman's ample bosom and tried not to stare. By all standards that stained bodice was several sizes too small to contain breasts that large. She tried not to gawk, but those mounds of flesh were difficult to dismiss.

The bar-maiden ignored Suna. Her attention locked onto Feran's sword. In a flash, her frown morphed into an ugly scowl. Trouble always followed when law-abiders such as the Elite Guards or Guardians showed up. To be sure, they'd be searching for someone who broke the law and the end result was a brawl, which meant damage to the establishment.

In a place like this, Suna couldn't imagine it getting any worse.

Feran's infamous grin beamed as he strode toward the woman. "A good evening to you, love. I'm looking for a friend," he said, flashing his pearly whites.

The bar-maiden snarled something under her breath as her face contorted with contempt beneath the many layers of rouge. "You ain't got no friends here, feller." She eyed Suna up and down worse than Carin had done. Suna's hand inched toward her sword.

"You ought to be giving that man a wee bit of respect, Zara."

Suna turned with Feran toward the sound of a voice that had come from across the room. The stranger sat hidden in a small alcove veiled in deep shadow.

Feran stared hard at him for a moment. Then his grin widened and became genuine. He made his way toward the stranger's table with Suna following close behind. The man stood and greeted Feran with a forearm-to-forearm grasp, which she recognized as a foot soldier's greeting.

"Viktor! How in damnation are ya?" Feran gave the man a painful cuff across the shoulders that made Suna flinch. He then turned and pulled a chair out for her. As she sat, she saw surprise pass fleetingly over the stranger's face.

With his nondescript clothing, Viktor looked at ease in the shadows, and perhaps it was just as well. His face was a map of battle scars. One of his eyebrows was completely gone, but the most prominent wound was thick and jagged, long since healed, that ran over his left eye, down the center of his mouth to end at the base of his throat. It's a wonder he hadn't lost his sight.

He wasn't a pretty man, but she sensed why Feran liked him. Viktor's aura consisted of honor that blazed in many hues of golds and yellows combined with pigments of red and pink. Her viewing depicted bravery and blood in abundance, but the many shades of gray she ventured no closer to. She sensed he was a good man doing a dirty job.

"I should be asking you that, you big lummox." Viktor slapped Feran's back so hard, it jarred Suna's teeth. "Where in devil's lair have you been? I thought for sure you'd come back and visit, but not a word did I hear after you left." He then aimed his attention at Suna, as if drawn by her silence.

"I've been doing some tracking for Sainsgarth. You know, a little bit of this, a little bit of that." Feran trailed off when he realized his friend wasn't paying a speck of consideration to him.

"Well, who might this shy thing be?" Viktor asked. The mischievous sheen in his eyes dulled.

She opened her mouth to answer, but Feran was quicker. "This is Sena, my, um, my wife." He rolled his shoulders as if to say 'she's no one important'.

Suna stiffened. Feran's edginess confused her. This had been his idea. Viktor was a friend, wasn't he? She'd promised she wouldn't go gallivanting in his thoughts, and she intended to keep that promise, however difficult it was. *So why is he so uneasy?*

Shock puffed out every scar on the veteran's face. "Wife? So you went and dun it. Feran, ol' boy, you're one lucky man. And to your lady here, my condolences."

Viktor leaned across the table and snapped up Suna's hand before she had a chance to pull away. He turned it over palm up and placed a sloppy kiss onto its center and released her just as quickly. He sat back in his chair sporting the same infuriating grin that Feran could manifest in a blink.

She eyed both men, wondering what just happened. She wanted to wipe the saliva off, but didn't want to appear rude.

Feran introduced him with a dramatic wave of his hand. "Sena, meet the incorrigible, but highly talented, Viktor Bossa."

It's a pleasure to make your acquaintance, Lady Sena. You know...?" With lightning speed, he leaned across the table again and flipped back the cowl of her cloak. She hadn't time to react. For his age, the man was impressively fast.

As he resumed his seat, Viktor's smirk widened. "Now I can see that pretty face of..." He stopped, his eyes rounding. Ashen, he turned and faced Feran, his hairless eyebrow arching.

Suna slid her hood into place and scrutinized the man. Awkward silence filled the small space between them.

"I hate to blow out the flame of yer candle, ol' boy," Viktor stated, narrowing his eyes dangerously in her direction, "but she ain't who she says she is." His gaze darted between them, his forehead furrowed, waiting for an explanation.

A mesh of memories flooded from Viktor's mind into Suna's. One of the strongest was of Viktor barely old enough to read, his face young, innocent and scarless. She'd ridden past him on a street in Dunkerk, but failed to notice the boy standing forlornly by the side of the road as her attention was centralized on the carriage filled with several highborn children under her charge. Pealing voices filled with excitement and rambunctious laughter rang out from the topless gilded coach.

Sitting in this ragtag tavern, the strength of Viktor's memories made every moment feel as if it were just happening. Young Viktor had paused to look down at the rags he wore before hiding in the thorny brambles of a rosewood hedge as her coach passed by him.

Her heart ached at the emotions emanating from him. Rejection. Shame. But the unworthiness was the worse. It cut through her like a dagger.

First Mollster's memories. Now Viktor's. She never imagined that she'd had such an effect on people. Perhaps if she had, it might have swayed her to stay.

"You look exactly the same," Viktor whispered. He shook his head and straightened in his chair, his voice no louder than a hush. "The rumors were true."

Saying nothing, she marveled at how these people had viewed her. She despised the fact she hadn't seen it herself. Heat flared in the apples of her cheeks as she peered down at her lap.

"I'm quite aware of that fact, Viktor," Feran whispered back with cutting sarcasm. "And I would appreciate it if you would take that look off your face."

He checked over his shoulder to ensure no one else was watching. In a place like this, it was rare to find someone who wasn't paying close attention to something. The positioning of Suna's chair had thankfully kept her face hidden from the other patrons, as well as the nosy shrew behind the bar.

Suna pulled the cowl of her hood lower. Unruffled, she scrutinized Viktor and wondered what he would do with this newfound knowledge.

The spy bent his head closer to the table. "Well, it's not every day that something like this happens. Ya mind explaining things?" He directed his question straight at Feran, but his agitation encompassed only her.

She leaned as close as the table would allow. "We're looking for someone. A rather small, gnarled and offensive creature."

Viktor's scar puckered as he grimaced. "You just described half the population of the west end, Lady Suna."

"Your memory serves you correctly, but in here, call me Sena. Please."

As he peered cautiously around the drinking room, the scars deepened on his face. "Spit me onto a fire and cook me well done. I'm not leaving here 'til one of you tells me what in bloodfires is going on." He leaned into the back of his chair and locked his hands behind his neck, preparing to wait all night if need be.

In a kingdom this big, she knew they needed all the help they could get in finding Ilio. If two eyes were better than one, then Viktor's network could do more than she thought possible. According to Feran, Viktor commanded the underground, a network she'd once thought was nothing but gossip. He knew all the comings and goings of Dunkerk's poor *and* elite. If anyone could help them, this was their man.

Feran waited for a concurring nod from her before he began telling Viktor everything that had happened.

The spy listened without saying a word, although his eyes widened every once in a while to a fact or event Feran relayed. The name Isafel and the explanation of Ilio made Viktor choke, but he recovered quickly and continued to listen without interruption.

Zara kept glancing their way, intrigued by the secretive conversation taking place at one of her tables. Thankfully, she didn't venture closer.

When Feran finished, Viktor let out a shrill whistle. "Blood and guts, boy! Just what have you gotten yourself into? No offense, Lady Sena," he added with an apologetic bow of his head.

"I would appreciate it if you'd stop acting like that."

"Well, it's a little difficult knowing who you are, my lady." The jagged scar on his face whitened as he grinned.

The sound of Feran's deep-chested laughter filled the small alcove. "Believe me, Viktor, I know exactly what you mean." He quickly sobered when he caught her scowl. "Look, we need help to find this little fiend and bring him to us. Better yet, find him and tell us where he is. We'll retrieve him ourselves."

"How do you expect to find this key when neither of you knows where it is?" Viktor scratched the silver stubble on his chin, his questioning gaze bouncing back and forth between them.

Suna pushed her chair closer to the table. "Because I have a sense Ilio knows where it's located. He's been birthed to serve a single purpose. To find the Kruthos key to set his master free. In some arcane way he seems to be following an obscure trail to it. That's why we have to find him."

"What if Ilio finds the key before the two of you do?"

"Do you know any of Etharia's histories, Viktor?" she asked and instantly regretted it. Boys like him were never given the opportunity of schooling. "If Ilio finds the key first, nothing in this world will matter."

Ominous silence followed as she leaned back to study the spy, allowing the ramifications of her words to sink in.

Viktor's shoulders slumped forward. "I may not be the brightest gem in a bag of baubles, but I do know what you mean. Feran, my boy, you left Dunkerk to leave all this horse dung behind. Now you're returning with the biggest pile of all. No offense, Lady *Sena*, but when it rains on ol' Viktor here, it's usually a downpour. Right now, I'd say we're past that and into torrential flooding."

Feran moved closer. "What do you mean?"

"I know the two of you obviously have enough in your buckets, but..." Viktor lowered the timbre of his voice even more. "I've just heard some news that's going to rattle your bones. Greth's going for the throne."

Feran fell back in his chair and stared long and hard at her. Suna knew that the questions she'd posed to him on the ship had led to this. She couldn't explain the hunch she'd felt then any more than she could explain why her heart thumped the way it did whenever he looked at her.

"Okay," Viktor stated skeptically. "Obviously, this isn't a surprise to either of you. Lady Allena has called the Council of Regents to convene tomorrow."

"Tomorrow?" Suna immediately sensed the bar-maiden's inquisitive stare boring in between her shoulder blades.

"Yes, and she'll be placing her nomination for Lord Tobas Greth to take the throne. Apparently the covenant means nothing now," he added with a disgusted twist of his lips. He was about to spit his distaste on the filth-infested rushes littering the tavern floor when he remembered she was present.

He swallowed hard and continued. "Wendel, Greth's nephew, has been quite persuasive about putting his uncle forward. In more ways than one. If you ask me, this stinks of Greth. Wendel doesn't have the brains to pull something like this off."

Their conversation halted when the bar-maiden's screeching voice reverberated from across the room. "If yer gonna sit there and not drink, y'all leave my tavern. This ain't no place for dolly-wallowing."

Viktor raised his head and peered over Suna's shoulder. With the cockiest grin she'd ever seen, he hollered back. "Gimme a pitcher of your finest mead, Zara. These are old friends who've come for a visit. I'd like to celebrate in style. And do me a favor, love? Give us some glasses you haven't spit shined, will ya?"

A loud snort sounded from Zara as she busied herself with their order. When the barmaid waddled her oversized bottom to their table, Suna could sense the woman counting the coins in her head. After slamming down three chipped mugs and an overflowing pitcher of watered down mead, the woman ignored the foam that spilled and pooled beneath the decanter. She placed her gnarled hands on her ample hips and waited, tapping her foot in the process.

The barmaid seemed to take too much interest in her, so Suna hid further into the folds of her cloak.

Feran looked up and flourished the hag with a grin that matched Viktor's.

"Many thanks, Zara." Viktor tossed several coppers in the air. The woman snatched the money with astounding speed and dexterity. She left satisfied, but still curious before shuffling to her usual place behind the bar.

The light in Viktor's eyes danced with amusement. "That should keep her content for a while. He grabbed a glass and began pouring himself a drink. He stopped when he realized that neither she nor Feran had taken the lead to do the same. He leaned close. "Pour yourselves a mug or she'll get suspicious."

Suna grabbed a chipped mug and examined it for signs of disgusting phlegm. Reluctantly pouring herself a glass, Feran did likewise, although both drinks sat untouched. Viktor had already downed his and was pouring another when the door of the tavern swung wide and a brute of a man stormed through.

"Amos!" Zara's greeting was loud enough for every patron to hear. To Suna, it rang out like a warning rather than a greeting.

Viktor groaned and slid several inches down in his seat.

Suna turned slightly in her chair.

"I'm looking for that maggot, Viktor Bossa. Is he here?" the man growled through the thickness of a black, matted beard.

"Ain't seen him for days. Try Marriot's place up the street," Zara snapped.

With a grunt that may have been an acknowledgment, Amos' sullen stare swept over the room for a moment before he turned and left, slamming the tavern's door behind him. Suna heard the crack in the front window widen.

The shrew shot all three of them a baleful glare, but said nothing. In this end of town, keeping your business to one's self was a means of survival.

Viktor groaned under his breath.

"Been making friends again?" Feran managed past a sheepish chuckle.

"With friends like that who needs nemeses," Suna countered.

"It's just a bet that's come due." Viktor muttered something incoherently as a pinkish hue spread across the bridge of his nose. "Now I'll have to owe Zara. Toad testicles."

Lowering his head and voice at the same time, he took one last swig of the mead and wiped his mouth with the back of his calloused hand. "You get outta here and make yourselves scarce. You'll need a place to stay for the night. This news? I'll have to call in some favors." He paused to stare with blatant unease in her direction. "If Greth takes the throne, there's gonna be changes. And they ain't gonna be pretty. Stop that from happening and I promise I'll help ya find this Ilio. You'll be hard pressed to find an inn with available rooms with this festival going on, so go to the Whitlambe Inn. It's reputable. And they always save a bed for me. I'll find you there in twenty-four hours."

He stood and extended his forearm out to Feran, who took it and embraced his friend with heartfelt warmth and camaraderie. Viktor worked under extreme dangers. The task they'd appointed to him was by far the most perilous. If Ilio sensed Viktor was searching for him that imp wouldn't hesitate to kill him outright.

The scarred veteran turned to her. Uncertain how to bestow a proper goodbye, she held out her hand and grasped his forearm in a manner identical as Feran. He stared back in stunned silence.

"Thank you, Viktor. We'll be waiting for you at the Whitlambe. Time is short. If you don't show by mid-morning tomorrow, we'll have to think of something else, but I make this promise to you. I'll do everything in my power to ensure that Lord Greth will not take the throne while I breathe."

"Then let's hope you just keep doing that. An imp like you described can't hide here. Too visible."

Feran grimaced. "He can glamor."

"And just what that might be?"

"Mage'ic to make himself look different, but he can't maintain the spell for long," she explained.

Viktor shook his head. "I wish him luck with that. I have people everywhere. With a little embellishment, news like this will spread like wildfire. Be careful. We don't want anything to happen to that pretty head of yours." He winked a shameful suggestion. Suddenly remembering who she was, he stumbled back a step. When she smiled her thanks, his apprehension disappeared. "Until then, stay safe you two. And outta sight."

Viktor stopped long enough to flourish a wave toward Zara, accompanied by an incorrigible wink that said, 'I'll repay my debt to you later'. He was out the front door before the barmaid began a tirade of indignant profanity.

CHAPTER TWENTY

The moon had disappeared by the time they came upon Whitlambe Inn. Although morning was still a few hours away, the day had disappeared far too soon for Feran's liking.

He heard Suna sigh of relief when she caught sight of the frilly lace curtains covering the clean, beveled windows. Above the door, a jade-colored sign depicted a lovable lamb sleeping on a golden bale of hay. The inn was a welcome sight since leaving the slipshod establishment of Ratty's Grin and neighborhood that went with it.

After climbing a small set of stairs, they opened the green door and entered. Behind a burnished receiving desk with two flanking wooden chairs, which was the only other furnishings that made up the cozy foyer, a short, heavy-set man with ash-colored eyes looked up as they approached. "Mr. Kipley at your service," he said.

When Feran inquired about a room, the man's featured softened with regret. "I'm sorry, sir, but the inn's all booked."

At the mention of Viktor's name, Mr. Kipley smiled. "Well then, we do have a room to offer. Viktor pays monthly and we keep it reserved just for him. I'll see to it that he's reimbursed for the nights you and your lovely wife will be staying with us."

In keeping with their ruse, Feran signed the inn's register as Mr. and Mrs. Lam.

"The room's small and it overlooks the stable. Hope you don't mind," the innkeeper explained with an apologetic dip of his head.

Feran didn't care. It was a room with a bed and a roof. And it wouldn't be the first time they had to share accommodations. *But we'll be fully clothed.*

He pushed aside his disappointment and followed Mr. Kipley as he led them up the narrow staircase. Clusters of wildflowers neatly arranged in simple blown glass vases sat on tiny wall-tables that stood at intervals in between each room. They made their way down the dimly lit hall to the very end. When he opened the door, Feran saw a small bed pushed up against the far wall covered by several clean, hand-sewn blankets. A small vase of wildflowers sat on the end table by the door.

He moved to the window that overlooked the stables across the street and stared out into the night.

"What the room lacks for in comfort I'll make up for with a hot meal and a bath. On the house, of course," the innkeeper offered.

Thank the gods for Viktor's connections, Feran thought.

"Thank you. You're most kind," Suna said.

"I'll be at the front desk should you need anything."

When Mr. Kipley exited the room, Suna flung herself on top of the bed. Several loose feathers escaped and fluttered down to the immaculate floor. "A hot meal and a bath," she murmured as she placed an arm over her eyes.

Feran stood quietly by the window and scanned the street below. At this hour, only a couple of lantern tenders were out. The majority of Dunkerk's population were asleep, resting for the festivities scheduled to start later in the day.

His thoughts drifted to the decree none of these people knew was coming. How would the good citizens of Dunkerk react to Lord Greth as king? He'd despised that pompous lord from the moment he'd first been introduced. The man had dismissed him like a servant, but his personal opinion meant little when it came to ruling a kingdom. Judging by the rumors he'd heard coming from Carberra, Greth's interests had changed over the years.

Perhaps Viktor was right. He too sensed a torrential storm coming their way, and the nomination of that lord was going to be a mere afternoon shower before the tempest.

It was bad enough they'd been chasing that imp halfway across Etharia or that the fate of so many lay upon their shoulders, but involving other people, and friends at that, didn't bode well with him. It wasn't that he was averse to asking for help. He just didn't like the prospect of endangering anyone because of it. True, Viktor Bossa was a cunning man. Even a wise and seasoned veteran, but Ilio was gifted with dark mage'ic. He couldn't help but regret his decision of involving his friend in this. Though left with few options, he had to hold to the hope that Viktor's network would find that imp well before events spiraled more out of control than they already had.

He turned toward the bed. "Who's first for the bath? Your choice. Eat first or bathe." He stretched his arms to the ceiling to ease the stiffness in his back

Suna peered at him from behind the crook of her arm. "I'll eat first, if you don't mind. You look like you could use a good soak."

"What do you mean by that?" He didn't mean to snap, but he was exhausted.

"Nothing," she mumbled as she pulled herself off the bed.

They made their way downstairs in silence. When they stopped at the front desk, he asked where the baths were located. Suna inquired about the kitchen. Mr. Kipley pointed to a spacious, vacant room across the hall from the foyer, telling her he'd be back to take her order once he showed Feran to the bathing rooms.

* ~ * ~ *

At this late hour, the empty dining room felt ominous. An eerie quiet hummed in the air as Suna sat at one of the many round tables and waited. When Mr. Kipley returned, red-faced and out of breath, she gave an order of goat cheese and bread, insisting there was no need to hurry. Before he turned away, she added a glass of mulled wine hoping it would help her sleep. Mr. Kipley nodded and left in the direction of the kitchen.

When she finished eating, the innkeeper led her to the bathing rooms. She passed Feran in the hall, but said nothing, exchanging only the briefest of nods. From the corner of her eye, she realized Mr. Kipley kept sneaking odd looks at the cloak and hood she refused to remove, but he never questioned her about it. *Dealing with Viktor, he's probably seen some strange things.*

When they reached the door to the baths, she said her thanks and entered.

The bathing room was dark and full of mist. A number of lit candles stood in melting pools of wax that lined the entire wall of the bathing trough.

After sliding the bolt through the metal hinge which secured the door, she removed her clothes and shook her hair free. She sank her entire body into the hot water and held her breath as long as possible before surfacing, sputtering water out through her nose and sighing in pleasure as the dirt from her travels washed away. A bar of sweet-scented cocoa soap sat on the ledge of the tub. She lathered herself from head to toe. By the end of her bath, her skin glowed pink, her body tingling clean.

The inn was still dark as she made her way back to her room. When she opened the door, the pungent fragrance of Feran's pipe tobac wafted through the small space.

He'd lit a single candle on the end table situated beside the bed. The diminutive glow felt warm and safe and seemed to enhance the smell of the small bouquet of wildflowers. Feran lay sprawled across the blankets in his clothes, his boots placed neatly on the floor beside his scabbard and sword, which leaned next to hers.

He looked up when he heard her enter and held out his pipe in her direction. "I hope you don't mind."

"No, it's fine. It's rather comforting, actually."

His brow folded into an unspoken question.

"It reminds me of someone I once knew." It made little difference that King Markes had also enjoyed a similar sweet pipe tobac, but she was in no mood to discuss such things. The wine she'd drank earlier was doing its job. Exhaustion seeped deep into her bones.

Her damp hair hung loose, curling upward at the ends as it always did when it dried. She shivered, but it had nothing to do with the dampness from her bath. The intensity in Feran's stare unnerved her. Again, she fought to slow the erratic beating of her heart that occurred whenever he looked at her like that.

He mumbled something, acting as if she'd caught him doing something wicked. Discomfort settled between them.

He rose from the bed and proceeded to tap out the ashes from his pipe into a dish on the table beside the one and only burning candle. "You take the bed. I'll sleep on the floor."

She crossed her arms and waited. Once she had his attention, she arched an eyebrow and pursed her lips.

He threw both his arms up into the air. "Now what?"

"There's enough room for both of us in that bed. You don't have to sleep on the floor. I won't allow it."

"You won't allow it? Really?"

The amusement in his eyes coupled with that grin of his couldn't have been more infuriating. She strode to the bed, trying her best not to stomp, and snatched back the covers. She settled herself closest to the wall. When he made no move to join her, she balanced up on her elbows and glared at him. *He can be so galling*. "Look, Feran. There's more than enough room for both of us. I really don't have the energy to argue about this."

Saying nothing, he placed his pipe down beside the vase and made his way to the side of the bed. He extinguished the candle and sat for the longest time on the edge of the mattress before finally sliding beneath the blankets like an ill-maneuvered marionette.

To her dismay, there wasn't as much room as she'd first anticipated. Or perhaps she was too aware of the leanness of his body next to hers. The muscles of his thigh and the warmth of his arm and shoulder through the blanket brought a flush of heat to settle in the base of her womb. Controlling her breathing became a struggle. She shifted closer to the wall and forced her thoughts elsewhere. Feran didn't move an inch. Suna closed her eyes and tried to sleep.

Minutes, perhaps hours later, when she'd finally found the cusp of sleep, an eerie cold began to permeate in their room. When she heard Feran mumble, "Hellfire, not again," she knew it wasn't a dream.

Both their scabbards leaned against the end table, but when she went to move toward them, she discovered her limbs were frozen in place. Feran's strangled moan confirmed her worst fear. He was in the same predicament.

"Suna?"

She sensed his presence before it entered their room.

Coiling strands of black mage'ic slithered through the cracks in the windows, chilling the marrow in her bones.

"You were to be mine, man-thing!"

Isafel's malicious voice oozed through the recesses of her mind with numbing depravity. His touch on her élan made her shudder. Still, she fought to free the restraints the demon had bound around her. Feran's frantic panting told her that he was in the same quandary as she was. However, knowing he was in danger brought forth a rage unlike any she'd ever experienced. She'd protect him at all cost.

Suna attempted to take hold of her mage'ic in an effort to shield them, but merely touching the demon's evil proved difficult. When she heard Isafel hiss, she knew that his control could be weakened.

She blocked out what was happening around her and delved deep into the source of her power—her élan. In her mind's eye, she saw the spectral apparition floating several feet above the outer walls of the city, his emaciated face stretched grotesquely by a mocking grin. The demon ventured no closer to the bright lights and people. The distance would make it a difficult battle.

You will not have him, witch. He's mine.

Her mind lurched in shock. *He means Feran! And he knows who I am?* She immediately shielded her thoughts.

Feran moaned. "It's my dreams coming to life. Hellfire! That's who wants my body? That's Isafel? He's worse than my nightmares."

Cruel laughter sliced like razor sharp claws through Suna's mind.

Master knows who you are too, Divenean bitch.

The fiend that he was, Isafel struck first at the one who could do him the most harm. Her.

Show yourself, demon! Show yourself NOW.

Feran's body convulsed. She'd forgotten about his connection to the monster. And to her. The force of her thoughts would have reverberated in his skull just as powerful as in Isafel's. It was a way of weakening the demon, but at the same time she was injuring Feran.

Sensing a sudden lull in Isafel's spell, she broke free of his hold and jumped from the bed before he could reinforce his mage'ic. She grabbed her sword and crouched. Muscles burned as she struggled to maintain her balance.

In the next instant, Feran was beside her in an identical stance, wide-eyed, panting, and ready to fight. She sensed his horror and distress, but also his conviction to beat the demon.

Her bare feet burned from the cold now seeping through the wooden planked floor. More black ice slithered its way up and over the walls and ceiling. From between her lips, her breath billowed out as thick mist.

"Where is he?"

She barely heard Feran over the crackling ice formations. "Outside the city's walls. I can't reach him yet, but I can still hurt him. Start slicing through the ice. It'll weaken his powers. Then I'll show him just what a Divenean bitch can do."

Ruthless laughter raced around the room.

Feran began hacking at the walls of ice that continued to grow and thicken around them. It was as if Isafel was attempting to seal them into a bitter cold cell of death.

She focused outside the frosted window, matching swing for swing of her blade with Feran's. She sensed the demon cringe at every strike they made against the ice, but it wouldn't be enough to stop the evil entity.

As Feran advanced toward another tendril, he became airborne and landed hard on his back on the floor. In a blink, he was up again, straining to find his footing. He swayed slightly and held a hand to his head. Blood trickled down his neck.

Trying to watch over Feran and concentrate on Isafel was depleting her energy too quickly, but she soon realized that it would take a lot more than this demon to stop the former general.

Moving with staunch determination, Feran continued scything at the black ice.

However, mage'ic needed to be fought with mage'ic—not a blade.

She dropped her sword and closed her eyes to better pinpoint Isafel's location. An image of a hunched, hooded creature with skeletal features came clearly to her mind. She mouthed an incantation she refused to speak aloud and raised both her arms into the air.

Twisting ribbons of crimson light rose from her feet and encircled her body. When she was completely cocooned within the fire spell, she fed her mage'ic with her anger, building it until her body became one with the flames. Then she let go of her fury.

Like an erupting volcano, the conjured fire shot upward to the ceiling and began to spread. It entangled itself within the slithering coils of Isafel's foul ice. Red mage'ic fought for supremacy within the demon's black.

Encased in heat that rushed through her veins, she soaked in the reprieve from Isafel's depravity. She could no longer see Feran, but she sensed him moving closer to her warmth. The evil in the frigid air was sucking the life from him.

When her spell reached a volatile level, she gathered the flames to herself and flung both arms out toward the window—straight in Isafel's direction.

Their room lit up like an exploding star before an unnatural darkness settled around them. Then a bloodcurdling shriek rent through the night.

She heard Feran fall to the floor. Her worry over his safety immediately released her from the spell. She rushed to his side where he lay crumpled with his head cradled in his hands. Blood seeped from both his ears.

As abruptly as it had started, the malevolence that had taken residence in their room disappeared. The darkness receded and soon, only the sounds of dripping water broke through the quiet.

* ~ * ~ *

Feran fought to remain conscious, but all he could hear was Isafel's horrid scream vibrating through his skull. The vile sound filled every crevice of his body with a foulness he couldn't describe. His guts churned. He dry-heaved. His head felt as if someone had split it into two. When he finally managed to look up without retching, Suna was beside him on the floor.

"A-y-urt?"

Only the din of distorted syllables reached his brain. Her eyes, wide and filled with concern, drilled into him. He struggled to sit, awestruck by the magnitude of power this small woman had just wielded. "I don't think so." Damn. He couldn't hear his voice. His ear drums felt shattered. And the pounding in his head? It was as if every hangover he'd suffered in his lifetime had returned as one major agony.

Suna helped him to stand. The burning in his fingertips reminded him he was alive, thanks to her.

The sound of pounding was the first thing he heard at a normal level. Feran opened the door a crack and peered out. There stood Mr. Kipley with his robe wrapped protectively around him and his pale face carved in panic.

"What were those screams? What's happening in there? And why is there blood on your shirt?"

He made an attempt to push his weight inside their room, but Feran placed his foot at the bottom of the door and blocked his entrance. *Great! And probably a name he shouldn't have heard either.*

Throwing a disparaging glance over his shoulder at Suna, he loosened his death grip on his sword and leaned the blade against the doorframe safely out of sight. "I do apologize, Mr. Kipley. My wife suffers from debilitating nightmares. She smacked me in the nose by accident in the throes of one of her dreams. I've given her something to help her sleep. I promise it won't happen again." *How loud was she? Or me?* Isafel had conjured himself through thought alone. In Suna's defense, hadn't they both screamed?

Mr. Kipley nodded, but fear blazed in his eyes. "Please ensure it doesn't occur again. You've disturbed the other patrons. It won't be tolerated."

Feran noticed several inquisitive guests had poked their heads outside their doors to watch their exchange of words.

The innkeeper went to leave, but shifted around to face him again. "I hope she feels better. Soon." The tension in his voice more than hinted that he refused to tolerate any further disruptions.

Feran closed the door, relieved to hear the man's footsteps fade down the hall. The remaining pieces of black ice were shriveling up and melting down the walls to form large puddles on the floor.

An invisible wind suddenly entered their room and gathered every drop of foul water into a ball that hovered in midair. Suna opened the window without lifting a finger and sent the water out to land safely on the empty street below. A resounding splash followed as she closed the window.

"Are you sure you're all right?" she asked. Worry pinched the corners of her eyes.

With a groan, he dropped to the edge of the bed and placed his head between his hands. "Besides the burning in my fingers and the pounding between my eyes, I'll live. I think. Just so I know what's going on here, I take it that was Isafel in the flesh. Sort of."

She positioned herself next to him. "Yes."

As he peered around the room, he noticed that the bouquet of flowers on the side-table had withered and died from the cold.

"That's who wants my body?" He hoped to be wrong.

"Yes."

They sat in silence while Feran's thoughts wormed around that demon and how much time they had left to find this damn key. He knew it'd been a bold move for Isafel to attack them here. But more importantly, why was Balthazar's minion *and* the imp both in Dunkerk?

Is that demon trailing after Ilio? Or is it me? he worried.

Suna went rigid, which told him she'd read his thoughts and had been thinking the same.

What isn't she telling me? The more Feran thought about the implications, the more discouraged he became.

CHAPTER TWENTY-ONE

They sat side-by-side on the edge of the bed for the remainder of the night, watchful and wary for another attack from Isafel, but all was quiet. When the inn awakened to another day, Feran knew they were safe for the time being.

Dunkerk suddenly came alive. The opening and closing of doors as the inn's staff and guests arrived and left echoed down the hallways. People using the privy accommodations resonated through the walls;

the streets below vibrated with the arriving and departing of carriages amidst the echoes of excited voices.

Everywhere merchants and citizens prepared for Dunkerk's Corn and Apple festival.

With a resigned sigh, he rose off the bed. "It's probably best to get some food. Hopefully Viktor will show soon." The throbbing in his skull hadn't abated in the least, and he hoped that by eating something it might lessen the pain.

Suna nodded and followed him out the door, stopping long enough to ensure the hood of her cloak was in place. She hadn't said a word for hours, which made him more than a tad uneasy.

After disposing the frostbitten flowers into the nearest waste bucket, they made their way downstairs.

From behind the front desk a plump woman with a kind face looked up from beneath her spectacles. "Good morn' to ya. I'm Mrs. Kipley." There was no doubt her husband had told her who'd caused the earlier ruckus. "Go find yourselves a seat before the dining room fills up." The caring smile creasing the corners of the woman's eyes was unpretentious and heartfelt.

Suna stepped closer to the desk. "I wonder if you could direct me to an herbal shop nearby."

"What is it you're looking for, dear?" Mrs. Kipley asked as she stooped to grab another drying sheet from the basket at her feet. The front desk was covered with neatly folded linens.

"Some malezia."

Feran shifted in uncomfortable silence. Merely speaking hurt his head. Besides, such wizen stuff was better left to women.

Mrs. Kipley let the sheet drop into the basket. "My husband told me you were having trouble sleeping. Look no further. I grow plenty out back in my garden. In our line of work, it's a godsend."

She gave a wink and shooed them away toward the dining room. "Sit yourselves down. I'll be right back, and I'll steep it strong, too."

Suna nodded. "Thank you."

Feran forced a smile and headed into the dining room.

Even at this early hour guests occupied the room to near capacity with bright, expectant faces looking forward to the upcoming celebrations. He wished he had one iota of their excitement, but the hollow feeling left by Isafel's visit wouldn't go away.

After finding a small table by the entrance, it wasn't long before Mrs. Kipley arrived with a steaming teapot. She placed it down next to a single cup.

When she turned to leave, Suna stopped her with a timid touch. "May I have another cup for my husband? I kept him awake as well."

"Of course." Mrs. Kipley hurried back into the kitchen.

In seconds, the aroma of fruity cinnamon mixed with ginger filled Feran's nostrils. After returning with an extra teacup, Mrs. Kipley scurried away to attend to the endless chores that needed her attention.

Suna grasped the porcelain handle of the teapot with a tea towel. "This is fresh. It'll be strong."

"Just as long as it stops the pounding between my eyes. If given a choice, I think I'd rather stomach another one of your traveling spells. Even blinking is like knives slicing through my skull." He placed a hand behind his head and kneaded the row of knots in his neck.

She poured a cup and slid the saucer toward him. "Drink it while it's hot. Mrs. Kipley has added some ginger to it. Personally, I prefer it with nothing added, but the ginger will ease your aches."

After burning his lips twice and the roof of his mouth once, Feran drained the cup. The tension in his neck loosened. Soon his headache became nothing more than a dull thud he could live with. "Is it always like this?" he asked as he rubbed his fingers over his tender eyes.

"For nulls, yes. Be it good or bad mage'ic, the frailty of your bodies can't tolerate much of it. It's like mixing your blood with something volatile. You managed to endure more than I thought possible."

He could barely keep the revulsion from his voice. "What kind of mage'ic was last night's?" He shuddered whenever he thought of that despicable presence inside him.

"The worst kind." She lowered her head and pretended to blow into her cup as she spoke in a hush. "That demon is Balthazar's favorite minion, not because he likes him, but because of his strength and power. There's no one stronger than Isafel except his master. You know the saying? Hold your friends close and keep your enemies as lovers?"

Frowning, he pushed the cup back and forth in between his hands. "What about Ilio then? I mean, look at the destruction at Carberra Ferry. Is he as powerful as Isafel?"

Suna's steely gaze scanned the crowd in the dining room before returning to him. "Ilio was defending himself against something. Someone." Worry deepened the lines on her forehead. "Perhaps this isn't the best place to talk."

He glanced up and realized how many people surrounded them. He'd been so engrossed in his misery to notice the growing crowd waiting by the door for a table.

"Let's go to our room and wait for Viktor there." She stood and poured two more full cups before leaving the empty teapot. When they passed the lineup of people packed into the foyer, it became obvious the Kipleys ran a delicious kitchen as well as a tidy inn.

Feran watched Mrs. Kipley dashing about. She no doubt could have used a cup or two of malezia herself. The morning had just begun and the poor woman was attending to two, sometimes three chores at once. She attempted to keep the mass of people at the entrance of her kitchen neat and orderly, while at the same time fold laundry from the basket on the floor and direct guests to the many activities scheduled for the festival.

"My goodness it's busy, isn't it?" she called to them over the crowd.

One of the cooks hollered from the kitchen. Something about a cracked pot. Mrs. Kipley managed a roll of her eyes as she went to hurry past them, but then stopped. "I almost forgot. Here, dear. I cut a few buds of malezia for you," she said as she slipped a small handful of brown leaves into Suna's palm. "Just in case," she added before scampering away.

Suna murmured her thanks and climbed the stairs. They passed a disheveled looking Mr. Kipley as he darted by them, all the while trying to pull up bright red suspenders over his shoulders, no doubt off to help his wife with the onslaught of extra guests.

* ~ * ~ *

After returning to their room, Suna wrapped the dried malezia into a handkerchief and slipped the package into one of the pockets of her jerkin. She listened to the constant banging of the front door as patrons entered and left the inn. Feran ventured to the window and stared down at whatever was happening below.

She'd forgo the braiding of her hair and combed out the knots with her fingers instead. "What if Viktor doesn't show up?" she asked. She didn't want to talk, but the burdensome silence between them felt worse.

He shifted around and peered at her over the rim of his cup as he sipped the malezia and swallowed. "To be honest, I was just thinking that myself. But for some reason I believe you already have something up those sleeves of yours."

She stood and began to pace. She always thought better when she moved. After analyzing half a dozen scenarios of options, she made a decision. "If Viktor doesn't show, you'll have to."

"I'll have to do what?" he murmured over the sounds filtering through the windowpane.

"You, *General* Feran, will have to make an appearance at the Council of Regents. We have to delay Greth's announcement so we can deal with Ilio first. They must be told what manner of creature is walking in their city. Although I don't think we should mention Isafel's little visit. It may cause them to disbelieve our story altogether."

He turned and gawked. "And just how in hell's bells am I supposed to accomplish that?"

"I don't know, but we can't sit around here and do nothing." She hesitated. "By the way, why did Viktor kiss me on the hand like that?" Intuition told her not to ask, but curiosity won the gambit.

Feran's grin was wider than any she'd seen before. "Why? Have you taken a fancy to him?"

She took a second to glower at him before returning to her pacing.

"It was a sign of respect," he said in a voice drenched in weariness. He walked to the bed and splayed himself across it.

"Respect?"

"And a congratulation of sorts. On our marriage. It was his way of saying he approved. Now how in the devil's lair are we going to explain those?"

She followed his gaze up to the ceiling. Water stains left by Isafel's black ice had discolored the wood paneling. Flowers were one thing, but water stains on the ceiling?

Ignoring the damage, she focused on Feran while trying to keep her voice even-keeled. "Approved? You need validation from a foot soldier?"

"No," he snipped. "Viktor is more than a foot soldier, Suna. He's also a close friend, and extremely talented at what he does. That was his way of saying that in his opinion I'd made a good decision." He closed his eyes.

I wonder what Viktor thinks of me now? Stunned, she stopped pacing. *Why would I care what he thinks, for goodness sake?*

* ~ * ~ *

Not long after, the inn fell quiet, but outside buzzed with activity.

Feran stood from the bed with his guts tied tighter than a maiden's legs. Viktor was a no-show. Another thing to place on his worry list. "We better get ourselves to the castle."

His Guardian instincts screamed that something had gone wrong, but sitting here doing nothing wasn't helping their situation. He personally knew certain members of the council, and he wasn't holding out much hope they'd listen.

How they were going to tell them without revealing Suna's identity would be a definite challenge, but the longer they delayed, the worse their situation got—and the less time they had to search for the imp and the Kruthos' key.

It's far better to face the torture sooner than prolong it, his mother was fond of saying.

"I'll make my presence known at the Council of Regents. Maybe, just maybe, I can get those thickheaded louts to listen without being thrown into the dungeons. The city will reel at the announcement of Greth's nomination anyway. Adding you into the mix will only add tinder to flame. As you said, your identity has to remain secret."

He hoped Lord Mollster had convened his own council and advised the underlords of the danger. That would make their job a whole lot easier, but he'd learned long ago wishing didn't always make it so. How much power did an ex-general hold? And one who'd left his post by his own volition? *Well, we'll soon find out, won't we?*

He knew that interrupting a meeting of the Council of Regents could very well get them both arrested. With Viktor not showing, their choices looked slim to nothing.

In silence, Suna donned her cloak and pulled the hood low over her head. With heads bowed, they exited the inn.

When they reached the front door, Mrs. Kipley's cheery voice called after them. "Enjoy yourselves."

Feran reciprocated with a dour nod. *If she knew what we're about to do, I'd bet a silver dellion she'd be choking on her words.*

* ~ * ~ *

Overnight the city had become a whimsical playground for all sorts of entertainers. Illuminators exploded their unique forms of mage'ical fireworks into the air, much to the delight of the children who oohed and ahhed over the spectacular sights. On every street corner an assortment of unsophisticated mages drew crowds as they performed rudimentary slight-of-hand mage'ic.

A couple of human puppets dressed in black skintight outfits followed like starving dogs on their heels. Their ridiculous antics annoyed Feran to no end. The bells that hung like crowns around the performers' heads tinkled like vexatious butterbees. No matter how many times they crossed the crowded streets to lose them, the two entertainers hounded their every step hoping for some coppers or even a silver dellion. It took several growls and him reaching for his sword before the two realized there'd be no collection of wealth. Both performers scampered away and disappeared into the crowds.

Feran continued to push his way through the throngs of people standing in long lines purchasing roasted cobs of fresh corn or the numerous array of apple dishes. Vendors lined the curbs of every street they ventured down.

As he passed a group of screaming children, a sticky apple fritter landed squarely on his boot, resulting in a child's wail of anguish. Several other children laughed and pointed their fingers at him. Exasperated, he grabbed Suna's hand and tugged her past the mass of people toward the back lanes where traffic was sparser.

Everywhere they went, shouts of merriment and squeals of children's laughter mixed with the boisterous calls of shop owners trying to draw their attention. It was a haven of jocularity, but not one bit of it touched on him.

Some time later, they stood before the stairs that led up to the castle. A row of Elite Guards stood in an impressive single line across the forefront of the entrance. This was standard duty for any Elite when a Council of Regents convened, and mainly for show. No one was allowed inside or out for any reason until the council meeting concluded.

Usually the lowest ranked and youngest of the sentries were given the task. Staring with impassive sternness out at the street below, the men seemed as impervious to the festivities taking place around them as Feran was. Each guard stood at rigid attention. Every buckle and piece of metal on their uniforms gleamed in the noonday sun. The red and white coats with black, starched pants that made up their uniforms showed sharp creases. All scabbards hung at perfect angles from their hips.

Standing at the bottom of the stone steps, he studied the regiment of men he'd once commanded. An ache gripped his heart when he realized that he missed his role as their general. Those feelings vanished when a slight touch on his arm broke through his melancholy.

He looked down at Suna's upturned face and realized that some things were fated to be. If he hadn't left, in all likelihood he would never have met her.

As he studied her face, he saw her eyes were bright and unassuming, but he sensed her ambiguity.

Mesmerized by the gray-blue brilliance in her gaze and the beauty shining off her flawless features,

Feran offered a small smile. "Here's hoping I don't land in the dungeons."

"You won't be alone," she whispered.

The true meaning of her words resonated through him.

Together they started the long climb up the steps. Two massive wooden doors stood behind the brigade of men, the wood carved hundreds of years before by famous artisans. Made for the first king of Dunkerk, the doors represented the standards that flew overhead, symbols of hope, prosperity, freedom and justice, but today the doors stood closed as if in mockery of their attempt to keep such things alive and well.

A low ranking officer stepped forward to bar their approach. "State your business."

Feran almost laughed at the inexperienced expression of adolescent contempt. "I'd like to speak to your general," he said, stiffening his back and staring down the insubordinate who dared to speak in such an insolent manner. These men were unfamiliar to him, and judging by their many hairless faces, they'd probably had been wearing nappies when he'd commanded the regiment.

The young guard narrowed his eyes. "General Heratio is not available—"

"What seems to be the problem here?"

Feran and Suna turned in unison. When the man caught sight of Feran, his mouth dropped open.

Feran placed two fingers to forehead, lips, and heart, and extended a deep bow of respect before he straightened. "I'm relieved to see that they've replaced me with someone of equal valor," he said with a chortle. His memories of General Heratio went back to when he was nothing more than a knobby-kneed lad trying to figure out which end of the arrow went into a quiver. The older man was clearly shocked to see him on the steps of the castle. His old friend and mentor's last words echoed through his mind. *I don't understand why you're leaving, Feran. Soldiers remain soldiers until injury or death claims them and not before.*

Although their parting had been on good terms, he sensed Heratio's misgivings at finding him on the steps of the castle before the convening of a Council of Regents. And he'd have felt no different if their roles had been reversed.

"Feran? When did you…?" Catching himself, he cleared his throat. "What are you doing here?"

"I need to gain entrance into the Council of Regents, Heratio. I mean, General. It's of the utmost importance that I, um, we do so." He dared a glance in Suna's direction.

The man paused to stare at the woman's shadowed face before turning back to him and hissing through his teeth. "Hell's bells, man. You know I can't allow you in there."

Peering past Feran's shoulder, he growled out an order to the Elite Guard still blocking his path. "Step back and resume your post."

Returning to his place by the doors, the young guard stood as unperturbed as ever.

"You can't deny me. It's more than important," Feran urged.

"No. I can't allow it. If I do, you know as well as I that they'd discharge me faster than blowing out the flame of a candle. Moreover, you'll probably land yourself in some dark hellhole, along with your lovely lady friend there. Probably me as well. Things have changed in your absence." With a shake of his head, Heratio made a move toward the doors.

"Then you shall permit *my* entrance, General Heratio."

Suna's voice rang out with authoritative defiance. Pulling apart the bow that held her cloak closed, she flung back her hood and allowed it to drop to the stone steps. Standing in the brilliance of sunlight, every man's head turned her way as she shook her hair free. The guards watched as enthralled as Feran at the halo of dark copper that slipped around her shoulders and down the length of her back.

General Heratio stood dumbfounded at the ghost he saw before him. Like Viktor, shocked recognition blazed across the older man's face.

Feran tried not to smirk. *Now this should be interesting.*

"You shall announce Lady Suna Di'Viao, last of the Diveneans, as proper dictum allows, General." Her tone left no room for argument. Stiffening her back, she straightened her sword so that it fit more comfortably against her left thigh, and in full view. The red cloak she'd worn lay on the steps like a repugnant enemy as she carried herself up the stairs with as much grace as any queen and stopped at the row of Elite Guards that still hadn't moved an inch.

Feran followed two steps behind. When he reached her side, several of the men made for their swords.

Heratio bellowed, "Halt!"

Thankfully the order was directed at his men and not them. Several confused soldiers turned to their commanding officer.

"Stand aside," Feran ordered the guard who'd first questioned them.

Frozen with uncertainty, the poor lad's gaze bounced between his commanding officer and him. General Heratio merely stood there gaping in shock at the woman before them.

Suna's voice moved languidly through Feran's mind. *I had to do this or we'd never get into the castle. Now let those who hinder us pay the price.* The conviction of her promise raised her chin higher in the air.

No one moved.

No one spoke.

The air crackled with tension.

She glanced at Heratio before facing the door again. With a wave of her arm, the line of guards parted like tumbling dice. Men bounced against each other which created an opening for them to walk through. With another flick of her wrist, the doors swung open.

Suna and Feran entered the castle unhindered.

No one stopped them as they strolled down the capacious main hall, but soon their presence began to cause a stir. Several older servants fell to one knee when they recognized her. The younger servants stared about in confusion, wondering who they were and why their presence was having such an effect on others. Moreover, why were these newcomers allowed entrance?

From the upper balcony overlooking the main antechamber, unified gasps of shock and surprise mingled with hushed whispers trailed them.

From his peripherals, Feran saw Suna's features soften into sadness, but she continued forward, her head held high.

Surprisingly, his presence seemed to cause somewhat of a flurry as well. The hall whispered with muted voices of 'the Lady Suna', but here and there he heard 'General Feran returns'. It wouldn't take long for the rest of the city to hear of their arrival. Servants' tongues wagged like wildfire, but it didn't matter anymore.

They had one purpose. To stop an inferno they knew was about to ignite.

* ~ * ~ *

The Regent's Gallery was an exclusive chamber situated at the back of the main castle where vast gardens led to the cliffs below. Fifteen Guardians stood at attention, each one of them recognizing Feran as he approached. If the Elite Guards had looked impressive at the front entrance, these seasoned soldiers made those men look like boys.

The Guardians were an imposing wall of strength, dignity, and dangerous intent, and every one of them a Sword Dancer. Many of them started to salute before stopping halfway, forgetting that Feran no longer commanded them. Their eyes swam with confusion and shock.

Feran glanced over his shoulder and heaved a sigh of relief when he didn't see Heratio through the throngs of people that had followed them. The last thing he wanted was to cause trouble for his friend. They were in it knee deep as it was.

Just before the colossal arched door leading into the gallery, they stopped before the Guardians. Bestowing the men a formal salute, Feran clasped his hands behind his back and stood with his feet slightly apart. "Stand aside, Captain Fletcher," he ordered the Guardian closest to the door.

"General. Feran. Sir?" Fletcher's face bled crimson as he fumbled to find words. The Guardian standing next to Fletcher kept jarring his arm with repeated annoyance. The captain turned and followed his comrade's gaze to Suna's sword. Every man stood slack-jawed, Feran's presence now ignored.

No matter where she goes, she causes a stir, he mused.

Standing her ground, she eyed the Captain of the Guardians with her usual aloof manner. "Stand aside, Captain Fletcher." Although cordially presented, her eyes flashed like burnished steel.

"But—"

"I'll take full responsibility for this. Now stand aside," Feran added, his stern carriage adding further weight behind the request.

Confused, the captain shuffled back from the entrance. The rest of the Guardians stared at one another and did the same. None dared to refuse her request.

Grasping the door handle in one hand, Feran peered briefly at Suna. She gave him a weak but courageous nod. They knew what lay before them.

At the last second, Feran shifted to the side to see Heratio had indeed followed, but was now surrounded by a group of High House members who'd thankfully delayed his approach by demanding answers to their presence.

Suna flung open the door and together they entered the Regent's Gallery.

CHAPTER TWENTY-TWO

Massive beams of polished snakewood lined the walls of the gallery to create a beautiful flying buttress effect across the expansive ceiling. Each beam lent a continuous arch to the room to establish an elegant but spacious meeting area. On the walls between tree-trunk-sized wood partitions hung a different colored pennant that symbolized each council member's High House.

The majestic beauty of the Regent's Gallery was not only contained in its elegant wood and furnishings, but also the floor to ceiling windows that made up the entire back wall. A picturesque view of the castle's gardens filled the area with natural light, making it appear as if the occupants of the gallery were outside rather than in. It was the focal point of the meeting room, and quite a breathtaking sight, particularly with the Kasprian Sea flowing out over the horizon. The garden's foliage was so thick and vibrant that no one noticed the shadow of a man eavesdropping just at the fringe of one of the windowpanes.

Beneath the center expanse of the cathedral ceiling stood a hollowed out round table made from the same polished snakewood as the beams, with a four-foot opening that allowed entrance into its center. Fifteen overstuffed armchairs flanked the outside rim, each covered in expensive silk that matched the hues of the pennants on the walls around them. These denoted each council member's place at the table.

After Suna and Feran entered, they saw that more than half these chairs stood vacant. In the center of the hollowed out table was a one-step dais. There sat Lady Allena. She stood in outrage at the two who'd had the audacity to interrupt such a formal meeting.

Her shrill voice rang out for every member in the room to hear. "What's the meaning of this? You both shall leave now. Guards!"

Suna stepped closer to ensure everyone had a good look at her. Gasps of surprise and whispers of awe from the elder members chased around the gallery.

"You call a Council of the Regents and yet?" Suna swept her arm around the room. "I see no quorum here."

Feran turned to close the door on the stunned faces of the Guardians who stood behind it and saw Heratio still trapped by even more High House members. The man's vexed expression cleaved through Feran's conscience. He closed the door with a heavy heart.

Allena should have been just as surprised, but her tone dripped with frost. "Lady Suna? You cannot come in here and dictate—"

"And you cannot force a change of the laws to Etharia either, Lady Allena," Suna shot back. "You dare to make propositions here today that go against everything Dunkerk stands for. You are Head Regent, yet you bring dishonor to this room. And council."

Without a hint of fear, she stepped through the small opening in the round table and climbed the single step toward the heavy-set woman.

Allena resumed her seat and scowled back. Apparently, seeing a Divenean was an inconsequential matter to the woman. That fact alone was more than a little disconcerting.

"You sit there like some pompous hypocrite and cite that I have no right to be here? I stand before you as a representative of King Markes and his legacy. How many of you can say the same?" Her anger matched Allena's word for word.

Feran feigned a cough to cover up his erupting laughter. Suna sensed he was enjoying this exchange a tad too much.

Allena gasped. "How dare you. You have no authority here. King Markes is dead!" Her very ample, and visible, bosom heaved with indignation.

Suna stepped closer. "You, Lady Allena, dare to defy the memory of our king?"

"Guards! Guards!" Allena screamed, her face puffing out more than her breasts.

Grabbing a chair from the corner of the doorway, Feran propped it up under the doorknob and used his foot as further leverage. Pulling forth his sword, the expanse of the room filled with the sounds of pounding fists on wood and muffled shouts of alarm from the men behind the door.

The Regent scowled at him with a hatred that burned deep in her kohl outlined eyes. "You?" she shrieked like a banshee. "You have no right to be here. This is for council members only. You're nothing but a freelance monger. A milksop who can't commit to his duty. You have no business being here whatsoever, *Feran*."

He smiled with as much sweetness as he could muster. "Be that as it may, Lady Allena, but here we are." His flippancy caused her to turn a deeper shade of red. "And just so you know, I'm here at Lady Suna's request, so don't mind little ol' me." He glared back.

Suna turned her attention to the occupants around the table, pointedly ignoring the Regent's theatrical huffs and puffs of ire. In a loud, clear voice, she spoke with calm candidness. "Do you know why *Allena* has called this council?" she asked, staring at each House member as she walked by them.

She'd just shown the severest sign of disrespect by omitting 'lady' from Allena's title. In the past, such an insult might have caused the stripping of a High House's title, but Allena had struck a nerve by treating Feran as nothing more than swine dung beneath her slipper. She refused to tolerate such disrespect—from anyone—and least of all from the High Regent who professed to be a representative of all the people of Etharia.

The question Suna posed caused several of the lords and ladies around the table to turn and look at their neighbor. Some still reeled in shock by her presence, but there were a few much smarter and slyer who were probably conspiring with Allena.

The boisterous voice of Lord Marshall Benne boomed through the gallery. He stood to speak, as formal edict dictates. "Lady Suna, what in damnation is going on here? You suddenly show yourself after all these years and interrupt a Council of Regents by throwing around insults and innuendos?" He turned an accusing glare on Allena. "I, for one, demand answers."

"And those you shall have. And more, Lord Benne. I assure you." Suna's gaze followed his to the High Regent's chair. "Do you wish to explain or shall I?" Allena opened her mouth, but Suna was quicker. "A nomination is to be put forth today. A nomination for the next king of Dunkerk. Do any of you know who this might be?" She circled the inside circumference of the table, hesitating for a moment on each face she passed.

Snickers sounded and the muttered name of Wendel raced around the room.

Allena rose, her knuckles white on the ornate armrests. "Now see here—"

With a dismissive wave of her arm, she forced Allena back into her chair with a subtle gust of air. Terrified, the older woman shivered in stunned disbelief.

The gallery again filled with gasps of wonder and shock. With that single act of mage'ic, the elusive rumors of her Divenean lineage became truth instead of speculation.

"I ask you all again. Do any of you know the nomination that is to be placed forward today?"

Some heads shook, while others looked away.

"Allena is soon to be married to Wendel Greth, nephew to Lord Tobas Greth," she continued, thankful for that tidbit of information Viktor had shared. "With the union of their marriage and using her position as Head Regent, her nomination is to place Lord Greth upon the throne as family kindred to the crown."

The announcement brought mixed reactions. Some revealed dismayed confusion, while others sat motionless. Obviously, not news to some.

"By marriage to the House of Greth, Allena thought to persuade you to place the Underlord of Carberra on the throne." Suna's anger bubbled just below the surface as she faced Allena. "If memory serves me correctly, the covenant prevents this from occurring, does it not?"

"It's my choice whom I place as nomination for king," Allena retorted with a defiant toss of her head. Her chin jiggled like jelly.

Lady Lessa Vandemont stood and squared her thin shoulders. "Personal choice is one thing, Lady Allena, but you cannot go against the covenant. Such a law can't be changed by a mere nomination. You know that no female or underlord can ascend the throne. Nor can a Regent dictate such a change without majority of council *and* people."

Usually a shy and unassuming, Suna dipped her head in gratitude at the lady Lessa.

Allena gripped the arms of her chair with claw-like lacquered nails in an effort to stand. Pursing her lips, Suna arched an eyebrow and dared the woman to move.

The Regent shuddered and remained seated, albeit with a childish pout. "The covenant is null and void," she argued, her voice thick with rage. "It was an agreement signed for King Markes and King Markes alone. No other who has ruled Dunkerk ever forced the five underlords to sign such a document. King Markes is gone, so why would a piece of aged parchment preclude a reasonable choice for the throne? These lands have been kingless far too long."

Allena was striving to gain power over a situation spiraling rapidly out of her control.

"Do you remember the purpose of the signing of this covenant?" Suna asked the assembled members.

"To prevent a monopoly of power. I know the laws, *Suna*," Allena snipped, repaying insult with insult.

Unperturbed, Suna carefully chose her next line of questions, but the incessant pounding at the door had become a distraction. "Feran, do you mind opening the gallery? I don't think we're to be arrested." She stopped and spread her arms wide before the gathered assembly. "Unless all of you feel it's just. However, I shall leave that decision in your capable hands. If that happens, you shall not hear of my news and you'll be left to your own fates."

Feran didn't move.

"Please open the door," she repeated.

With a resigned sigh, Feran removed the chair and stepped away as the door burst open. General Heratio stormed inside followed by every Guardian under his command. He stopped short and bowed before the Council of Regents, but his line of vision centralized on Suna. He appeared to have recovered from his shock. Now he looked uncertain and ill.

"Arrest them. Arrest them both," Allena screamed as she leapt to her feet.

Heratio didn't move. Nor did the Guardians, who stood behind their commanding officer; a tense wall of strength, they waited for his orders and his orders alone. The prospect of arresting their former general was daunting enough, but they looked far more curious about the woman who carried a Sword Dancer's blade like themselves.

Suna was sure rumors had filtered through their ranks. Now that they'd had an opportunity to see her for themselves none appeared disappointed.

Several council members stood looking as disconcerted as General Heratio.

"Do you dare defy my orders, General?" Allena's eyes smoldered with fury.

Suna gave a blasé shrug of her shoulders and strolled toward the dais where Allena stood perched like a vulture. "You do as you see fit, General Heratio." On the bottom step, she shifted and looked straight at the General, pointedly ignoring the High Regent. "But before doing so, I would suggest a vote from council. I place this decision in your capable hands. You will decide our fate. Not Allena."

The Regent looked ready to lunge at her with her bare hands. Breasts that overflowed the snugness of her bodice heaved as she tried to rein in her anger.

Council heads swiveled, each staring wide-eyed at the other. This, by far, was most unconventional. All but one looked unruffled.

Lord Benne stood. "Nay. I want to hear what Lady Suna has to say."

Lady Lessa followed. "I concur with Lord Benne."

Several other members stood and gave affirmations by nodding. Only a few remained seated, peering with ambivalent unease in Allena's direction.

Feran sheathed his sword and waited.

Heratio peered briefly at him before turning to leave. As he passed through the door, Suna heard Feran mutter, 'dismissed' to the other Guardians. Some stared with ambiguity at their former general when walking by, but Feran kept his head down, refusing to look at any of them.

When the door closed behind the departing soldiers, Suna took a moment to offer a condescending jeer at the Regent. If Allena could turn any redder, she would have matched the hue of Lady Lessa's cardinal banner.

Suna's voice dripped with forced honey as she moved off the dais and addressed the assembled audience. "Shall we begin?"

"This is an outrage!" Allena cried. "You cannot conduct this Council. You have no authority here."

Lord Stinley Moren rose from his seat and gave an impassive flick of his fingers. He raised his head and stared down his nose at Suna. "I find that I must concur with Lady Allena."

Dressed in his usual flamboyant manner, Lord Moren appeared unconcerned over the generated excitement. Gold mounted jewels sparkled from his many layers of colorful silk and expensive black wool. His penetrating blue eyes held loathing as he attempted to stare Suna down—just like another of his kin tried to do so many years before. She couldn't help but notice the uncanny resemblance between father and son.

Feran growled at the pompous man who'd just spoken. Apparently she wasn't alone in her dislike of the man.

"Those of you who do not wish to hear my words may take your leave. But know this. It is for the sake of this realm and all who live within it that I'm here. As council members you are held to these same obligations. What you do with this information after I leave will be left in your hands. And leave I shall."

Suna tilted her head toward the exit before returning Lord Moren's icy stare. Her memory of the

House of Moren wasn't fond. His father had been one of those in attendance with King Markes on that fateful hunting expedition. She'd always held the belief that those who were there that day had been somewhat responsible for his death, but no evidence was ever found to prove otherwise. She'd left Dunkerk shortly thereafter. She'd never liked the Morens, and after all these years her feelings hadn't changed.

When Moren bit the corner of his lower lip and cocked his head, she knew it was to disguise a sneer. His father had had the same habit, but he resumed his seat without a word. Steepling his fingers, he reluctantly dipped his head, his cold and calculating eyes watching her every move.

Allena's annoying, whiny voice cut through the silence like a knife. "Will none of you stand for me?"

A squat, balding lord stood and tugged nervously at the expensive lace hanging from the sleeves of his frocked coat. "Perhaps it'd be wise if we give Lady Suna an opportunity to tell us why she's returned. We'll find out nothing by continuing this irresponsible quibbling." Strangely, Lord Nevil Hawkin's squeaky voice had a calming effect as the tension in the gallery seemed to lessen.

From the corner of her eye, she saw Allena rise from her chair and begin to proceed down the dais. "You seek to exit this council, Allena?" she asked with feigned innocence.

The woman stopped and pivoted, her hands clenched into tight fists at her sides. "I seek to end this show of disrespect for my sovereignty. Thus, this Council of Regents is adjourned."

Pale and ill at ease, Lady Lessa's fearful gaze darted between the two warring women. Some lords and ladies bent their heads and whispered behind their hands, but the next words spoken silenced the room.

"A meeting of this magnitude is not adjourned because you say it is so. Council members are free to leave, but you are not. Many respected citizens of Dunkerk sit here before you. Your responsibility is to them, or have you forgotten your High Regent's duty that you so aptly recite to me? I suggest you take your seat." There was no denying the threat in her tone. She would keep that woman here, even if she had to lash her to the chair herself.

Taken aback, the woman hesitated, her face paling beneath the angry scowl etched deep on her face.

Suna raised her hand slightly. "I have asked you politely. I won't do so a second time."

With a fearful gasp, Allena resumed her seat. For several seconds she glared back. Then she spat out with more venom than necessary. "If you demand the power of this council, so be it, but in keeping with dictum, *he* shall be removed." She pointed a pudgy finger in Feran's direction. "He has no authority here and attends as a mere commoner."

Feran glanced in Suna's direction. Anger sparked in his eyes, but he looked more than compliant to bend to the request.

Allena's demands were exhausting. Suna lowered her head and grasped her hands in front. "The honor of retired General Feran Lambert is not to be excluded from this meeting. His role in all of this?" She paused for effect. "Is similar to Aires Bricken."

All eyes turned to him. Feran fumbled with the chair he'd used against the door and sat. As unflustered as possible, he stretched out his long legs and concentrated on something outside the window.

Lord Benne stood. "You've come here under obvious urgency, Lady Suna," he said, his voice heavy with undercurrents of worry. "I would ask, nay, *we* would ask that you please continue."

Straightening her stance, Suna drew a deep breath and began. "I am a Divenean, as you have all now surmised. My duty is to protect this realm and all living things within it, which included King Markes and Queen Saliste, with mage'ic or my life."

Lord Moren offered an icy smirk. "It would seem that you failed miserably to fulfill that task, Lady Suna." Allena's snicker ricocheted in the background.

Suna stared him down, refusing to tolerate another outburst. Breaking away from her cold stare first, the gangly lord shrugged at Allena and promptly snapped his mouth closed.

"It would seem there's much presumption in this room," Suna replied. Her gaze encompassed the entire assembly before settling back on Moren. "If I recall correctly, your father, Norres Moren, did nothing to succor the situation either. King Markes ordered me to stay behind with his queen or circumstances would not have transpired as they had, I can assure you. I, unlike some others in this room, revered my king. How many of you can say the same with a clear conscience?"

Flabbergasted silence followed. With her point made, she began again. "I bring ill tidings to this Council of Regents. Isafel has been freed."

A mixture of outrage and denials mixed with cries of horror erupted.

"Preposterous. What proof do you bring that this is true?" Allena demanded, her face now ashen.

In slow motion, Suna stepped closer to the Head Regent. "You dare question a Divenean?"

Allena pushed back into the cushions of her armchair. Like Moren, she snapped her mouth closed and averted her gaze.

Suna turned back to the council. Even though she had initially thought it unwise to mention Isafel's name, she had to make the council listen. If frightening them achieved it, so be it. More importantly, she had to make them believe the danger facing them all.

"Isafel is free," she repeated. "He paid us a visit last night here in your city. He's been following us. Watching. Waiting. While another searches for the key. Do you know what key I speak of?"

Frightened gasps raced about the room coupled with a host of confusing expressions from those too young to understand the significance of her question.

She continued. "Balthazar is still secured within the prison created by the Diveneans eons ago by the Kruthos, but the lock has been found. The key to set him free has been lost for far longer than I have walked these lands. However, Isafel doesn't search for it. For the time being, he's busy with another task. Balthazar has created an underling he's birthed from the bowels of his prison world to serve his one purpose. To hunt and find the key and bring it back to him. He attempted to shape this being into something human, but that he is not. We have been tracking this imp since Odarian. He's led us here. That vile creature is within this kingdom's walls as I speak, searching for the object that will unleash unspeakable horror across these lands. Somewhere in Dunkerk the Kruthos key is hidden."

No one spoke.

"There's a small thing to be thankful for," Suna added.

"Thankful? What in the seven shades of Hell can we be thankful for?" Lord Benne rumbled without rising to his feet.

"Isafel has not yet taken human form."

"Oh!" Lady Lessa's tiny hands gripped the edge of the table.

"It's something to be grateful for. We had an inclination as who his target was to be—"

"You k-know who it was?"

Tears welled in Allena's eyes, but Suna felt no compassion for the shrew. Of course, her position as Regent would have made her the logical choice, and everyone in the room knew it.

"That's none of your business," Feran cut in.

From the distance separating them, Suna saw him turn two shades darker. He mumbled a quick, "never mind," and returned his attention to the back window.

Lady Allena wiped a tear that had strayed down her cheek, smearing the black kohl around her eyes.

Suna continued. "I'm sure news has reached your ears about the destruction of Carberra Ferry. It occurred because of this minion. His name is Ilio. He's small, deformed, and smells like death crisping over hot coals. Make no mistake. He may not be as strong as Isafel, but he's still a spawn of Balthazar's and is gifted with dark mage'ic."

She stopped and studied the faces around her before delivering the worse part. "I believe Balthazar has been busy since his banishment. He's forming an army of his own. And Ilio? He's but one of those creatures. I'm not familiar with the mage'ic used to devise his prison, as it was created by the Diveneans of old. Unfortunately, those secrets are lost to me. How Balthazar has been able to do this is also unknown, but he's managed to create one that escaped the Divenean wards of his oubliette. How many more can do so? If this imp finds the key and sets him free, our lands, our lives, our very world will be no more. Nothing we have ever seen, even in our darkest nightmares, will compare to what he's been preparing."

Lord Benne paled. "I thought those prisons holding both Isafel and Balthazar were indestructible. Are they not still enforced by the mage'ic of the Diveneans?"

She paused a long moment before answering. "The Divenean race is gone. I'm the last of my kind. It's for this reason I believe that the mage'ic in the walls that had held Isafel had deteriorated over time, allowing him to escape. A thousand years is a long time, but Balthazar's prison is enforced with stronger, more ancient mage'ic—and the Kruthos. Thus, his need for the key."

Intuition made her turn and see Feran rise from his chair. Something in his expression troubled her. *What is it?*

I don't know. I thought I saw something at the window. It could be the sunlight and a breeze playing tricks. Through their silent connection, she sensed his Guardian instincts flare to life.

Then all hell broke loose inside the Regent's Gallery.

CHAPTER TWENTY-THREE

In the quiet of his bedchamber, Mollster read and re-read Conac's words until he memorized them. A hastily written message in cryptic script, the Lord of Laspeth confirmed Lady Allena's intent regarding Greth's nomination as the next king of Dunkerk.

The three underlords now had substantive proof of those two rogues' true motives and the real reason why they'd refused to amass their armies at Mollster's request. Instead of fighting for Etharia's future, Greth sought to place his own selfishness above all those he'd sworn to protect. It went against everything the five of them had vowed to uphold. At least three of them still held to those original tenets.

Still, Mollster had to hope that in some way the covenant still meant something and that the other council members would see it as well. However, he nurtured a nagging doubt that tugged at the corners of his mind like a spoiled child. He also knew Lady Allena could be quite persuasive when she had to be, but it would be a snowy day in the devil's lair before he acknowledged Tobas Greth as the next King of Dunkerk.

And, thankfully, he wasn't the only one.

Mollster's thoughts meandered to Lady Suna and Feran. When word had reached him about the destruction at Carberra Ferry, his blood had run cold, but there had been no reports of a woman or ex-general among the dead. Because of that, he clung to his hope. The message he'd received from Feran's falcon mentioned nothing except that he and Suna were on their way to Dunkerk via Carberra and nothing else. *They should have arrived there by now, but still no word from them.*

Mollster rose from his armchair and made his way to the window overlooking the bailey below. His troubled thoughts plagued him as he stared at nothing in the distance, his thoughts driven on the Divenean and Feran and their precarious journey. He sensed those two had bigger roles to play yet, though he knew not why. Knowing their gifts and courage did little to ease his restlessness.

The sound of pounding hooves on the flagstones below brought him out of his miserable trance. He rubbed his bleary eyes and squinted at the rider in the courtyard. Karvelle's insignia on the left arm of the uniform caught the sunlight. "One of Fenwick's Infers. I'd wager my crown it's not good news," he mumbled. His shoulders slumped as he turned from the window and made his way downstairs. Good or bad, he had a duty to know and to do whatever was necessary.

As he passed one of his house mards, he stopped the man. "Samuel, I need to call a meeting of every member of my house. Please circulate the message. I'll receive everyone in the Grand Hall in an hour's time."

The servant dipped his head. "As you wish, my lord." He went to scurry away, but Mollster stopped him again.

"And send me my scribe in an hour's time. I have scrolls that must be sent," he added wearily.

"Certainly, Lord Mollster." Samuel dashed down the corridor.

After dismissing the cleaning staff from the Grand Hall, he waited to receive the Infer, his palms sweaty, his stomach tumbling.

Karvelle's soldier ambled in, his head held high, and approached the throne. Placing his fingers to forehead, lips, and heart, he bent to one knee and held out a sealed scroll. "For Lord Mollster's eyes only," the soldier announced solemnly.

He took the rolled parchment and tried his best to keep his hands from shaking.

"With all due respect, my lord, I must take my leave. Lord Fenwick requested my immediate return to Karvelle. I cannot delay. He advised that you would understand once you've read the message."

He observed the Infer's dusty cloak, mud splattered boots and black circles that lay beneath his eyes. This man had traveled nonstop to ensure delivery of the message. Whatever news Fenwick needed to convey was urgent—and most assuredly bad.

"You are welcome to rest. I can arrange for some food or whatever necessities you might need before taking your leave. You look exhausted, man."

The Infer shook his head impatiently. "Thank you, but no, my lord."

"What's your name?"

"My name?" Confusion swam in the soldier's weary eyes, but he straightened his carriage. "Captain Dungas, my lord."

"For your due diligence, I thank you, Captain Dungas. I will be sure to mention the expedience of this message to your liege." With a kind, but sad smile, Mollster placed the scroll onto his lap.

Momentary surprise flashed over Dungas' face. "Thank you, my lord." Puffing out his chest, he flourished a final bow and formal salute before exiting the Grand Hall.

For a long time, Mollster stared at the unopened scroll. He then grasped the parchment, and with a fingernail, broke open Fenwick's royal blue seal. Unrolling the parchment, his fingers tensed as he read Fenwick's words:

The snows are coming, and yes, it will be extremely cold in the north, but we will prevail. Listen carefully to the east. Storms are brewing, so tread carefully. The waters of Carberra are running too swiftly. In two days' time they will swell to Valhallen's Gates and beyond.

To ordinary eyes, Fenwick's words were as mysterious as Conac's, but he knew their meaning. Shaking his head, his jaded sigh was the only sound in the empty chamber.

Mollster left the Grand Hall and proceeded outside where sapphire skies and the warmth of sunshine did little to ease the heaviness in his heart. In his lifetime, he'd been fortunate never to see strife of this kind.

When he was but a lad, he'd served time at Vansgaard, training as most young men of High Houses are destined to do. Skirmishes with Barbs were nothing compared to real battle, or so his father had often lectured.

A suffocating sense of turmoil hung in the air around his castle. Whether he wanted to admit it or not, war was on their doorsteps—and Greth and Ethbridge were fanning its flames.

He crossed the bailey and followed the path that led to the back of the castle, surveying the activities of the men and women of his staff. As he passed a small building supported by three walls and a gray slate roof, he paused to observe the numerous blacksmiths who had been working nonstop since the Divenean's visit. His secret preparations for war had kept the forges running at full capacity. Sweltering blasts of dry air hit Mollster like a slap in the face. He cringed at the heat. Sweat instantly beaded on his brow. *How can men work under such conditions?* he wondered as he scrutinized the strength and perseverance needed to perfect such skills.

Since Lady Suna and Feran had left his city, the smiths had worked day and night preparing for a war he now knew loomed closer than he thought. The consistent pounding of metal upon metal rang out through the castle's courtyard, grating on his already thinly stretched nerves.

He turned away from the blacksmiths' shack and realized he still grasped Fenwick's scroll in his fist. Stuffing the parchment into his frock pocket, Mollster continued down the path until it forked sharply to the right, leading him straight to the Elite Guards' practice yards.

There were over a hundred men working with various lances of silver, spiked maces and an array of swords and rapiers. Men jousted without horses, learning the finer techniques of balance and tension needed to perfect a rider's stance. Some sparred in pairs or in groups of ten to fifteen. The yard was like a child's playroom scattered with weapons instead of toys. His guards had been diligent in training for war, as his blacksmiths, and the determination and fervor he saw on their faces both pleased and saddened him. With a glance across the yard, Mollster squinted against the bright sunshine, his weathered eyes seeking out the only man standing stone still.

General Darrow scrutinized the groups of soldiers with seasoned veteran eyes. Sometimes he moved in between the men to give quick instruction before stepping back to watch their improvements.

Today was no different from any other day—Darrow looked to be in need of a shave and bath. Small ears peeked out from beneath a shaggy mop of black hair speckled with silvery grey that sparked in the sunlight. He'd have been handsome once, but for the nose that had been broken far too many times. It lay flat against his face, making his cheekbones more prominent and his eyes further apart. His leather jerkin, soaked with sweat from the heat of the midday sun, clung like a second skin across his wide chest. Standing almost seven feet, Darrow was a giant of a man. Some whispered that Barb's blood ran through his veins, but those who had the nerve to say it close to his ear were usually left unconscious by either a left or right of his bear-sized fists.

Darrow studied the men training with eyes so dark they were almost black. As if sensing someone's gaze upon him, he looked up. With long, even strides, he crossed the practice yard and stood beside Mollster. He offered his friend a weak smile. Saying nothing, Darrow crossed arms that could shame a blacksmith and waited for Mollster to speak.

The underlord shielded his eyes from the relentless glare of the sun. "Beautiful day, isn't it?"

"I'm quite sure you didn't come all the way out here to talk about the weather, Mollster." Darrow ran a calloused hand over the silvery speckled stubble on his chin. They'd been friends for many years and formality had become unnecessary between them.

He blew out a laden sigh. "No, Darrow, I didn't."

"Any word on what really happened at Carberra Ferry?"

"Nothing. Just that there was an unfortunate fire. Carberra has been tightlipped about the entire incident, most likely to quell the fears of travelers heading to Dunkerk's festival."

Tedious silence filled the space between them.

Finally, Darrow asked the question he'd been dreading. "So when do we leave?"

"As soon as possible. Lady Allena is placing Greth's name before the council in two days' time. I want to be on the road by first light. How many men do we have?"

Darrow frowned. "Almost two thousand strong. And what do you mean *I*?"

"I'm riding as well." He sensed the giant stiffen.

"You know better than any that you must remain here. Doctrine states that you can't leave your kingdom, even in war. It will be taken as abandoning your realm. And...?" He trailed off as the corners of his eyes tightened.

"And?" Mollster pressed.

Darrow turned and fixed him with a daunting stare. "You're not a young man anymore. Odarian needs its underlord. It goes against law and covenant. You can't go to war." His hard features softened. "That's what generals are for."

"So Greth's actions are law abiding? He goes against the covenant that he signed and swore an oath upon? That we all did? He seeks to deceive our people and sway the balance of power to him. The lands will need another underlord to repute this. What makes my decision any more unlawful?" He shook with fury.

Shaking his head in resignation, Darrow turned his attention back to his men, refusing to take his bait. "I understand that, Mollster. It seems everything has been turned ass-over-belly these days. Nonetheless, I can at least try to reason some sense into that thick skull of yours."

Mollster studied the sparring techniques of several foot soldiers. "Not on this you won't. I'll take the risk of losing my kingdom if it means the people of these lands learn the truth. I'm dispatching Infers to Lords Fenwick and Conac. Fenwick's army is already marshaled and waiting. They'll meet us at Valhallen's Gates in three days. Then we ride to Dunkerk." The words sounded blasphemous when spoken aloud.

"Dunkerk's walls have withstood every enemy that's gone against it," Darrow murmured. "If Greth is crowned, we fight the King of Dunkerk. Has this possibility crossed your mind?"

"Of course it has," he snapped. He shook his head to chase away the ever lingering doubts. "Fenwick and I know what we're getting ourselves into. I can't abandon Dunkerk to that, that wretch of a man. On top of this we leave Conac alone to battle whatever Ethbridge has up those slimy sleeves of his. Nothing about this bodes well with me, Darrow. Nothing."

To his surprise, and relief, his general nodded. "So be it. At first light our men will be assembled and ready to ride. Four of your Elites will surround you at all times—"

"Let's not—"

Darrow shifted and stared him down. "You may be Underlord of Odarian, but come Hell and flood waters, *my* duty is to ensure *my* lord remains safe. Your Elites will be by your side at all times, even during privy breaks. This may be your kingdom, Mollster, but this is my war, my men. And my rules," he added dryly.

Mollster snorted with indignant annoyance. "Now see here—"

"Above all else, my duty as your general is to protect you. And protect you I will. Even if I have to tie you up and stuff you into a crate. If you insist on riding into war you'll do so under my course of action. Never underestimate me. Wasn't that the reason you saw fit to appoint me as your general?"

"You wouldn't dare?"

"Try me. I'll protect you by any means I see fit."

Mollster opened his mouth to retort, but closed it just as quick. Arguing with Darrow was pointless. *Here is yet another man who refuses to shirk duty.* "At first light then." He turned and left, mumbling, "Damn, man. He'll have me in nappies before we reach Dunkerk's walls."

Darrow's shouting of orders faded as he walked back to his castle. Once inside, the underlord dispatched an Infer to Conac. When he discovered Dungas on the verge of leaving. Mollster managed to pen a hasty message for the soldier to take back to Fenwick.

Then he broke the news to members of his House that Odarian's troops were riding to war. Amidst cries of dismay and panic, he explained that *someone* was attempting to usurp the sovereignty of Dunkerk, although he mentioned no names, even when they demanded to know who would do such a horrendous thing. He said nothing of Isafel or Ilio. His subjects were frightened enough, especially with the news of war. As their underlord, he had an obligation to protect them from as much worry and fear as possible.

When he was alone in his room, he called in Malenda. "Please take down my armor." When her eyes widened and filled with tears, he turned and left her alone. His heart was too full of angst to deal with any more.

CHAPTER TWENTY-FOUR

At first light, Odarian's army stood assembled outside in the courtyard. Almost two and a half thousand mounted men, restless steeds and attendants waited. As he walked down the steps of his castle, Mollster's silver armor reflected the vermilion hues of an early morning sunrise. Upon his head he wore the crown of Odarian—a single strand of twisted gilded silver embedded with one flawless agate emerald. Four towering Elite guards surrounded him as soon as he mounted his midnight-black destrier.

Pursing his lips, he threw Darrow a disparaging glare, who acknowledged his disapproval with a respectful dip of his head and an infuriating grin.

As the procession moved through the streets, Odarians lined its walkways and windows, waving and tossing garlands of blakenberie at the feet of the men. Some of the passing soldiers caught the flowered garlands upon their swords. Tradition held that it would bring the catcher good luck and a safe return.

It took most of the morning before the last of the army passed out of Odarian's gates. Darrow sent a quarter of his force toward Jorja Ferry. Those men he ordered to supervise the supply carts carrying the blacksmiths, fletchers, farriers, healers, and the siege machinery. Darrow had explained the evening before that it was never wise to proceed to war with your entire regiment. Surprise was the key to a successful battle. Supply carts would only hinder the speed of the rest of the fighting men. And it would give them ample time to prepare outside of Dunkerk's walls.

Let Greth think Odarian comes unprepared, Mollster mused.

The rest of their regiment thundered toward Carberra Ferry, where the building of new ferries was taking place. Would they be ready in time was another burden he had to contend with.

What weighed even heavier on Mollster's mind was knowing every man under him raced to face a war they had little hope of winning.

* ~ * ~ *

Ethbridge paced the gleaming floors of his bedchamber with harried, nervous steps. He'd bitten his nails down to little more than bleeding nubs. The massive hearth by his door blazed with a roaring fire, but it did little to warm his bones, especially on nights like this when the mountain winds blew so strong that the piercing cold turned the very breath in your lungs to ice. The close proximity of the Zamin Mountains always kept the stone of his keep miserably damp and cold.

Gads, how he despised this place.

It'd been several days now, and he'd heard nothing from Greth. His anxiety grew like the early winter ice forming around his keep. The guards under his rule were getting antsy, not to mention bored. He'd given them no logical reason as to why their patrols of the mountain borders had ceased. Without daily tours men got lazy, and to ease their boredom they turned to drink, gambling and fighting. Ethbridge was sitting on the cusp of a boiling cauldron of goose fat, and he knew it. A timid knock sounded outside his door.

"What is it?" he barked, his mood as dark and foul as the night outside.

"My lord, an Infer has arrived from Lord Greth. He's dismounting as we speak," Denneck, his personal mard, called out.

Moving with lightning speed toward the door, Ethbridge opened it and shoved the servant aside to see behind him, but the cowering man stood alone.

"Show him to the dining hall," he snapped. He then returned to his room and poured himself a healthy shot of abazine. He gulped it down and raced to the dining hall. He'd embarked on a dangerous journey with Greth, but he was prepared to do anything to get out of this miserable stink-hole of ice.

Various housemaidens and scullery maids were in the process of preparing the hall for breakfast when Ethbridge stormed through the doors. Several women jumped and shrieked in fear.

"Leave. Now!"

Every woman gathered her skirt and ran for the nearest exit. They knew better than to dawdle when their liege was in this dangerous mood. Glancing over their shoulders, they ensured every door closed behind them.

Ethbridge paced as he waited. At last, Denneck showed up with Greth's Infer in tow.

"Give it to me," he demanded and held out his hand.

Denneck was already running down the corridor in the opposite direction before any more was said.

Carberra's Infer's eyes thinned into slits. Stiffly walking forward, he handed Ethbridge a rolled scroll that blatantly revealed Greth's unbroken gold seal.

"Take your leave," Ethbridge mumbled absently. He dismissed the Infer like a mere servant, his attention altogether focused on what lay in his hands.

The Infer turned and left, giving no regard to a proper salute, which, thankfully, Ethbridge failed to notice. With trembling fingers, he broke the seal and read the single line written upon it.

It's time to move the mountains.

He grinned. The news was better than he'd anticipated. *Let Conac think I'm a fool.* He barely refrained from dancing around the room like a jester. All three daft underlords would soon come to know the true strength of Nyles Ethbridge.

He left the dining hall to announce to his men that they would be riding to war, but not just any war. They were going to seize Odarian whose dimwitted underlord had just abandoned his people.

* ~ * ~ *

After Fenwick returned from the council meeting in Odarian, he'd spent every waking moment searching his library for information about the prisons that had held Isafel and the one currently holding Balthazar. There was little documentation, as most records had been either lost or secretly hidden by the Diveneans who'd initially recorded it. He did find a passage that puzzled him, however.

Upon the seal of banishment shall remain the intrinsic power of the Diveneans. Should this falter, only one thusly gifted can reinforce its ancient mage'ic. Free will shall cause its ultimate demise.

Fenwick had studied the passage until he had it memorized, but try as he might, its true meaning eluded him. He knew little about the Diveneans' powers, and far less about mage'ic, preferring his studies to battles that had been won and lost. Further searching of his library proved futile.

When his network spy from Dunkerk had shown up at his castle with the news of Lady Allena's intentions, Fenwick's decision had been made for him. He'd sent out Infers to advise both Mollster and Conac. He didn't relish the thought of going to war, but as Mollster had so aptly pointed out, only a united front could give them an advantage to winning this battle. And even if the nomination failed, Greth would do something underhanded to change it. He knew firsthand how devious that brute of a man could be.

Lost in time in his library amidst towering piles of yellowing parchments, dusty scrolls and thick leather-bound books, he failed to notice when one of his mard's came running into the room.

"My lord, my lord," the man cried, gasping for breath.

Fenwick looked up from his reading and jumped to his feet. "What is it, Seamus?" he asked past the pounding of his heart.

"M-My lord," he panted, "Infer Johan has… He's just returned. He has news."

Johan rounded the corner and entered the library unannounced. Fenwick sank into his chair easily reading the grimness on his soldier's scarred face. *So it begins*. He lowered his head. "How many men?" he asked, surprised his voice sounded so calm.

Johan looked dead on his feet. "They've split into two segments. At least two thousand ride to Dunkerk. The others are scattered at the ferries."

"And Carberra?"

"We have our workers there, along with several of Lord Greth's men helping to rebuild it."

"Dungas will be returning from Odarian shortly. Take your rest, Johan, for you'll have little of it in the days to come."

With a curt nod Johan departed with Seamus, leaving Fenwick alone with his troubled thoughts.

We ride to war against a kingdom whose sole purpose was to unify these lands. What will be our fate? Worry gripped his heart and refused to relent.

* ~ * ~ *

The imposing figure of Lord Tobas Greth at the head of two long columns of men made for a spectacular sight. The gold of his armor shone in the afternoon sun, announcing to the lands that a new king was about to arrive, or so that was the impression he tried to convey.

Carberra's embroidered standard fluttered in the breeze above his head. Sitting tall and proud on his sable destrier, Greth was confident in the knowledge that in a few days' time a crown would rest upon his brow. He brought no siege machines, just many heavily armored men. The sounds of their clinking mail and numerous hooves pounding across the land filled the air like a thunderstorm, although it didn't mask the conversation he'd eavesdropped on between two of his Elites.

"Seven shades of Hell," spat one soldier as he'd wiped the dust from his eyes and leaned closer to his comrade riding beside him. "Here's hoping there's a rebellion."

The older soldier eyed the other man's leering sneer in cold contempt before replying. "Lord Greth brings us as a show of honor. To ensure proper leadership is undertaken. The people of Dunkerk must know that what we do, we do for the rightful choice of a king."

The first soldier's face creased into a toothy grin. "And let's not forget the title of 'Guardian' that some of us might gain. To serve Lord Greth as such? Blood and guts. I could die tomorrow," he boasted.

The other soldier had sniffed indignantly. With a quick snap of his reins, he moved closer to the head of the column, and the man he honored more than his life.

Greth grinned as he heard the words spoken between the two of them. *Such ambition makes many of these men dangerous indeed*, he mused. Once Dunkerk accepted his nomination, his army would replace the former Elite Guards and Guardians in Dunkerk's employ. His imbecile nephew had all but guaranteed it. Still, a streak of uneasiness slithered inside. He'd left a man's job in the hands of a boy.

When the Lord of Carberra first saw the billows of black smoke curling upward above the main castle like a sacrilegious stain on his future, he and his army had just crested a small knoll about a league outside Dunkerk's impressive walls. He reined in his horse so hard, his mount reared. Greth brought the animal under control and stared in mortified disbelief at the destruction of his destiny.

A fireball suddenly lit up the sky over a section of the castle. Then something big and flat spun up and out of control before splintering into pieces that rained down to the ground.

Without hesitation, he drew forth his sword and pointed it in the direction of the city.

Angered and dismayed at what he was seeing, the underlord spurred his warhorse forward, his voice roaring for those close enough to hear. "Dunkerk is under attack. We ride to battle. We ride to my future kingdom's defense.

CHAPTER TWENTY-FIVE

Suna faltered as Feran moved cautiously toward the back of the gallery. It was then she sensed not one, but two individuals outside. In the next breath, the picturesque window imploded with a deafening *boom*. In horror, she watched Feran fly through the air and land hard to skid several feet across the floor. Massive shard-like spears of glass shot into the interior of the room. Suna fell to her knees with just enough time to place a protective shield over herself.

Everything happened so fast, she had no time to pinpoint and ensure the safety of the other council members.

Then the chamber fell unnervingly quiet. Without thought of anyone else, Suna jumped to her feet and ran to Feran. Fear lodged in her throat. But before she reached him, she saw him attempting to get to his feet. His hair shimmered with pieces of glass, but he was uncut and unhurt, as far as she could tell. Relief filled her to the core.

Suna faced the back wall where just a moment ago there'd been beautiful landscaped gardens. Now chunks of rubble and stone collapsed from its gaping hole. Billows of dirt and dust settled around the mass destruction.

Ilio walked through the cloud of debris levitating the mangled body of Wendel high above his head. How unfortunate that Greth's nephew happened to be eavesdropping where he shouldn't have been. The imp threw the man like a skimming stone across the floor of the gallery. The crumpled body landed at the entrance of the council table. Even from the distance between them, she saw Ilio's face contorted with maniacal glee. His bulbous head angled grossly to the left which reminded her of the kick she'd administered to him when they'd first met.

Ellena's sorrowing scream ricocheted throughout the gallery.

Suna sent her thoughts to Feran with such force, he fell to the floor. *Stay down and take cover. This isn't your fight. The pull of mage'ic is guiding him, drawing him closer to the key.*

She did her best to assess the injuries of the council members. Four lords had perished instantly. Much to her chagrin, Lord Moren was attempting to pull himself up to the table. His hands bled, and a large piece of skin flapped off his left cheek. The severity of the wound would be a permanent scar on a face he loved to stare at in a mirror.

Lord Benne's right arm had been severed at the elbow. Although in shock, he managed to remove his coat and use it as a tourniquet to bind his arm against his torso. He helped Lady Lessa up, who had somehow ended up beneath the table. Both moved in a stupor.

Suna discharged a telekinetic warning to the remaining council members. *Those of you who can hear me, move! Get out of here.*

Several of them stumbled and fell from the impact of her warning inside their heads, but either by dragging or running, those who still had the ability to move hurried as fast as they could towards the exit. Including Lady Ellena.

Ilio's malicious laughter echoed through the gallery as he watched the few trying to escape. Large pieces of glass rose off the floor. Ellena was the last to try to make it to the door. A sword-sized shard flew through the air and embedded deep into the base of her throat from behind. Her glazed eyes stared at nothing as blood bubbled from between her lips and dripped down the front of her bodice to pool into her cleavage. The impact of the jagged piece of glass had been so severe that it had almost decapitated her.

She fell to the floor with a sickening thud.

Ilio raised his arm to stop the rest from escaping, but Suna was faster. The imp had grown more insane since she'd last seen him. The evil running through his blood was taking control. All this destruction could have been avoided, but he was intent on torturing and killing.

Conjuring a dense wall of air, she threw her spell. The imp soared through the air and out of sight into the gardens.

She opened the gallery door with a gust of air and pushed those who remained alive to safety before slamming it closed and locking it behind them. Even the Guardians couldn't help them now. Too many lives had been lost already, and she was determined to lose no more.

Only three High House members remained. Lords Hawkin Reese, Telfer and Harding. They lay unconscious, scattered at different sections across the floor, their lives flowing out in bright puddles of pooling blood. She gathered each man, including Allena and Wendel, into the grasp of her mage'ic and floated them to the far end of the room. If they were lucky enough to survive this fight there was still a chance some of them would live to see another day. However, she wasn't too optimistic, judging by their wounds.

It's time, she thought with grim resolve.

She heard Feran dragging himself across the floor toward the door to place himself out of Suna's way. Rage ignited at the thought of Feran being harmed.

Ilio suddenly reappeared. An elongated gash across his forehead bled profusely, the blood glistening black, not red. He was paler and far gaunter. His harried pursuit to find the key was taking its toll, and the evil running through his veins was breaking down his body.

When the imp moved nearer, she noticed several of his teeth were gone, creating a gruesome, more asymmetrical dimension to his already hideous features. His body may have been deteriorating, but he was still as strong as ever.

She stepped to the center of the Gallery and faced the ill-begotten foe.

His gaze leered up and down her body. "You seemth to be following me," Ilio lisped through the gaps in his teeth. "Suth prettyneth. A thame to kill you."

If she could goad the creature into making that one mistake that would end his pitiful existence on this plane of life, then she'd put an end to him now and forever. Key or no key. "What is it you want, Ilio?"

He brandished a wicked grin. "You know what I theek. Tho much easier if you move and leth me path."

His beady eyes glowed red before returning to their depthless black. Worse was the malevolence emanating from him, but it only reinforced her resolve. She'd rather die than allow Ilio to possess the Kruthos' key.

Her mind raced with the implications as to why he was here at the castle in the first place. She followed his repeated gazes to the wall-walk connecting the Regent's Gallery to the Palace of Kings.

Before she could think more about his interest in the palace, a blast of mage'ic hit her full force. She flew through the air and connected solidly with the wall several yards back.

Shuddering uncontrollably as his dark touch roiled through her, she realized the miscreant's mage'ic had strengthened since their last meeting. *So the more powerful, the more deteriorated his appearance.* Soon, he'd become what her visions had revealed—a black wraith wielding the dark gifts.

Something warm and wet trickled down her arm. A piece of glass had embedded deep into the hollow of her arm and shoulder. She felt no pain as she grasped the end of the shard and pulled.

Then the air suddenly *whooshed* from her lungs. Ilio pinned her against the wall in an attempt to crush her life. She pushed back with a wall of fire. His spell began to falter. At last, she gained some footing.

Sucking in lungfuls of air, Suna kept her eyes on the target and lifted both her arms. *Will I be strong enough to defeat him?* she worried. Slithering bands of yellow and red mage'ic ensnared the imp.

Ilio rose several feet off the floor and dangled in midair. He twisted and turned in an effort to free himself, but she gritted her teeth and enforced her spell. She had to be careful. Ilio was adept at escaping her snares.

Keeping the net tightly bound around him, she catapulted him to the ceiling with her right hand, while her left crushed his putrid body against the wooden beams. Several pieces of wood split wider and fell from the impact as she added more of herself into the spell. Then she let him free-fall to the marble floor.

Ilio landed solidly to the marble. Hard enough to hear several bones crack. He struggled to his feet with labored wheezes coming from his chest.

She'd hurt him internally, maybe even crushed a few vital organs, but he was still breathing. Balthazar had forged his culpable child to withstand more abuse than what she was conjuring.

Feran called out, but she was too late. An orb of dark, vile mage'ic surrounded her. The smell made her retch. Despair sapped at her strength. Ilio's spell raped across her skin before soaking into every pore to eat away her will like ravenous maggots. She panted, desperate to free herself.

Through the murky haze of the sphere that had trapped her, a regiment of Elite Guards and Guardians raced through the hole in the back wall. Their movements caught Ilio's attention too. It was the distraction she needed.

Suna delved deep into her élan and took from the deepest, darkest vessel of her being a power completely alien to her. She grasped the strange mage'ic and bound her quickening to the pulsing energy. The bubble of evil surrounding her melted and hit the floor like molten lava.

As the soldiers took defensive positions outside the rubble, she realized their foolishness. They thought to defend against an enemy they couldn't bring down. Several archers shot an array of arrows into the room. Every one of them curved and angled in chaotic directions, missing Ilio by several feet.

"Put down your weapons. There's still people alive in here. I beg you. Come no further."

She threw a spell of conjured iron to ensnare Ilio as he'd done to her. Again, the imp's speed and stealth saved him. He leapt out of harm's way, her spell soaring past him like an innocuous breeze.

Ilio shifted toward the gardens. Horrified, she watched the demon select several guards, one of them Fletcher, and suspend them in the air. The captain thrashed against the invisible bonds which refused to yield.

She had to save those men. Too many had died already. She teleported her body into the air and landed close to the imp, but still a safe distance back. He turned his head with a chuckle, the sound like stone grinding on iron.

Her fingers twitched around the ball of hot, white light she'd summoned in the palm of her hand. She took a step forward, and then pushed her body up, propelling the spell directly above the imp's head.

The air detonated. A thunderclap of power counteracted Ilio's.

The soldiers fell like dead weight to the ground, some still shrieking. They bounded to their feet and began jumping up and down while smacking different parts of their bodies as smoldering strands of good and evil mage'ics coursed over them like crackling fire.

The imp eyed the dancing men before narrowing his attention on her. Disbelief stretched across his repugnant face.

Other soldiers scrambled to grab the frightened men who'd been caught in Ilio's mage'ic. They pulled their comrades back through the wall. In seconds, the horrid, choking sounds of retching followed.

Ilio lifted his nose. He sniffed and grinned.

She sensed movement by the entrance to the gallery and turned, praying that not all the common sense had been knocked out of Feran's stubborn head.

Suddenly, a loud *crack* raced around the gallery. She twisted around to see the council table splinter and lift off the floor. Thick, viscous bands of black mage'ic lifted it up and over her head. She'd seen that mage'ic before. The imp was getting outside help.

Isafel!

The table began spinning. Faster and faster until it was nothing but a whirling mass. She crouched, waiting for the inevitable. From the corner of her eye, she saw more guards arrive. Again she propelled the same warning into their minds, ordering them to come no closer. She had enough blood on her hands.

Her concern was palpable, but what she hadn't realized was that Ilio had sensed it too. He shifted toward the gaping hole and the soldiers outside, whirling the table like a windmill caught in a raging storm. His toothless grin widened. Small bolts of lightning sizzled and flared from beneath the wood's flat bottom. With flicks of both his wrists, he hurled the table out to the gardens. Streaks of lightning danced in the air and ignited everything they touched. Soon human torches ran blindly about. Agonized screams filled the gallery from the men on fire, and with it came the dreadful smell of burning flesh.

She tried to exhaust Ilio's mage'ic to break his hold on his spell, but as soon as her élan touched him, she recoiled. Isafel's mage'ic combined with the imp's was too nauseating to touch. She fell to her knees and tried not to throw up.

He sneered over his shoulder at her. "You don't like tuthing me? I've not been promiseth you, but I thor do like your tuth. Esthpethily when you're tho warm."

Suna rose and laced her fury with her powers and aimed her mage'ic in his direction. The force of her spell knocked him clear across the room. Disorientated, Ilio attempted to pick himself up.

She pounced.

Dousing the lightning with a cloak of midnight, she gained control over the table and sent it soaring into the sky before releasing her hold. Wood exploded and rained harmlessly downward to the ground.

Shrieks coming from the men still engulfed in flames tore at her heart. Others tried in desperation to help their friends burning before their eyes, but terror had created mayhem. Tortured howls unlike any she'd heard before filled the expanse of the gallery. She gathered whatever water had been soaked into the ground from the destroyed fountains and strove to douse as many men as possible. Feran's voice suddenly resonated in her mind.

Suna, if I can distract him...?

"*No!*" But she was too late. He raced directly at Ilio.

The imp turned at the last minute, his eyes wide. With Ilio's attention off her, it was the moment she needed.

Suna closed herself off from the world and delved inside herself. Deeper than she'd ever gone.

Gods, hear my plea. I haven't asked anything from you since you took everything from me, but I beg of you, give me the strength now to save these people.

An instantaneous maelstrom began roaring in her ears as a mass of ancient mage'ic boiled within the core of her élan. It was a volatile source of power that wasn't her own, yet it was. Instinctively, she laced it with her quickening.

She became a seraph of blazing energy. She rose higher and higher off the floor. Still, the occlusion of mage'ical energy built.

Stronger than any she'd ever sensed.

Purer than any she'd ever touched.

She smelled the earth, the wind. She basked in light so bright it burned her eyes. She touched the elementals of this world and became one with the universe.

Undulating swells of power stroked her system. She began spinning, caught in its throes. She allowed the power to take control. The whirlwind amplified. Faster and faster. Dust and dirt rose from the floor, caught in its tailwind.

Through it all she saw Ilio standing transfixed. Feran gawked. Then she came to a jarring stop. A voice escaped her lips, but it wasn't hers.

"Whence you came, so shall you return."

An eruption of power erupted from the crux of her élan directly into Ilio. The blast terrified her. Never had she constructed something so destructive. So virtuous. Blinding and powerful, the force of it flew her backwards into the wall.

The imp's scream pierced her ears like blades.

Beams cracked overhead.

Men cowered on the ground outside and pressed hands over their ears.

Feran fell on his face, his body curling on the floor.

Isafel fled.

Caught within the darkest realms of her mage'ic, she saw it all and sensed the damaging nature of this kind of power. This was no Divenean mage'ic. From that part of her mind that was still her own, she realized Feran was situated too close to Ilio. Separating the flows of energies, she shielded him.

Ilio began quivering. Then shaking uncontrollably. His shrieks increased in volume and clarity.

She floated to the floor like an angel of death, but all she could think about was Feran. She rushed to his side and adjusted the shield over both of them. Then she placed an invisible barrier between the guardsmen outside.

Spellbound they watched the evil entity that had caused so much devastation begin to change before their eyes.

His tremors intensified.

His cries grew in crescendo.

His soulless eyes rolled.

White foam frothed at the corners of his mouth.

Bones cracked.

Ilio threw back his head.

His petrified scream shook the very foundation of Dunkerk. Like melting wax, the imp's features began to disintegrate. His skin dripped and pooled in disgusting lumps around his dirty, bare feet. Soon, sporadic patches of grayish bone could be seen poking through his decaying flesh. Rancid smoke rose from his heels. His strangled howls worsened, never once stopping in momentum or pitch. The rancid smoke thickened and shrouded the rest of his grisly transformation. Flames shot straight through the ceiling of the gallery to disappear into the sky.

More debris rained down around them.

Suna reached for Feran's hand. His warm fingers enveloped hers. When she felt him squeeze back, the world felt somewhat normal again.

Silence fell, broken only by an occasional whimper or groan. When the smoke cleared, all that remained of the imp was a smoldering pile of dark ash and the lingering stench of something vile that had been cooked over an open flame.

Feran stood and pulled her up next to him. They moved toward the heap that had once been Balthazar's child. With the toe of his boot, Feran kicked at the remains as if to reassure himself that the demon wouldn't rise and attack again.

In the corner of the gallery lay the other council members. She let go of Feran's hand and rushed to the men she'd placed out of harm's way and discovered not one of them had survived.

Out in the gardens, the unharmed guards tended to their wounded comrades. Others meandered about, too shocked to do much else except gape in her direction.

Fletcher stumbled over piles of stone and staggered toward them. Green at the gills from being caught in mage'ic, he moved far better than Feran had.

Suna stared in horror at the senseless loss of lives. Drained of energy, she was otherwise fine, except for a stitching her shoulder needed.

That voice. It wasn't mine. However, it had been the same as she'd heard in her dreams. His guidance had helped her forge that spell to destroy Ilio and sever Isafel's hold. The imprint of that strange mage'ic stirred through her still, like hands kneading and soothing away the wounds and aches she'd suffered. The duplicity in the blinding white strands she'd detected at Carberra Ferry confirmed that something more was at work here.

The words "*you are not alone*" echoed like a soft-spoken promise. She peered over at Feran with renewed hope.

He walked to her and crushed her hard against his chest. The erratic beating of his heart thrummed through her.

"Don't ever do something like that again. You could have died," he whispered.

She melted into him. Never had she felt this for someone. Not even King Markes.

With a quiet sigh only Feran could hear, she leaned into him and returned his embrace, feeling the same way. *He will never know,* she vowed.

* ~ * ~ *

Karel had sensed Suna's urgency enfold him like a blanket of dread. He was almost at the base of the mountain when he'd heard her prayer to the gods. It was a connection he'd placed there when she'd been his charge so many moons ago. So much squandered time.

Immediately drawing a shroud around himself, he'd infused it with his spirit, strength and quickening before propelling it straight for Dunkerk. Through her eyes, he saw Ilio one last time. He had delved deep inside her and searched for that which she didn't know she possessed—a power he'd sensed in her as a child. Now he'd awakened it. It would be up her to understand it and use it wisely.

After he unleashed the mage'ic, Karel fell in a heap to the ground, drained by the expenditure of using his powers over such a far distance. As he watched the demise of Ilio through Suna's sight, he worried about the key, but he had other things to contend with first.

Balthazar would have surely have sensed the enormous amount of mage'ic expelled here. He had to cover his tracks or all would be lost.

Emptying his mind of all thought, he concealed his élan and became one with the mountain.

CHAPTER TWENTY-SIX

Suna pushed away from Feran's embrace. She couldn't show weakness. Not to him. Not to the soldiers. Not to anyone.

She saw the hurt on his face, and he knew she saw it.

He focused on the floor and mumbled, "That shoulder of yours needs some darning."

A thousand questions had swirled in his eyes before he dropped his gaze. Questions she had no answers to. She pushed aside a strand of hair from her face and shivered as vestiges of that strange mage'ic finally subsided.

"So you're just going to bleed all over the place?"

"I don't think it'll make much of a difference, do you?" she snipped.

He glanced bleakly around the gallery.

"I'm sorry. You didn't deserve that." She hung her head, unable to look at him. More emotions threatened to unleash, but she battled them as unwaveringly as she had Ilio and Isafel. Not just for herself or Feran, but for everyone who had witnessed this atrocity. As a Divenean she *must* maintain.

With a shrug, he turned his attention to a large regiment of Elite Guards and Guardians who'd just swarmed through the gallery's door. They first checked the council members who hadn't survived before skirting around the grotesque pile of what was left of Ilio to attend to the wounded they could help. Confused glimpses drifted their way more than once, but no one approached.

Despising the attention, she followed Feran to the only chair still left standing. From the pouch at his waist, he pulled out a needle and thread and sutured her shoulder with a row of neat stitches.

It hurt like hell, but she refused to show any reaction for fear of unleashing the tidal wave of emotions churning too close to the surface—emotions that went deeper than any she'd ever experienced before.

She sensed Feran's need to talk, but whether it was because there were too many ears that could listen, or he had too many questions, he stayed thankfully quiet.

One of the most daunting aspects was the voice that had come from her. It hadn't been her own. *Then whose was it?* she wondered.

The more she thought on it, the more her head hurt.

Balthazar's spawn was no more. Unfortunately, so was the key's location. Why had Ilio come to the castle? What was so important that he'd take such a risk to come here? And with Isafel's help?

Her thoughts scattered when scores of additional guards hurried past them to retrieve the dead. They moved like puppets toward the back wall of the gallery, which didn't exist anymore. And the bodies of the dead lay everywhere.

The horror of this day would not be easily forgotten.

The once gleaming marble floor was now smeared with dirt and sickening trails of blood. Mottled walls striated with smoke were grim reminders of what had just occurred. Two main beams that had lined the gallery's ceiling were splintered. One in particular hung at a precarious angle that almost hit the floor. Soldiers were busy wedging a support for it.

Chunks of stone lay scattered about and earth from the gardens covered everything with a dusting like devil's snow. Outside, broken portions of the council table still burned and crackled from Ilio's deviant mage'ic.

Everywhere she looked was devastation and blood.

The intense stares of every man there pierced into her. Some in shock. Others remorsefully. Word of her arrival had most certainly spread throughout the city, and with it would come embellished recounts of what had happened here. As a result, she'd become a savior—or monster.

The Guardians stood to one side supervising those soldiers who'd come to help. They also glanced more than once at her and Feran, but in quiet speculation, not fear.

"There shouldn't be too much of a scar," Feran murmured. The stiffness in his body and the tight set of his jaw revealed his dislike of the attention they were receiving. She too sensed a whirlwind of emotions brewing inside him.

Suna turned away, hoping the guilt she harbored didn't show on her face. She failed.

Feran spoke for her ears only. "This wasn't your fault. Ilio didn't come here for you. He came for the key. Like you said, death follows him wherever he goes."

"I know, but perhaps I could have done something differently. Something to prevent this."

Aren't you carrying enough guilt already?

On hearing his thought, she clenched her teeth. Damn his blunt but ever logical way of putting things. She should have been able to push these emotions aside and deal logically with the situation, but she couldn't.

At the sound of approaching boots, they looked up to see General Heratio standing in front of them, his features etched like stone.

Feran stood and saluted.

At that moment three Elite Guards carried the portly body of Lord Hawkin past her. The dainty lace he'd so nervously tugged on when standing for her was soaked with his blood. One piece of glass was embedded deep into the side of his neck close to the jugular. Hawkin had been alive for most of the battle. Sadly, he'd bled out before Ilio's demise.

Regret threatened to overcome her. She rose on shaky legs and stumbled a few feet away. No one would see her tears. No one! A Divenean was supposed to be immune to emotional travesties like this, but no matter how hard she tried, too many things about her had changed of late. The lacerations inside caused by such reckless losses of lives cut deeper than any of those shards.

Heratio's somber tone matched their moods. "Feran. Lady Suna."

She half-turned and gave a bare minimum nod.

"General," Feran replied softly.

She peered down at her hands and the blood stained upon them. Even under her fingernails. It was her blood, but it was a glaring reminder of the others who'd died today.

"What happened here? I mean, I know what I saw, I think, but... Who was that devil?"

Feran ran a hand through his hair and winced when he touched the back of his head. "His name was Ilio. We've been tracking him from Odarian. He was one of Balthazar's—"

At the mention of that name, Heratio drew back with a hiss and grabbed the backrest of Suna's chair.

The low hum of both generals' voices moved through her, but she was in no mood to participate.

When Heratio plopped down into the chair Suna had vacated, Feran began to tell him how this had all come to be.

Now she could be alone with her thoughts. She maneuvered herself over a chunk of debris to stop at the wall-walk entry of the gallery that led into the Palace of Kings. Other than the main doors out front, it was the only other entrance. Seals placed the day King Markes and Queen Saliste died secured both this door and the front leading out to the streets. The imp's interest in this place troubled her.

She pondered Ilio's ill-fated visit until her head felt as if it were splitting in two. There was only one way to find out why he'd taken such a risk to come to the castle.

When she turned, she realized the Guardians standing close by had been inconspicuously eavesdropping on their commanding officers' conversation. Feran had just finished chronicling the events that had led them to Dunkerk. Heratio's pallor now looked a lot like Fletcher's. Balthazar's name was a disturbing one to mention in any conversation, but if they'd taken the time to explain this on the steps outside, she knew his reaction would have been one of cynicism instead of believability.

"General Heratio?" she called out.

Feran and the general approached her.

"Please clear the gallery."

The large man's eyes rounded. "What do you mean clear the gallery? My men are doing their jobs."

"There's something more that can be done, but in private. Let's not allow the lives lost here today to be in vain." She moved closer to his ear. "I need to enter the Palace of Kings."

Heratio drew back with a scowl. "No one gains entrance into the palace. You know this. It's been sealed as dictum states."

"I am quite aware of the laws of Etharia, but does it truly matter now? Do you dare deny me entrance into what had once been my home?"

The seals on the doors were to stay undisturbed until a future king came forward, but they'd come too far and had lost so much. Everything that had happened here went far beyond regimental laws. In any event, they could explain any damage to the seals as being caused by Ilio.

When Heratio didn't answer, she slipped a bitter edge into her voice. "I plan on getting into the palace with or without your permission. Here's our conundrum, General. We can do this with an audience? Or without. The choice is yours."

He was about to protest, but she forced him quiet with a glare. She'd advocate her request by whatever means possible, even if it meant for everyone in the gallery to see and then have tongues talk about it later.

The general turned to Feran.

"Arguing with her is like hitting your head with a mallet. There's just no point in doing it."

"This is—"

Suna stepped closer to Heratio. "If you wish to do nothing, General, I'll leave it in your hands to explain why I've breached the seals. If we do it my way, no one will be the wiser. It's imperative I gain entrance. I believe it's why that demon-spawn came here. Do you want these deaths to mean nothing?"

Heratio studied her for a moment and grunted something unintelligible before turning on his heel. His authoritative bellow reached every corner of the gallery. Perhaps even the street. "Everyone out!"

Heads turned and soldiers jumped, but no one moved.

When Heratio turned back at her, she thinned her lips and waited.

With a bellowing sigh, he faced his men again. "I said move it. Now!"

As if waking from trances, men began exiting the gallery. Except the Guardians. They drew their swords and planted theirs blades tip first onto the floor, staring in quiet contemplation. And defiance.

Fletcher's left side of his face was red and swollen, which juxtaposed his sickening hue, but the staunch determination in his eyes reassured her. Even while suffering the ill effects of Ilio's mage'ic, he wasn't to be deterred. He stood steadfast. A true Guardian refusing defeat.

He took a small step forward and bowed his head. "My Lady Suna, as Captain of the Guardians it's my sworn oath to guard this city and its occupants. I'm not leaving. Nor will my men."

He peered briefly at General Heratio, who reciprocated with a concurring nod. Fletcher moved nearer and whispered so passersby's couldn't hear. "We have no quarrel with you entering the palace. We'll remain here and ensure that the wall-walk and entrance into the gallery is properly guarded. Our thanks to you for our lives. We serve you, my lady."

Several Guardians moved to stand at their captain's side.

Touched by Fletcher's loyalty, she dipped her head. Guardians bestowed such honors only to a king or queen. The desolate hole left inside her by so many deaths eased and her damaged spirit lifted somewhat. "Thank you, Captain Fletcher. Allow no one entrance. No one is to see what I do. Too many have already," she added under her breath. She gave the other soldiers a tight-lipped smile of thanks.

Fletcher and his men moved toward the wall-walk entrance. However, many soldiers still milled about in confusion.

Suna turned to Heratio. "General?"

The large man growled as he shifted to the middle of the gallery. "If this room isn't clear in the next two heartbeats, heads will roll."

It took longer than a couple of heartbeats, but the gallery eventually emptied, leaving Feran, Heratio, and the fifteen Guardians. Only then did Suna approached the entrance to the private wall-walk.

Four strips of gummy red cloth sealed the top, sides and bottom doorframe. With a twist of her wrist, the material split and the door swung open.

When Feran moved beside her, she resisted the urge to grab for his hand. She doubted he knew how thankful she was that he was with her. The palace had once been her home and the only one she remembered well. Memories would be difficult.

But was it only gratitude she felt?

General Heratio joined them, but an urgent pounding sounded outside the main door. In a blur of activity, the Guardians took defensive stances in front of the main entrance, their swords drawn.

"General Heratio. General Heratio!" a terrified voice cried out from behind the wood. "You're needed at the gates immediately. Oh, by the dark stars! GENERAL HERATIO."

The older man faltered, uncertain as to which emergency he should attend to first. Suna sensed his desire to see inside the Palace of Kings, as was many of Dunkerk's citizens, but duty called him elsewhere.

"I know my way, General. You must go." She wondered what the urgency was. It was daylight. Isafel's powers were weak, but not ineffective. After what had happened here, she was confident it wasn't him creating the mayhem that needed his immediate attention. *Most likely some spirited ruckus from festival-goers enjoying themselves too much,* she mused.

With a reluctant nod, Heratio hurried out of the gallery. Once their commanding officer slipped through the door, the Guardians barred the entrance with a piece of a shattered beam. Four men stood guard there; eight took positions at the back, while the others, including Fletcher, returned to where she and Feran stood.

Suna peered down the gloomy wall-walk corridor and spoke for Feran's ears only. "Ilio's interest in the palace is not a coincidence. I sense it as strongly as I sense the honor in you and your Guardians."

"They're not *my* Guardians."

"They're your men. Not Heratio's. That's easily visible. You'd be a fool not to see it too."

He mumbled something she couldn't hear.

"Not many have been granted passage into the Palace of Kings, Feran. You'll now be considered one of those lauded few."

"Why are you so fixed on the palace?"

"Ilio."

"I still don't understand."

"When he came into the gallery, he kept looking toward the wall-walk. I have a feeling—"

"—the key is somewhere in the palace."

"Yes." She glanced over her shoulder and addressed Fletcher. "No one else enters here. Please understand that I do this not for selfish reasons. There's more at stake here than you know."

"We understand, Lady Suna." Fletcher and his men took stances on the opposite side of the wall-walk door. When Feran and Suna passed them, every one of them saluted and issued a low bow.

She stopped. "That's not necessary."

General Fletcher's head rose a fraction. "No. It's not. Just appropriately bestowed."

Her cheeks burned as she moved by them. Feran murmured an 'at ease' without realizing it. *Once an officer, always an officer. Perhaps when this is over, he might reconsider his role as their commanding officer.*

The thought saddened her for some reason, but she promptly dismissed it. She had no desire to think about the future. The present was all that mattered.

After Fletcher closed the door behind them, they stood alone. Sunlight glinted off the glass ceiling canopying the long wall-walk leading to an unmarked door several hundred yards in the distance. Intricately cut stone bricks worked their way upwards to support the glass. An azure sky dotted by an occasional cloud was mired by intermittent wisps of gray smoke still rising from the destruction of the gallery. The glass allowed smattering patches of sunlight to sneak through which created sprinkled beams of light that danced across the stone floor.

Disquiet transcended over them; a spiritual sacredness of being where only kings and queens had walked before.

Suna peered at Feran from the corner of her eye. An array of emotions emanated from him, most of them confusing. Without a word, she made her way down the corridor. The brass handle carved into the likeness of a lion's head in the center of the door that led into the palace beckoned. She reached for the lion's maw, but Feran's slight touch on her shoulder stayed her hand.

"Do you think this is right?" His words echoed ominously down the empty corridor.

"Ilio's interest in the palace?"

"Yes?"

"My senses tell me the key is somewhere in there. I can't describe it. It's a stretch, I know, but we have nothing else."

His features stretched into that infamous grin of his. "Well, we've had a lot of nothing to go on since we started this quest. So I'd say you're doing a grand job with those senses of yours."

Only he could be flippant at a time like this. "I'd include *we* in that, Feran. It'll take years to rebuild the gallery back to its original beauty. But the loss of lives?" She hung her head.

"Without you a lot more people might have died. It could have been worse and you know it. Several of those guards owe you their lives, not to mention those snooty High Houses you helped get to safety."

She pursed her lips.

Feran held up his hands in defeat. "Okay, okay. The *council* members."

"What is it about the High Houses that causes this anger in you?"

The green in Feran's eyes deepened before he looked away and focused on the aged mortar encasing the stone. "Let's just enter, okay?"

Stunned by the veracity of emotions rolling off him, she considered them. A tumult of humiliation, hurt, and bitter anger raged about him like a hurricane. Memories of his life filtered through her mind with resounding clarity.

An image of a dainty woman dressed in commoner's clothes filled her inner sight. Then came a younger version of Feran, the son of a scullery maid. The strain of a mother who worked hard to put her son through military school was evident on the woman's face. He, in turn, made her proud by being the best soldier he could. Whispered innuendos and misgivings filtered through the scenes. *Where's his father?*

She sensed Feran had asked the same question his entire life.

The vision changed. He was still young, but on the verge of manhood, questioning his mother consistently about the father he'd never known. Suna heard whispers of 'highborn' and 'a member of a High House'. She couldn't see the man's face, but there was power and strength in whoever his father had been. And something else. Something that touched at her consciousness and fled.

Her connection to Feran suddenly intensified. He believed his mother had consummated some sordid love affair with a member of a High House and he was the result of that copulation. Certain that his father was a man of wealth who'd abandoned his mother, he hated everything that society didn't do for her. But there something more. Something she couldn't see.

The vision changed. She saw Feran as he is now, sitting beside the bed of his ill mother. A horrid disease had ravaged her body to a mere shell of bones. They spoke softly together. Suna instantly drew back. The moment felt too personal to bear witness.

The images disappeared with an abrupt jolt. All she sensed from him now was raging anger, which he tried to hide. "Are you all right?" she asked.

Concerned, but also perplexed by what had just occurred, she needed him to know that she would never judge him. His visions had been so powerful that he'd unwittingly brought her into the memories surging through him.

He said nothing.

She placed her hand onto his arm. "Feran?" Although not the time or place, she wanted him to know he could talk about it. The strength and vividness of his past had touched her. He carried a lot of scars. Almost as deep as her own.

He tried to grin away the lie. "Just a bout of dizziness. My head isn't as hard as I thought it was." Staring at the door, he waited for her to open it. "This is a once in a lifetime opportunity, right?" His half-hearted attempt at a joke fell short.

She wouldn't push him. She respected him too much.

Suna grabbed the lion's head. The dusty metal felt cool against her palm. She stopped and whispered, "Personally, Feran, I can't think of anyone more deserving of this honor."

Ignoring his stunned expression, she pushed open the door and entered the Palace of Kings.

CHAPTER TWENTY-SEVEN

Suna halted halfway into the antechamber of the palace. Feran, paying more attention to his surroundings than what was going on in front of him, narrowly missed colliding into her back and sidestepped at the last second. The smell of aged dust and a room closed off from sunlight and fresh air assaulted his nose.

When he turned to her, he saw she'd closed her eyes. A haunted nostalgia softened her features. She took a deep breath, but didn't move.

The scent of hardwood oil permeated through the dust-covered muslin sheets lying like ghosts over the opulent furnishings. Enmeshed with this was the taint of hardened beeswax from the forgotten candles in the many wall sconces lining the walls of the foyer. Beneath all of this was the faint but poignant aroma of lives that had once dwelled here.

Humbled by the fact that they were the first to step inside this building since the servants had sealed the palace thirty-odd years ago, Feran strolled further into what was the throne room and stared about in wonder.

Layers of thick draperies shrouded the beautiful beveled windows. At some point in time, the fabric had been white, but age and housekeeping neglect had made them a dingy gray. Dismal gloom and sadness imbued the entire hall.

Like the beauty of the Regents Gallery, massive beams of snakewood partitioned off sections of the room with each beam buttressing up and over the dome-like ceiling. The left wall was bare, and like the drapes, time had marred the last whitewashing to a dull yellow.

Standing as silent sentinels of past preeminence, a fleet of various shields and matching armor lined the right wall opposite the windows. Each had once belonged to every king who had ruled Dunkerk. A blood-red, black and gold suit of armor with a matching kite shield looked the newest, and Feran surmised it must have belonged to King Markes. Thick sheets of silvery dust covered the metal adding to the desolation that had swallowed this once stately residence.

All this beauty left to the ravages of time, he thought sadly.

His line of vision followed Suna as she approached the raised dais. With shoulders slumped, she climbed the seven steps to the throne platform, each step alternating between black and white marble. Unlike the other furnishings, mere muslin didn't cover the grandeur of the thrones of Dunkerk. Ruby-red silk draped the twin chairs, its gossamer fabric falling in elegant folds to the floor mired only by a thin film of dust.

Those chairs stand as silent wardens of past kings and queens who'd ruled here. And the future ones yet to come. The thought brought a lump of humility to lodge in his windpipe.

On the left and right behind the thrones, two arched staircases with thick balustrades of bleached snakewood branched upward like welcoming arms. "Where do those stairs lead?" His voice rumbled in the stuffy silence.

"There's a grand ballroom on the second floor. And a library. There's other floors."

As she moved gracefully onto the dais, Feran could have sworn she floated. She appeared decorously comfortable in these aristocratic surroundings. He had no idea why he found it surprising, but he did. The sheer veneration emanating from her and the palace seemed to be as one.

When she shifted to the side, he saw her eyes glistening with tears, but she was quick to turn away.

"Do you know the Diveneans are distant descendants of the Elves?" she whispered.

He shook his head. It seemed that whenever he opened his mouth, something inane came out of it, so he said nothing. This was not the time or place to intrude on the intimacy of this moment for her. She had things on her mind—things, he sensed, she needed to say.

"Although we look like ordinary Etharians, our annals revealed it was because the gods made us this way to better blend in. Unlike the Elves, we felt too much. Cared too much. We were more human than elf. When the Elves left Etharia more than a thousand years ago, they left the human race to their own devices. No one remembers them anymore.

"Sadly, my people have followed the same path. Be it for selfish reasons or not, I don't know why they left. Our two distinct nations had lived in harmony with all things of these lands, but the Elves chose to cross the great sea and never return. The Diveneans refused to leave their place here. They took it upon themselves to carry on the traditions instilled between our races and the gods that created us. Our diktat was to protect and give aid to any and all that would be subjugated.

"King Markes used to dream of the day when the Elves would return and the balance of the lands, as he called it, would be restored. He'd begged me for information about them, but I knew little myself. Our Elders held that knowledge. I found it strange that he'd ask me such questions. I always assumed it was out of curiosity. Months before his death, he'd stopped asking. He never lived to see that day, Feran. Neither did my kin."

From the moment he'd first laid eyes on her, he'd noticed her resemblance to the Elven folk. He'd only read about them. The descriptions depicted small bone structure, mage'ical abilities and wills of iron. The Elves were folklore to the people of Etharia. No one could boast ever seeing one themselves. Like the Diveneans. But Feran did. Or thought he had.

Shortly after his appointment as general, he'd traveled to the kingdom of Carberra to meet with Lord Greth. The night he'd left to return to Dunkerk, he had stopped at the water's edge on the outskirts of the city to rest. By the shore of a desolate inlet, he happened to see three men boarding a boat. They were slight of height; lithe in their movements. When the moonlight hit upon them under the cover of night, they seemed to glow. He'd always wondered who they'd been, but secretly, he'd hoped that they had been Elves.

Suna was just like them. Tiny and slender, yet tougher than angler leather. Deep down, some part of him had always believed that what he'd seen had been real. *I swear a day will come when I'll learn nothing new about her.*

"In my years here," Suna continued softly, "King Markes was engrossed in learning about the Elven and Divenean histories. More specifically, why the Elves chose to leave our lands. He studied everything he could get his hands on. I know that in our time together, he never found the reason why. I also know there's ancient script purporting this knowledge, but none but my Elders knew of it. I fear those scrolls are forever lost now.

"The Divenean way of life is sacred. We're forbidden to share who and what we are, but the king knew. It wasn't just curiosity. I know this now. I tried my best to help him better understand by giving him a sense of who I was, but keeping my Divenean lineage secret. He knew what my duty here consisted of. Protection. I didn't divulge that information to him. A Divenean never discloses their duty, yet he knew and kept it in confidence. I played the role as their wizen and advisor. And teacher of children. Even though I never shunned my duty as their protector, it turned out that I failed nonetheless. How did he know about me? A dream? A vision?"

She stopped to run a hand across the silk resting on the armrest of one of the thrones.

Feran stood transfixed. This was a history lesson he was pretty sure no one else had been privy to. "Perhaps the gods thought it wise to tell him." He saw her back stiffen like granite.

"The gods?" she spat. "They don't meddle in the affairs of humans, even when they're begged to do so."

She'd said it with such vehemence it made his heart hurt. Out of respect he refused to say anything more.

"King Markes held to duty as fiercely as I do. And you. His determination to make these lands a better place held no bounds." She paused and wiped her hand across her face.

She tried to hide it, but he knew she cried. A knot tightened in the base of his gut.

"Why is it that the gods seem so willing to take good people from us too soon?" She flung back the diaphanous cloth draping the thrones. The delicate material slipped from her fingers as a silver cloud of dust rose into the air around them.

It was obvious to him that the same artisans who'd carved the massive doors of the main castle had also engraved these thrones, and with the same attention to detail.

Crimson velvet covered the backrests and seats with gilded buttons sewn into an intricate crown pattern on the back. Sculpted above each headrest were lions' heads, their open maws roaring as if in defiance to all who stood before them. The legs consisted of three-pronged claws that rose up to oblong armrests. The small table that connected both thrones shone even in the muted light.

At seeing the chairs, Suna released a flood of tears he knew she'd been trying to hold in. From where he stood, they shimmered as they slid down her cheeks. As she cried, he sensed it was much more than the loss of an old friend and king. She cried for the people of Etharia. And for her own race. He couldn't help but feel like an intruder. Worse, he couldn't think of a damn thing to do to console her.

"King Markes' greatest wish was to have a son. An heir he could love and nurture. To guide and teach him to care for these lands and its people as he did." Her shoulders shook as sobs racked through her.

Feran shifted uncomfortably before taking a hesitant step toward the dais, but stopped. He felt like a trespasser on a sacred moment in time. Her pain was so palpable that he wished he'd personally known the man as she had.

"Where's King Markes' crown?" There was no denying the thorny sharpness in her tone. She whipped around. With the heel of her hand, she did an angry swipe at her tears. "A crown's missing, Feran. King–Markes'–crown–is–missing." Fury glistened in eyes mired by her tears.

"What do you mean missing?"

She sidestepped to the left to give him a better view of the thrones. There on the tiny table connecting the two regal chairs, he saw only a delicate circlet. A crown suitable for a queen. And nothing else.

Without a word, she raced up the left side of the staircase and disappeared from sight. She moved so fast, it took a moment to come to his senses before he bolted after her. When he reached the second level, he stopped. The echoes of her boots pounding against the wood on another set of stairs reached his ears. He searched the hallway and found a staircase hidden into an alcove on the right side of the wall. Taking the steps two at a time, he reached a third level with a wide corridor.

A collection of beautiful woven tapestries hung along the length of the walls. Then he heard the sounds of her running above yet again. Once more she'd managed to outrace him. *How big is this place?*

He searched various rooms, opening and closing doors on his left and right and discovered the level was servants' quarters. *In a palace? They're not off grounds?* He'd heard stories of how wonderful the king and queen had been in their time, but he thought they'd been embellished tales concocted by the lords and ladies of the High Houses to keep the monarchy untouchable to peon people like him.

At the end of the corridor, he saw a floor to ceiling tapestry move as if caught in a subtle breeze. He approached and pushed it to the side. *Hidden stairs?*

Shaking his head, Feran climbed the narrow staircase and arrived on at fourth level. He stopped to catch his breath and take in his surroundings. The hallway was narrower with no windows. To his surprise, the floor was rather ordinary. Nothing hung on the walls. The tongue and groove flooring looked immaculate, as if it had been polished that morning.

"Suna?" His whisper carried down the hallway like a shout. When he received no response, he went a little louder. "Suna?"

"I'm here."

Her faint voice came from one of four doors standing ajar.

Poised in an elegant armchair in what looked to be a sitting room, Suna faced a doorway leading into a bedroom which displayed a beautifully crafted four-poster bed canopied in delicate black lace netting. The massive hearth cut into the stone beside the bed was empty of logs and looked as if it'd never been used. Unlike the throne room, none of the furnishings here held muslin sheets. Just a slight powdering of dust covered the unprotected wood.

"I went to search King Markes rooms, but... This used to be my bedchamber." She looked up with eyes filled with haunted longing before concentrating on something in the other room. She braced herself in her chair. "Do you see what I see?"

He followed her line of vision into the bedroom. In the middle of the bed was a bundle covered with a satin cloth in the same hue as the coverlet that covered the mattress. No wonder he'd missed it.

Suna entered the bedroom and pushed aside the delicate netting hanging from the bedposts. She lifted the package and carried it back to the sitting room as if it were a newborn babe. Placing it on a table beside the chair she'd vacated, her brow furrowed as she resumed her seat.

Feran sat in the armchair directly across from her as she pulled away the fabric. There was a crown. As she stared at the gold circlet, time seemed to stop.

"I'm taking a guess here and say that's King Markes' crown?"

She nodded slowly.

"Um, why is the crown of Dunkerk in your room?" he asked.

"I don't know."

Beautifully gilded in gold with subtle hints of silver, it wasn't as elaborate as he thought it would be. Since no king or queen had ruled in his time since his service, he'd never had occasion to glimpse such grandeur. He'd assumed a king's crown would be bigger, more elaborate somehow.

Similar in design to the one downstairs, it was a simple gold circlet with five elegant crescent arches.

On top of each crescent was a thumbnail-sized gem that depicted the exact colors of the five underlords' banners. A single twisted strand of silver encircled the bottom portion. Just below the crescents, a vine of thorns wound around the upper half. Hewed in the center of the gilded gold was the largest opal he'd ever seen. It shimmered with hues of pinks and greens amid traces of blues and purples.

The longer Feran stared at it, the swirling veins of colors seemed to come alive. It was hypnotic. By far, it was the most beautiful jewel he'd ever set eyes on.

Then he saw something else. Something only a trained soldier would notice. Cleverly nestled into the bottom of the crown was a pin attached to a miniature hinge set directly into the metal. Almost undetectable.

Suna noticed the same thing, but before he could stop her, she pulled out the pin. "Why is there a hinge on a crown that doesn't fold?" She examined the tiny piece of metal between her fingers.

He held out his hand. "May I?"

She transferred the crown into his hands. With a push of his thumb, a tiny square of malleable metal slid over the base. To the naked eye, it blended perfectly with the rest of the crown.

"What are you doing?"

"When I was a lad at the academy, a mentor brought in an old suit of armor to demonstrate a unique trick used by warriors in days gone by. Back then they sometimes forged a small hinge on the inside of armored chest plates. With a pull of a concealed wire, or pin like this one, a hidden metal plate slid open to allow access to a dirk. It proved useful in opening a throat or piercing the heart of an enemy in case of capture. Unfortunately, its application didn't become too popular because any direct blow to the chest sometimes popped the hinge, which meant your own weapon could end up killing you. This is identical in design to that old piece of armor, but much smaller."

On closer inspection, he found something else. He thrust the crown back to her as if it were a deadly viper.

Her hands shook as she pried the small parchment out, leaving it unrolled in the palm of her hand. It was one mystery as to why King Markes' crown was in her bedchamber, but this was something else entirely.

"Just my humble opinion here, but that note was meant for you to find."

"I didn't find it. You did."

"Be that as it may, it might be a good idea if you read it."

The blue in her eyes took on a luminous glow. "King Markes often mentioned that he didn't like wearing his crown. He said the weight always gave him a headache."

"But it's not heavy."

She aimed an unwavering stare at him. "The weight of the crown, he said, was always heavy." Placing the coronet back on to the table, she rolled the message back and forth along her palm.

"Would you like some privacy?" he asked, rising from the chair.

Before he took a step toward the door, she stopped him with a touch on his arm. He shifted around and almost drowned in the blueness of her eyes. Eyes that held vulnerability and need.

"I wouldn't have found this without your help, Feran. Please. I'd like you to stay."

He'd learned several sides of this woman, but what he saw on her face now stopped him dead. He'd never seen her look so uncertain about anything. He resumed his seat and waited.

Unrolling the parchment, she read aloud:

If this message finds you, all has been forsaken. The evil of others has come to fruition. My dreams have guided me to this end. Do not blame yourself for events that have happened and are about to happen.

"Even in death, I failed him," she whispered.

He winced. That small passage had lacerated wounds that should never be opened. In her mind, her failure to the king and queen had become inescapable. She drowned in the misery of memories. Her pain was so tangible, it scored through him like it was his own.

Without thinking, he took her hand and squeezed. She peered up at him through tear-soaked lashes and attempted a smile.

A distant rumbling vibrated beneath their feet. *Seven Hells! She makes the earth quake when she even tries to smile.* His heart did an odd dance inside his chest. "Did you feel that?" he asked.

"Illuminators' fire?"

"I guess. Are you okay to continue?"

"Yes."

He gripped her hand tighter. "Is that it? I mean, is that all he wrote?" His heart actually hurt seeing what this was doing to her.

"No, there's a little bit more."

It took everything in his power not to cup her face and kiss those lips. Every time he looked at her, he drowned in the tears in her eyes. They were like an ocean of churning waves beckoning him to fall into their depths. The spell broke when she looked away. He pushed his chair forward to read with her.

With a shaky breath, she continued.

I've done things of late I'm not proud of, but the reasons behind the act can outdo the nature of the wrongdoing. You always told me that a king must make difficult decisions. Crown my son, for it's the key to Etharia's salvation. Beware, Lady Suna. If all comes to be, no living creature will ever live free.

He took the parchment from her hands and re-read the message, except for the strange writing on the bottom. "What does this last part say?"

"It's ancient script. Strange. I didn't know King Markes knew how to write it, let alone understand it. It says something about a woman, but I'll need time to transcribe it."

"Obviously written before his death. 'Crown my son, for it's the key to Etharia's salvation? What's *it's*?'" He peered at the circlet, wishing he could force it to talk. "Seems too much of a coincidence that what we're looking for is a key."

"He knew his death was imminent, Feran. How did he know? He fell from his horse. How could he have predicted that? It's as I always suspected. An assassination. So much I should have done. Should have said. If he would have told me—"

A resounding *boom* resonated outside.

Feran whirled toward the door expecting Ilio to prance in. "What in the shades of Hell was that?"

Suna hurried to the large window and pushed aside the heavy curtain. From where he sat, all he could see were patches of the destroyed gardens below. She turned with a frown. "That sound was the main gates being closed. A lot of people don't know what happened here. They could have assumed it was part of the celebrations. Perhaps General Heratio thought it wise to close the city."

Thinking it unimportant, he shoved aside the interruption and began to pace. There were more important matters to contend with than a bunch of disorderly festival goers. "Okay, King Markes said 'Crown my son, for it's the key to Etharia's salvation… it's the key to Etharia's salvation'."

The heart of the opal's colors swirled in his sight. It was difficult to pull his gaze away. When he did, he felt lightheaded and an urge to stare at it again. "The opal? Is it mage'ic?"

She returned to her chair. "No. It's just a gem. Why?"

"Because every time I look at it, it's… well, I feel strange. I do have a head injury," he added with a grin. "By the way, who made these crowns?"

"Script purports that the Diveneans of old forged them as gifts to the first king and queen who'd ruled at that time. Why?"

When the gem caught his attention again, he forced himself to look away. "There's something strange going on with that stone."

"If it were mage'ic, Feran, I'd be able to detect it. Unless?" She picked up the crown and stared deep into the heart of the jewel. A sudden burst of light shot past her shoulder. The circlet slipped from her hands and hit the floor.

Feran moved, but she misconstrued his intent.

"Don't touch it!"

He had no intentions of touching that damn thing again.

Gingerly, she picked up the circlet by one of its arched crescents and placed it on the table. As her hand did a slow wave over the top, the colors in the opal began moving in a frenzied state. He tried to look away, but couldn't. The hues moved and blended together, almost like a living thing. It was so mesmerizing that when the stone glowed as bright as the midday sun, he failed to look away.

Momentarily blinded, he heard Suna's melodic voice. *"Sa'san mullio illiminious d'an n'to."*

The gem's kaleidoscope of colors moved in an even more frenzied dance until a brilliant beam of light shot out from its center.

He barely had time to duck as it came straight at him. It then shot to the ceiling and circled the room before traveling out the door and disappearing completely. His eyes burned and watered. "Blood and guts! What in the devil's lair was that?"

A ghost of a smile curled the corners of her lips. He was about to ask what she found so funny when he heard a gentle *pop*. The opal dropped from its mounting and landed on the table.

Her rare smile was now a victorious grin.

CHAPTER TWENTY-EIGHT

Feran attempted to lick his lips, but his mouth was as dry as the Menjio Desert. He plopped down into the nearest chair like a rag doll, gawking at the jewel. Black spots still filtered through his eyesight and he had to blink several times to get rid of them.

"How strange that I couldn't detect the concealment spell until you mentioned it… but you could." She picked up the crown. "Do you see that?"

"I don't know if I'll ever see right again." Still, he shifted closer to the table and focused.

In the hollow where the jewel had once been, she pried the object out and placed it in the center of her palm. The key was small and insignificant, yet Feran sensed the power it held permeate throughout the room.

"'The crown of Dunkerk is the key to the land's salvation'. This is what he meant."

"He hid the Kruthos' key in his crown?"

"The king didn't hide it. The Diveneans who made this crown did. These crowns are a thousand years old. Maybe older. Divenean mage'ic concealed it all this time. They would never have told a null such a secret. So how did King Markes know?"

Feran looked down at the note still clenched in his hand and reread the message. "His dreams. He left this as a clue so we'd find the key. Maybe there's more. The ancient script on the bottom. What does—?"

A violent shuddering swept through the room. Suna jumped to her feet. Worry and confusion had dulled the excited glow that had lit up her eyes just before she closed them.

"What's going on?" he asked. An odd tingling vacillated in the air, which he recognized as her mage'ic.

She gasped. When he reached for her arm, her eyes opened. What he saw in them now chilled him to the bone.

"Dunkerk's under attack."

Joking was not a part of her nature, so what she'd just said was impossible.

"Dunkerk's under attack, Feran. Tobas Greth is leading his army through the first set of gates. Dunkerk's walls are about to be breached!"

Snatching the message from his hand, she slipped it under the front of her jerkin and raced out the door. He grabbed the crown with one hand and the opal in the other, and bolted into the bedroom. He forced the milky stone back into the hollow of the crown with his thumb and tossed the sheet over it. *We have what we need. Leaving it here won't make a difference.* He left the crown and ran from the room.

When he caught up with Suna, she'd already reached the bottom hidden staircase. "We have to get the key out of the city," he panted in between his strides.

"If there's a city left to leave."

Her ominous reply made him pick up speed.

* ~ * ~ *

They raced through the wall-walk and burst through the doors leading back into the Regents Gallery. Fletcher and his men jumped with their swords drawn and ready for battle.

"What in the devil's lair is going on out there?" Fletcher scanned the gallery before locking on the gaping hole at the back wall. Tense and alert, it was if he expected Ilio to make another appearance too.

They didn't stop running. Suna paused long enough to shout over her shoulder. "Dunkerk's under attack!"

When the full impact of her words sunk in, they followed on their heels.

Down the castle's main corridor they raced. Several servants collided with them but there was no time for apologies. Suna saw people weeping in corners, while others cringed in shock. No one knew what was happening.

Along the balcony that lined the upper level, various High Houses yelled down to them, demanding an explanation.

Confusion and terror gripped the occupants of Dunkerk's main castle. While many still reeled from the battle that had occurred a short time ago, seeing the fleeing backs of Lady Suna, their former general, and a host of Guardians running for the front gates only added to their despair.

Feran slammed through the front doors of the castle. No Elite guard stood there. However, hundreds of people ran straight at them seeking safety within the castle's walls. These people had likely been in the vicinity of the front gates when Greth's army attacked. Others followed in blind panic, not realizing what was going on, just that something dreadful was happening.

They search for safety in the first place Greth will overrun, Suna thought miserably.

Unknown faces flew by marred by terror, smoke and tears, but she focused on what lay ahead.

Feran shoved bodies aside to provide a path by which to get to the front gates. The Guardians behind her yelled out orders, commanding people to move, but panic gripped the city. Several times they had to stop and pull bodies up off the ground to prevent them from being trampled to death.

Why has Lord Greth done this? Was this orchestrated in case his nomination was declined? To add a war to everything currently going on? What's happened between the underlords? What madness has claimed these lands?

Trepidation coiled in her guts along with the multitude of questions she had no answers to.

When they reached the outskirts of the inner gate, the sounds of battle grew louder. Most of the citizens here had either fled deeper into the city or to the main castle. When they rounded the final corner, they stopped, stunned. They'd been here just one night before amidst the bustle of happy citizens. Today was total mayhem.

Coaches lay overturned across the roadways, some burning with flaming arrows embedded in their wooden carriages. Horses still tethered to many of the wagons ran in frantic circles. Suna tried to unfetter as many animals as she could with her mage'ic. The freed horses immediately fled from the fighting.

Feran raced to the wall and pushed his body into the stone. He raised his hand and spoke to Fletcher with Guardian hand signals.

After the captain gave three of his men specific signs, those men dashed in opposite directions.

Feran inched his head around the corner.

Fletcher crouched beside him. "First that demon? Now this? Who are we fighting?"

Feran growled. "Carberra."

"Why in the seven shades of Hell would Lord Greth be attacking Dunkerk? This doesn't make sense," Fletcher said.

The remaining Guardians mumbled in confusion as well.

Assumptions were not Suna's forte, but she had nothing else to offer. "He most likely saw the destruction being caused by Ilio. He believes Dunkerk is under attack from the inside. Dunkerk's soldiers know nothing of what has happened inside or out. They'll defend Dunkerk at all cost, even against Lord Greth."

"Your orders?" the captain asked solemnly.

Suna had seen what Feran had without having to look around the corner. Before he opened his mouth, she stepped forward. "Greth's soldiers are bottlenecked within the first and second baileys. Dunkerk had no time to seal the front gates before they stormed. These second gates are holding. For now. We just have to keep them there as long as possible."

Feran cursed under his breath. "It'd help if we knew how many men are out there."

She closed her eyes. The visual that came astounded her. "Nearly two thousand strong. Lord Greth brings no siege machines. Just every soldier under his command." *He was going to take the city whether his nomination was sanctioned or not!*

She pulled her sword from her scabbard on her hip. The sound of steel rang out.

Fletcher tried not to, but he gawked at the emblem on her blade. Feran's weapon, already grasped tightly in his right hand, matched hers. As did all the Guardians.

The captain's smile was more than a little rueful. "Lord Greth's betrayal to King Markes' legacy, to these lands, to our people, will be for naught. He'll regret what he's done. Today, we shall all dance with death." When he unsheathed his own Sword Dancer's blade cheers erupted from the other Guardians.

Feran pulled her close. "Promise you'll stay close to me."

The unspoken intensity in his eyes was something Suna didn't want to deal with. The strange thumping inside her chest made it difficult to breathe. She couldn't allow his worry over her put him in harm's way.

"I'm capable of taking care of myself. Watch your back. I'll watch mine."

She turned and ran toward the gates, holding his concern for her close to her heart.

She knew they had little hope. With Dunkerk missing more than a thousand men sent to Ethbridge a week prior by Lady Allena, the defenders of the kingdom were scattered. Lord Greth's nephew had had a hand in this attack. She hoped she'd be able to thank Viktor for that bit of useful information.

A regiment of that many men wouldn't have reached Vansgaard yet. Even if they sent Infers with messages for them to return, it would be too late.

Added to this was the many soldiers granted leave to attend the celebrations. With the inner and outer gates so poorly manned, the situation was bleak.

Carberra's men had already surrounded the outer walls. By sheer size, they'd managed to force their way through the main gates and first gatehouse and were now in the inner bailey.

Grappling hooks hung from the walls, their ropes trailing down like gigantic webs as Carberra's soldiers scaled down the stone like grotesque spiders. The bailey contained in the first and second fortifications already teemed with fighting forces. Utter chaos ruled.

She closed her eyes and concentrated on Carberra's force. *Grappling hooks and two battering rams. Greth came somewhat prepared. No siege machines, but arsenals enough should there have been dissention for his nomination.*

A twenty foot portcullis protected the rest of the city, but there weren't enough men manning it. It was here the bottleneck temporarily cut off Greth's men from overrunning the city.

Suna ran toward the fray and stopped several hundred yards from the portcullis. From this vantage, she saw Dunkerk archers make their way up along the crenellation of the inner gates, but there were too few to do any real damage except get themselves killed as human targets.

She also had a difficult time discerning friend from foe as the uniforms looked too similar. Whether that was by accident or not, she sensed Lord Greth had been planning this for some time.

The broad back of General Heratio caught her eye. He ran alongside the archers, bellowing orders. As if sensing her gaze, he turned and looked down. He gave a grim nod and dashed off.

Screams of the wounded and dying mixed with the metallic stench of blood that already hung thick in the air.

Like the Guardians behind her, she waited, poised for battle. Dust filled the air like a caustic fog. Adrenaline spiked. Slick with sweat, she gripped her sword tighter and counted the seconds. Then the sounds of a battering ram breaking through the inner bailey doors roared in her ears.

Carberra's forces had crushed the last stand of Dunkerk's defense.

She closed her eyes and brought forth her mage'ic, concentrating the spell on the front gates. Within seconds, the stone walls crumpled to the ground, stopping the rest of Lord Greth's men from entering. In her mind's eyes, she saw hundreds perish beneath the rubble, including some of Dunkerk's soldiers.

She kept telling herself she had no other choice in which to cut down the number of men entering into the second bailey, but it didn't lessen her grief at the meaningless loss of lives. It was only a matter of time before the inner gate was breached, but she'd ensure to make it as difficult as possible.

Grappling hooks flew through the air. Carberra's soldiers reinforced. Their reprieve was short lived.

When the surge came through the final gate, the soldiers stopped short, surprised at the small but defiant group of men and one woman who stood waiting for them.

She drew the most attention. As she'd hoped, the ruse worked. The men failed to notice the insignias embroidered on the lapels of the Guardians' uniforms. If they had, they might have reconsidered their advance. Only fools danced with a Guardian.

Suna cringed at the lurid thoughts coming from these soldiers. Battle lust burned in these men's veins, obliterating all common sense. If the worst were to happen, she'd ensure she was dead before they got their hands on her.

She ran straight for them. With a gust of conjured air, she pushed them back, but there was too many. Her sword ran through the first man's windpipe before the others realized what happened. Feran's presence beside her gave her a sense of security.

She swung her arm up in a clean arc, slicing open another man's guts. The urge to use her mage'ic became overwhelming, but Dunkerk's men would also be taken down. She'd use her powers as a last resort.

Carberra's soldiers fought for their lives, but for every one they put down, twenty more filtered through.

She ducked in time to miss a mace aimed for her skull. Swinging out a leg, she tripped the soldier. With fluid ease, she turned and thrust her sword down. The blade sank straight through the heart and lodged in the soldier's ribcage.

As she struggled to pull her weapon free, honed instincts sent her flat to the ground. The broadsword nicked her cheek. She rolled and looked up. The soldier stood stock still above her, his eyes round and vacant. In slow motion, he fell to his knees as if in prayer. Then his head fell off and rolled between her legs.

Feran stood behind him. He leaned and jerked her to her feet. With a touch of mage'ic, she yanked her blade free from the dead man's ribs.

Men fell in the midst of screams, fountains of blood and flying limbs. The Guardians fought as deadly as her and Feran. They hacked and sliced through Carberra's men until hundreds lay at the entrance of the gates, making it more difficult for Greth's men to gain entry.

CHAPTER TWENTY-NINE

Feran's worry for Suna was the worst feeling he'd ever experienced. He'd keep her safe, but his reasons had absolutely nothing to do with his oath to Mollster.

He stepped aside just as a backsword narrowly missed his sternum.

He swung his fist upward and connected with the soldier's jaw. Bones cracked. Blood and teeth flew. He turned his face as a molar hit his cheek.

Another attack came from the left. He swung his blade down and forward, but the blood splatter from the soldier's broken jaw caused him to lose his grip on his sword. The weapon slipped from his fingers.

He dived to the ground and pulled a stunted rapier from a side sheathe of his empty scabbard and sliced at the calves and heels as he rolled beneath the legs of Carberra's men. He crippled as many of them as possible while Guardians came from behind and finished them off.

He wiped his hands down his pants before seizing his sword and inching his way closer to Suna.

She worked her sword in her left hand and a dagger in her right, swinging both with deadly precision. She cut any who came at her. He studied her technique. Dark circles of exhaustion marred the skin beneath her eyes. Her hair was wild disarray and soaked with blood and sweat. She was weakening. "We have to get out of here," he screamed above the battle noise.

"I know. We can't hold them. There's too many."

To admit defeat was difficult, but to die trying was stupid. He looked up and saw the sharp edges of grappling hooks now being thrown over the inner walls. Greth's men were bypassing the chunks of stone from the inner gate Suna had destroyed and were climbing as they'd done with the outer walls. In no time the city would fall.

He searched the fray for Fletcher and the rest of the Guardians. Suddenly, the air filled with a familiar high-pitched screeching.

"Take cover!" he shouted.

* ~ * ~ *

With seconds to spare, Suna managed to place a shield of air over both herself and Feran. She tried her best to remember the other Guardians' positions as the sky darkened. Like an incoming thunderstorm, a volley of arrows rained down. They bounced harmlessly off her mage'ic, but dozens of men fell around them, including Carberra's men. Arrows protruded from bodies like porky-quills. Greth gave no regard to killing even his own men.

She looked up and saw General Heratio one last time. An arrow had pierced through his right ear. His eyes glazed over in death. He fell over the edge of the crenellation and disappeared.

"Feran, we have to get out of here. Now!"

Feran staggered and clenched his head. A Carberra soldier saw the moment of weakness and pounced from behind.

Instincts took over. Suna dropped her blades and flung out her hands. Mage'ic exploded the man's body from the inside out. Blood and guts cascaded into the air.

Her emotions were being driven by battle lust. There was no controlling it. She abhorred using her powers to kill, and in fact, a Divenean was forbidden to do so unless for the greater good.

Right now, this was far beyond the realm of the greater good. They wouldn't make it out alive if she didn't.

The tenets instilled in her to never use Divenean mage'ic to destroy shattered in that instant. Feran's survival was all that mattered. There was no greater good than that.

She stooped and picked up her dagger and sword before moving nearer to him, sheathing her sword as she went. Loathing filled her to the core. This had been an underhanded fight from the beginning. Now she'd use whatever means at her disposal to get them out of here unscathed, no matter the cost to her.

"Feran!"

Thrusting upward, he killed two men with simultaneous swings. The precision and strength behind his strikes was horrifying, yet mesmerizing. She discovered his death dance uncompromising. He feared nothing but one thing.

With all her heart, she wished he'd stop looking over his shoulder at her.

Another mace flew past her ear and nicked a piece of skin. She pivoted, forcing her dagger up to slice open the soldier from sternum to neck. The spray of the man's bowels drenched the front of her jerkin. *Feran, rally the other Guardians. We have to move to the inner city.*

From the corner of her eye, a rapier blade jabbed dangerously close to Feran's ribs.

Follow me, he said.

Stashing her dagger, she faced the gates and raised her arms with her palms pointing outward. She blasted anyone who came near. Showers of flesh and buckets of blood poured down around them as she imploded flesh and bone. Some men began running in opposite directions, terrified of her mage'ic, but others were quick to take their place in order to try to kill her.

She fought for Feran's life and those of the Guardians, but she couldn't keep this up much longer. Battle lust ruled her, but it was the only thing keeping her standing on her feet. With the mêlée she'd had earlier with Ilio and now this, she was expending far too much of her élan. They had to reach safety or she'd burn herself out completely.

Feran's fingers dug into her shoulder, pulling her back inch by careful inch. He hacked and cut an opening for them to follow. With her spine pressed against him, she faced the battle head-on while he kept attackers coming at them from the sides.

Dunkerk's soldiers had joined them, but they were far too few. It was a hopeless fight. Some soldiers eventually dropped their weapons and ran, although a few fought bravely on, prepared to die in defense of their kingdom.

Suna did her best to protect them, but the twisting and dividing of her energies only depleted her more.

Feran's arm wrapped around her waist. He half-carried her as he led their group deeper into the safety of Dunkerk's alleyways. Her hands flew in all directions as she aimed her mage'ic with murderous precision. Fletcher and what was left of his men followed close on their heels.

Greth's army began to thin as they headed deeper into the city center. Soon they were sprinting straight into the west end. When the noise of battle faded to distant screams, only then did they slow. Feran led them through the deserted streets until stopping in a dank alley to regroup.

A few stray horses wandered past, lost and confused, but otherwise unscathed.

Every man panted as they attempted to draw down the fire of battle lust flowing in their veins.

Only seven Guardians, including Fletcher, made it with them along with a handful of Dunkerk soldiers. Suna hung her head, dizzy from the expenditure of her élan. Feran moved to her side and placed his arm around her shoulders. She leaned against him, grateful for the support.

Fletcher growled. "What are we supposed to do now?"

"I don't command this regiment, Captain," Feran replied grimly.

"Someone must." Suna met their questioning looks, including Feran's. "General Heratio went down on the wall. I would suggest the rest of you hide."

Greth will pay for every drop of blood he's spilled this day.

She winced. Feran's thought blasted through her mind, but his vengeful promise mirrored her own. She also had a feeling Isafel would be doing their retribution for them.

He pushed himself off the wall, weary and blood splattered. "Find a place called Ratty's Grin. It's about fifteen streets north of here. Ask for Viktor Bossa. Tell him he bears a scar on his left shoulder in the shape of a mountain. He'll know I've sent you."

Fletcher's bloodshot eyes narrowed. "Just what are you asking?"

She heard the Guardian's teeth grinding. This was not the time to take on Feran. Anger and battle lust were a volatile mix.

Feran took several deep breaths. "Tell him it was me who put that scar there. He'll help hide you. If you're captured, Greth's men will kill you without a tribunal."

Fetcher snorted. "Let them try. We don't fear death. We fear failing in our duty. If we allow the city to be taken—"

"It's too late for that. And you won't be much good to us dead when we return," Suna cut in.

Several of the Guardians muttered amongst themselves. It wasn't their nature to run and hide, nor did they like the latter part of her statement.

Fletcher drew back. "What do you mean *return*? You two going somewhere?" He stared down both exits of the alley before locking his gaze on her.

She looked away. "We have to leave the city. It's imperative we escape."

"Dunkerk needs a new general, Fletcher. I believe you've more than earned the honor," Feran said.

The man's eyes widened. His mouth opened, but not a word came out.

With a laden sigh, she explained what she could. "We leave not because we want to, but because we must. There's matters more urgent than this. Isafel is here in the city. He's biding his time. I believe Greth's days are numbered. When he's crowned, nothing will hold that demon back from taking human form in the guise of a king. He'll bring forth unimaginable evil. As a human, he'll be undetectable as the demon he is except for brands around the wrists, ankles and neck. They'll be odd symbols that only a few can decipher. Isafel, or whoever he claims as his host, will try to conceal them. There are few who know this, so share this information with people you trust. Isafel will not be easy to hunt in human form. He'll still possess his powers. And far stronger than Ilio was."

She paused and stared at each Guardian in turn. "Ilio and Isafel? They're nothing compared to the danger facing Etharia. Ilio has been destroyed, but Isafel will be far more difficult to do so. He has one goal. To set his master free. We have the Kruthos key. It's because of this we leave. I'm hoping he'll follow us, but he desires a host first."

The Guardians nodded grimly, with a few of them muttering profanities under their breath.

Fletcher turned in the direction of the gates. He didn't seem surprised.

She made no mention of Balthazar's name, but she knew he'd eavesdropped on Feran and Heratio's conversation.

"What we're asking you to do is not a cowardly act," Feran added.

Throwing his hands up in frustration, the captain growled. "We're supposed to hide like rats in this hellhole?"

"What others call a hellhole, some call home. Remember that fact well, especially as Dunkerk's general. You represent *all* Etharians, including those more destitute. Hiding will save your lives so you can fight another day."

Fletcher's gaze darted between them. Then he stepped back. The glow in his eyes made her study her bloodstained boots.

"Barrin!"

A stocky, muscular man jumped forward. "Yes, General?"

"Consider yourself *Captain* Barrin."

The Guardian nodded.

"Get to the royal stables. Ready two of Dunkerk's fastest destriers and bring them to the wall-walk in the Regents Gallery." He turned to her. "You know of the secret passage into the throne room?"

She nodded.

The general shifted back to Barrin. "Take the alleys and back roads to the castle. Find a change of clothing on the way. Get the horses to General Feran and Lady Suna as fast as you can. Then meet us at this Ratty's Grin tavern."

Without a word, the Guardian saluted and sprinted around the corner.

Fletcher faced Feran. "I'll do as you ask, but I don't have to like it. I'm taking command in your absence. When you return, so will this title."

Suna hung her head. Fatigue had begun hitting her in small waves, but she couldn't falter now.

The new general stepped back and stood at attention. "You two will have an easier time blending in with Dunkerk's population than we will." He stopped, his eyes roving over their clothes stained bright with blood and mottled with bits of flesh. "Perhaps not. Look for changes of clothing, too. And may the gods give you wings."

Every Guardian stepped forward and saluted them before bestowing a low bow.

She and Feran conveyed the same honor back.

Feran took her hand and together they raced down the alley and out of sight.

* ~ * ~ *

Fletcher shifted toward his men. "Spread out and search for common clothing. We have to find this Viktor fellow. Meet back here in five minutes."
The Guardians and soldiers nodded and took off in different directions.

The general peered down the alley long after Suna and Feran disappeared. "Godspeed," he whispered. Then he went in search of garments to replace his blood-soaked uniform.

Suna and Feran's journey was as plagued with danger and the unknown as his was. He also knew the importance of what they carried.

How did the world come to this? He thought in between his running strides.

Fletcher glanced up at the smoke-filled sky and did something he hadn't done in a long time. *May you protect and watch over them,* he prayed. *And if it's not too much to ask, don't forget about the rest of us.*

THE END

ABOUT THE AUTHOR

D. Thomas Jerlo's novels inexplicably draws readers deep into mystical worlds where mage'ic rules and battles between good and evil are forever constant. Blending reality and illusion that leave indelible impacts on her readers, they are riveted to the spellbinding plots and unforgettable characters until that past page it read.

I am enough of an artist to draw freely upon my imagination. Imagination is more important than knowledge. Knowledge is limited. Imagination encircles the world.

~ Albert Einstein

Also available from Foundations Book Publishing

It's a helluva job, but someone has to do it... And for Rhune it's a small price to pay for his past sins. He's taken a new name and a somewhat normal life, except at night when he transforms into a hellhound to take souls to the City of the Dead for purgatories legions to deliver them to Hell. For fifteen centuries he's lived in happy solitude until Hanna, a paralegal with the most amazing eyes, rear ends him in the small town of Rio Morden. He's seen those eyes before, but it's been years since the last time. Now she's all grown up and involved in a murder trial that has its sights set on her becoming its next victim. What's a hellhound to do? Surely not fall in love—and certainly not with a Dreamwalker. And is that all she is?

Mix in a diabolical lawyer and his lover, some Voodoo magic, and it's a recipe for mayhem and murder.

Can Rhune keep Hanna safe, or is she destined to be Hellhound Bound?

Pity's Prelude
By Crighten Halbert

Stephen Bates is desperate. Paid by a foreign superpower to leave Earth and sacrifice his life, he finds that ritual suicide isn't that simple when the planet he lands on erupts into civil war. He and local war hero, Titus Sirocco, struggle to discover who's trustworthy and who's gunning for them. As two different wars rage around them, will Stephen and Titus find what's worth dying for, or will the rebels choose their fate first?

And what's with those shapeshifters?